THE WATERSTONE

THE WATERSTONE

REBECCA RUPP

CANDLEWICK PRESS
CAMBRIDGE, MASSACHUSETTS

Many thanks to all who helped so much in the making of this book: all the kindred spirits at Candlewick; Amy Ehrlich, who read the first draft and nixed the bulldozer; Cynthia Platt, my infinitely patient and creative editor, who saved the weasels; Ethan Rupp, who drew a map of Tad's world for my birthday; Caleb Rupp, who read every single rewrite; and my husband, Randy, who makes everything possible.

Copyright © 2002 by Rebecca Rupp

First paperback edition 2005

The Library of Congress has cataloged the hardcover edition as follows:

Rupp, Rebecca.
The waterstone / Rebecca Rupp. — 1st ed.
p.   cm.
Summary: Twelve-year-old Tad embarks on a quest to seek a powerful crystal that will restore balance to the world.
ISBN 0-7636-0726-6 (hardcover)
[1. Fantasy.] I. Title.

PZ7.R8886 Wat 2002
[Fic]—dc21   2001052939

ISBN 0-7636-2294-X (paperback)

2 4 6 8 10 9 7 5 3 1

Printed in the United States of America

This book was typeset in Columbus.

Candlewick Press
2067 Massachusetts Avenue
Cambridge, Massachusetts 02140

visit us at www.candlewick.com

For Josh,
who first invented Pondleweed

CONTENTS

THE WATERSTONE

Prologue

THE MAGPIE'S TREASURE

The young magpie collected things. Her shaggy nest was crammed with treasures, all lovingly sorted into heaps and piles. She had—she counted on her wingtips—a curly yellow ribbon, an orange butterfly's wing, six striped feathers, a handful of scarlet berries, two silver beads, a pink snail shell, and a glittery gold-flecked stone. It was an outstanding Collection—one of the best in the Flock, the magpie thought privately, though she was too well brought up to say so. Still, even the best Collection was never finished. Collecting was a way of life, and a good magpie was always watchful, searching for new and better additions for the hoard.

Today she had found a prize.

She had spotted it far below her—at first just a tempting glitter, a sudden flash in the sunlight, like a fragment of mirror glass. She dived toward it, heart pounding. There it was. A once-in-a-lifetime find. Half hidden in a little hollow littered with dead leaves lay a snow-white crystal the size of a robin's egg, streaked with shining threads of silver. Its facets captured and reflected the spring sunshine in a dancing dazzle, and from within, it glowed with a mysterious, soft cool light. Unable to believe her luck, the magpie stooped, deftly plucked it up, and rose triumphantly into the air. In her excitement, she barely noticed the approaching foe, until he squawked demandingly in her ear.

She had seen him before. A scruff-tailed bully from the other side of the forest. Because his own Collection was so paltry—crumbly gray lichens, a pinecone, and a few withered heads of red clover—he often tried to snatch finds from cleverer, more talented birds. Well, today he wasn't snatching. Not from her. She dodged adroitly, glaring fiercely at the interloper. But he wouldn't let her alone. He followed her, squawking greedily, deliberately bumping against her, trying to knock her out of the air. His wings buffeted her head. She screamed in fury.

The crystal was falling. It plummeted downward through the air, dwindling in an instant to a vanishing silver pinprick, and splashed, with dreadful finality, into the blue lake far below. Beneath the surface it fell onward, plunging down through the clear water, gleaming whitely and trailing a long comet's tail of tiny silver bubbles. Above it, unheard, a horrified male magpie fled, pursued by an enraged female with blood in her eye.

The crystal slowed in its long descent, drifting gently to the lake bottom. In its wake a shadow fell. Suddenly the quiet water trembled as if something better left sleeping had come awake.

1

THE VOICE IN THE WATER

Tad was beginning to hate the spear.

It was his first spear, and—when he had woken on the morning of his twelfth Naming Day to find it leaning against the wall beside his bed—he had thought that it was the most beautiful thing he had ever seen. His father had always pretended that Naming Day presents were brought each year by the Moon Elves, who traveled to Earth on moonbeams and brought gifts to well-behaved girls and boys. But it had been a long time since Tad had believed in the Moon Elves, and besides he would have recognized the handiwork of his father, Pondleweed, any-where. The spear had a broad chiseled flint point, a pol-ished wooden haft painted in red-and-black stripes, and a leatherleaf handgrip, just the right size for Tad's hand. There was even a decorative tassel at the end, made of braided silkgrass threaded with brightly colored seeds. No boy, Tad was sure, had ever had a finer weapon or a better Naming Day gift. Just owning it was enough to make him almost burst with pride.

Of course, it wasn't the way the spear *looked* that was the problem. It was the way the thing behaved. No matter what Tad did, the spear simply wouldn't do what he wanted it to. It acted as though some magicker had put an evil spell on it. It seemed to have a mind of its own, and that mind was mischievous, contrary, and sometimes just plain mean.

This time his throw should have been perfect. He had taken his stance just as Pondleweed had taught him: one foot forward, knees braced, back straight. He had taken his time, drawing back his arm, rehearsing every move in his head, taking careful aim. The target was a square of birch bark with a great round eye — the Owl's Eye, Pondleweed called it — painted with red berry juice in the center. A good spearsman, Pondleweed said, could hit that Eye with every throw — and every man of the Fisher Tribe, it went without saying, was an expert with the spear.

Tad just knew he had it right this time. It *felt* right. As the spear flew from his hand, he could almost hear the solid *thunk* of the stone point hitting home and the satis-fying hum of the quivering haft. He had even opened his mouth to give a delighted yell of triumph. And then, at the very last minute, everything went sour. The spear wobbled, veered sideways, and dived abruptly out of the air. It bounced once, slithered under the blackberry bushes, scooted across the ground, and splashed heavily into the pond. It floated there for a moment on the water's surface; then — deliberately, Tad thought — it sank, leav-ing behind a mocking trail of bubbles. Tad stared after it in dismay.

The pond erupted in a chorus of croaks from a bevy of startled frogs, followed by a raucous burst of what sounded like loud amphibian laughter. A blue jay, balanced on an overhanging branch, set up a derisive squawk. *"Ha! Ha! Ha! Ha!"* She sounded as if something were squeezing her around the middle. Tad wished it were him.

He glared at the blue jay furiously. It wasn't wise to pick a fight with birds, Pondleweed said; even seed-eating birds could be dangerous, with their knife-edged claws and their dagger-long beaks capable of pecking an unwary Fisher right in two. "If it's near as big as you or bigger," Pondleweed always said, in that serious voice that he used for things that were important, "chances are it's not your friend, and even if it's got no mind to hurt you, it still might. So don't you go worrying any birds."

The blue jay gave a last loud giggle and flew away. Tad clenched his fists and kicked angrily at the ground. *"Mudpats!"* he muttered under his breath. He looked guiltily over his shoulder, but there seemed to be nobody within earshot. He paused for a moment, trying to think of something even worse to say. *"Fish pee! Weasel droppings!"*

The red Owl's Eye seemed to be looking right at him with an expression of mocking contempt. Tad bent down, picked up a pebble, and threw it at the target as hard as he could. The pebble missed too. It was his seventeenth miss that day. Tad felt mad enough to pop like a milkweed pod. At the same time he felt like bursting into tears.

"Tad?"

Tad jumped. It was his little sister, Birdie. Birdie had turned nine on her last Naming Day, in the cold Moon of Bare Trees, and her present, Tad remembered, had been a willow-twig doll. Fisher girls were supposed to cook and sew and grow up to be good wives and mothers. Nobody expected *them,* Tad reflected bitterly, to perform impossible tricks with hateful mudsucking stone-pointed sticks. Birdie didn't know how lucky she was.

He turned and looked toward the sound of Birdie's voice. At first he saw only shifting shadows of brown and green. "Find the right place and stay still," Pondleweed always said, "and most things will pass you by, seeing no more than a bit of twig and leaf." The trick, of course, was figuring out which place was the right place and then remembering not to wiggle once you were in it. Birdie was better at it than Tad was. She was sitting cross-legged at the foot of a towering clump of dandelions, her small brown face and misty greenish-brown hair dappled with flickering stripes of shade and sun. The bright yellow dandelion blossoms—wide and flat as furry umbrellas—bobbed gently in the breeze high above her head. Her fringed green tunic—belted with braided linenleaf and stitched around the collar with tiny yellow seeds—was just the color of the dandelion stems.

She probably saw and heard everything, Tad thought. The missed target, the sunken spear, the kicking, the yammering about weasel droppings, that stupid bit with the pebble. He must have looked like a puddleflapping idiot. The pointed tips of his ears turned raspberry with embarrassment. He hated himself. He hated everything. He wished he'd been born a frog.

He scowled furiously at Birdie.

"Were you spying on me?" he demanded.

Birdie scowled right back. *Fisher girls weren't supposed to scowl like that,* Tad thought. Fisher girls were supposed to be serene and even-tempered and good at handicrafts. At least that was what Pondleweed said. Birdie was always being scolded about her temper and sent to sit on a rock in the garden until her thoughts were as peaceful as a still pool.

"I was *not* spying," Birdie said in an unpeaceful, offended sort of voice. "I don't *spy.*" She pointed to a tangled heap of woven pea vines beside her in the grass. "I was mending the fishtrap net."

She bit her lip, studying Tad's red face.

"Spear throwing just takes practice," she said. "You have to be patient. It's like Father says: 'Berries don't ripen overnight.'"

So she was *watching,* Tad thought. It was nice of Birdie to try to be comforting. But he just wasn't in the mood right now to hear himself compared to a green berry. He was sick of being a green berry. He wanted to be brave and powerful and admired, like the heroes and warriors in Pondleweed's stories. Like Bog the Weaselkiller who wore a collar of gold nuggets and weasel claws and carried a spear made of blood-red agate that never missed a foe. Or like Frostwort the Winterborn who fought the White Fox of Far Mountain with nothing but a slingshot and a magic silver pebble.

"I'll be right back," he told Birdie gruffly. "I have to get my spear."

He turned and ran toward the pond, darting out along a half-submerged log at the water's edge. He hesitated for a moment, judging just where his spear had fallen in. Then, in one swift fluid motion, he dived. The clear green water of the pond closed over his head.

Tad was as at home in the water as a fish. Like all Fisher children, he had learned to swim even before he had learned to walk, first splashing in the shallows, then paddling in the deeper water with a floatstick to hang on to, and finally gliding smoothly through the deeps, sleek and slippery as a young otter or a slim brown minner. His green-brown hair flattened slickly to his head, and flaps of skin sealed his nostrils shut to keep the water from going up his nose. He kicked expertly, his wide brown feet with their long webbed toes sweeping strongly through the cool water. He turned a somersault and then began to paddle slowly back and forth, his eyes searching the pond bottom for the spear.

The underwater world gleamed. Ribbons of sunlight wove back and forth across the sandy bottom, tangling themselves together, then untangling themselves and swiftly sliding away again. Silky strands of eelweed brushed Tad's legs. A fat spotted rock bass—twice as long as Tad him-self—poked a curious nose out from a cluster of water lily stems and goggled foolishly up at him. Its big bulging eyes were slightly crossed. It opened and closed its mouth twice, blew a bubble, and slowly withdrew, wiggling back-ward with a furl of fins and tail. Tad puffed his cheeks and blew a bubble back. Then, out of the corner of his eye, he caught a glimpse of red and black. It was the spear, resting neatly on a bed of mud and pebbles, looking somehow pleased with itself, as if it had never made a mistake in its life. He scowled at the spear resentfully and began to swim toward it, stretching out a hand to pick it up.

Then—suddenly—something about the pond felt different. Wrong.

At first it was only a nervous ripple and a creepy feeling between his shoulder blades. Then a thump of alarm. Tad twisted in the water, looking anxiously about him. Some-thing was *wrong*. It was as if something malevolent—a watersnake?—had suddenly turned its head and looked directly at him. Watching with angry little eyes. But where was it? No danger was in sight, but the peaceful and famil-iar pond felt hostile. The stems and leaves of the water plants were frightening forests; the rocks, dark lairs of lurk-ing terrors. His skin prickled, his heart began to pound, and the hair stood up on the back of his neck.

Watching.

There were strange toadstools and funguses deep in the forest that sometimes shone at night with an eerie green light, standing out like ghostly fires from their dark surroundings. Glowmolds, Pondleweed called them. Tad, hanging fearfully in the water, felt just like that—like a glowmold, helplessly illuminated, caught in a puddle of light with no place to hide. He felt more and more frightened. Something was watching him. He could feel it. He turned his head desperately from side to side, but nothing was there. Nothing he could see.

Are you the One?

The voice, cool and clear as spring water, echoed inside his head. It was an inhuman, somehow empty voice, the sort of voice that the wind or the rain might have if it could speak. It seemed to come from no direction and from all directions at once. At first it reminded Tad of bell music and chimes; then it grew colder and harder until it sounded like breaking icicles or like frozen pebbles dropped on a silver plate.

Are you the One? Is it you?

Whoever it was meant him no good, Tad was sure of that. He wanted to run and hide, but there was nowhere to go, no way he could tear himself free. A confusing swirl of images filled his brain, like pictures from half-forgotten dreams: a strange silver-eyed face framed in a cloud of pale green hair; a blue-lit chamber paved with pearls and patterned tiles; then—*where?*—a blaze of flaming torches and a great stone mountain whose cliffs mysteriously moved and shifted; and over all a thundering tide of dark water through which ran the sound of voices, many voices, singing some high sweet song.

What's happening? he thought frantically. *Who are you?* And the voice, like an icy silver dagger, answered.

Do you not remember? I am Azabel.

2

THE FIRST REMEMBER

Tad was gasping and choking, back on dry land again, lying facedown at the edge of the pond. Everything—mouth, nose, eyes, ears, lungs—was full of water. He felt like a sodden sponge. He coughed convulsively. His stomach heaved and he spat out a mouthful of pond water.

When he rolled over, he saw that Birdie was crouched over him, her face furrowed with concern. She was dripping wet. Her green-brown hair was plastered flat to her head and her tunic was dark with water. There were puddles around her feet.

"What happened?" Tad croaked.

"You didn't come up," Birdie said. She was breathing in hard gulps as if she had been running. "You didn't come up and then all the frogs started yelling their warning noises. So I jumped in to see what was wrong and you were just floating there under the water with your eyes wide open." She sniffed loudly and wiped her nose with the back of her hand. "You looked awful. I was scared. I thought you were dead."

"There was something in the pond," Tad said. He sat all the way up. Then he bent over and put his head down on his knees. He felt sick and dizzy. "Did you get my spear?"

"*No*," Birdie said. "I wasn't thinking about your *spear*." She stopped sounding upset and began sounding irritated. "If *you* found somebody drowning, would *you* go paddling off to pick things up off the pond bottom? Your stupid spear's still down there. I'll go get it in a minute."

"*No!*" Tad said. "Don't go in there, Birdie!" Even though the late afternoon sun was warm, he was shivering. He wrapped his arms tightly around his knees. Birdie looked at him in surprise.

"There's something...somebody...in the water. Something dangerous." His teeth began to chatter. "Not like a pike or a watersnake. Something else. I could hear it—her—talking."

"Underwater?" Birdie said. She looked skeptical. "You can't talk underwater. The words would all sound like this." She made a gargling sound deep in her throat. "You couldn't have heard talking."

Behind her a bullfrog gave a disbelieving *Glub!*

"Well, I did!" Tad said loudly. "Move over, Birdie. You're dripping on me."

Birdie took a grudging step backward.

"So what did it say?" she demanded.

"She told me her name," Tad said slowly. The cold silver voice echoed in his memory. "She said, 'I am Azabel.'"

"'Azabel,'" Birdie repeated. "Az-a-bel. It's pretty, Tad. Like a name in one of Father's fairy tales."

Tad shook his head. The sick feeling was coming back. "This was real, Birdie." *And it wasn't like a fairy tale at all,* he thought. He hesitated, trying to explain. "It wasn't what she *said* exactly. It was the way she said it. She's . . ." He gave another shiver. "She's nothing like us, Birdie. To her, we're like beetlebugs or something. I could feel her mind inside my head. It felt . . ." He paused, groping for words. "*Dark.* And old, terribly old. And cold. Like black ice."

And there was something else, Tad thought. *She said something else. What was it?* The Remember hovered annoyingly just out of reach.

"Tad! Birdie!"

Pondleweed was running toward them. He was carrying a flat woven basket. *He must have been blackberry picking,* Tad thought. Sick as he was, he noticed that his father hadn't found many berries.

"Has something happened? Are you all right?" Pondleweed dropped the basket and his hand went to the hilt of the stone-bladed knife that he wore strapped to his snakeskin belt. "Has something been here? A heronbird? A watersnake? A fox?"

Tad shook his head. He found to his dismay that his eyes were beginning to sting with tears. Pondleweed knelt down next to him and put an arm around his shoulders.

"What happened, son?"

"I dived after my spear," Tad said, "and I heard something in the pond." Falteringly he told his story: the search for the lost spear, the sudden terrifying feeling, the strange mind prying about inside his own, the cold hollow voice. *Azabel.*

"When I went to look for him, he was just floating there like a dead fish," Birdie said. She put her arms out to the sides, lolled her head, puffed out her cheeks, and opened her eyes very wide. She managed to look a lot like the foolish rock bass. Tad glared at her. "So I grabbed him and pulled him to shore and dragged him out."

"Voices in the water?" Pondleweed ran a worried hand over Tad's hair. "Are you sure you didn't bump your head when you dived?"

"Tad was drowning, wasn't he?" asked Birdie. "If I hadn't been here, Tad would have drowned, wouldn't he?"

"Thank Great Rune that you were here watching," Pondleweed said solemnly.

Birdie raised her right hand and drew a circle in the air in front of her face. That was Great Rune's sign; Tad had taught it to Birdie himself. He had learned it from their mother, who had died of winterfever when Tad was three and Birdie just a baby. The sign was supposed to keep you safe from danger, though Pondleweed always said it was best to dive in a hidey-hole first and make signs later.

Birdie doesn't have to sound so puddleflapping pleased with herself, Tad thought. *What about me? I was the one who was in danger, not Birdie. I was the one Azabel spoke to.*

And there was something else, too. She said something else. Something I ought to remember. Memory flickered, like a trout beneath the lily pads, but then darted away again into darkness.

"Well," Pondleweed said, "I don't like the thought of strangers slinking about. You children sit here and dry off. I'm just going to go have a look." Tad opened his mouth to protest, but Pondleweed shook his head at him reassuringly. "There's probably nothing there now," he said. "Look at the frogs—half asleep, the lot of them, the great green lazygullets. They'd all be bellowing if there were an intruder in the pond. But better to take precautions now than to patch up afterward, as my old grandda used to say. Where did you dive in, Tad?"

Tad told him, pointing, and Pondleweed strode briskly out along the broad moss-furred log. He stood silently for a moment, frowning and studying the surface of the water. Then he dived. His body cut the water so cleanly that there was barely a splash. Tad and Birdie, huddled together on the shore, stared at the quivering ripples where he had disappeared. Long minutes passed. Then, in a fountain of spray, he reappeared, swam in two smooth strokes to the log, and climbed out of the water. In one hand, water dripping from its braided grass tassels, he held Tad's spear.

He smiled at the children's anxious faces. "Nothing there," he said. "Not so much as a waterflea's whisper."

He sprang down from the log and strode toward them across the grass, water dripping from his brown tunic and silkgrass leggings.

"Time to go inside, the two of you. You need dry clothes and supper. And I could do with a mug of butter-nut beer."

Birdie leaped up to scamper beside him, but Tad, halfway to his feet, tripped and abruptly sat down again.

All in a rush, he was filled with a Remember.

He was diving, diving, deeper than he had ever gone before. He was himself and yet somehow not himself; his body was new and strange, a larger grown-up body dressed in a tunic of glittering fish scales. In one hand, he held a double-bladed sword—a metal sword inlaid with patterns of gold, the kind of weapon made by the Diggers who lived in the distant mountains. Tad knew what it was, even though he had never seen a sword before. His fin-gers—broader and stronger than Tad's own fingers—curled around it easily, as though it were familiar and often used.

He was in a vast submarine world, infinitely larger than the friendly pond, dimly lit with a flickering blue-green light. Great black cliffs and rocky crags arched over him, extending upward for unimaginable distances. All around him was a forest of ropy dark-stemmed plants with long slimy leaves that continually writhed and coiled back upon themselves like squirming nests of snakes. Beyond the underwater forest was a long flat expanse of pale sand, in the middle of which stood a black palace made of carved stones. The stones were stacked into turrets and towers of many different shapes and sizes, some topped with jagged rows of roughly pointed stones, others with conical roofs tiled with colored shells. The walls were richly studded with jewels: emeralds and rubies and deep blue sapphires. There were arched stone windows draped with ropes of creamy pearls and a great front gate made from the white jawbone of some enormous fish.

This was where he was going. This was where she lived. He had something to do here, something dangerous but terribly important—so important that if only he could accomplish it, it didn't really matter if he escaped alive.

What's happening to me? Tad thought again. This is someone else's Remember, not mine. *Whose?* Where did it come from?

And then he seemed to hear Azabel's voice again, that cold voice thick with hunger and desire.

She was saying *Water.*

3

DRYING TIME

"A palace all covered with jewels?" Birdie said. Her green eyes sparkled with excitement. She was eating a slice of sweet rootbread and there was a dab of blackberry butter on the tip of her nose.

Tad nodded. Now that he was warm and dry, with two bowls of watercress soup in his belly, the frightening part of the encounter in the pond was beginning to fade away. It was all beginning to feel more exciting somehow, more like an adventure. *If it happens again,* he thought, *I'll be ready. I won't just panic like some muckbrained minner. I'll be bold and dauntless. Like Bog the Weaselkiller.* It was a satisfying picture. Boldly, in Bog style, he reached across the table between the soup bowls for another piece of sweet rootbread.

"Don't reach, son," Pondleweed said, in a tone of voice that Tad was sure was never used toward Bog the Weaselkiller. "Your mother would say that you were behaving like wild Hunter. Ask your sister to pass the platter."

Birdie passed the platter.

"Why did she say *Water?*" she said. "Your pond lady. Didn't she say anything else?"

Tad shook his head. "I don't think so," he said. "Just *water*. As if it were the thing she wanted most in the whole world."

"Water," Pondleweed said. He pushed back his stool and set down his baked-clay mug. "We could use some more of that ourselves. I've never known the water in the pond to be so low."

"We haven't had any rain," Birdie said. "Not for ages and ages. The rain barrel is empty. I looked just this morning. It's dry all the way to the bottom."

"Well, let's hope we get some soon," Pondleweed said. He winked at Birdie, but Tad saw that his forehead was furrowed into little lines that meant that he was worried. "I saw three bluebirds flying in a row this morning. 'Three birds means times changing,' your Granny Thimbleberry used to say. And it's been fine weather for so long that what could change be but rain?"

Tad could just remember Granny Thimbleberry, a tiny wizened brown woman in a moleskin cloak, surrounded by pots and jars and grinding bowls and bundles of strange-smelling herbs. She had had a mole's skull on a pole beside her front door, and she kept a grass snake in a covered basket. Tad had been a little afraid of her.

"Maybe I'll be a magicker like Granny Thimbleberry when I grow up," Birdie said. "I'll be able to read the wind and tell the future, and I'll learn how to make spells that bring a good harvest and to mix healing potions." She took another bite of rootbread. "Tad can't be a magicker, can he, Father? It's just girls that have the Talent."

She wouldn't be so puddlejumping eager about it, Tad thought, *if she could remember that snake.*

"You can't just decide to be a magicker," Pondleweed said. "You have to be born with the Talent. Granny Thimbleberry—may she rest forever in Great Rune's garden—had a gift for foretelling and a touch for anything green and growing. Her potions were the finest in the forest, and when she wove a silkgrass cloak, she could whisper every strand of warp and woof so that whoever wore that cloak could walk almost invisible, safe from hawks and owls."

Tad, before he could help himself, made a horrible face. He remembered those potions. The very thought of them made his tongue curl.

Pondleweed was still talking. "Maybe you'll find that you have the Talent, Birdie, as you get a little older. But the Talent is nothing to joke about. It's a great responsibility."

"Is it really just for girls?" Tad asked jealously.

Pondleweed grinned at him. "The Talent does seem to favor the female folk," he said. "But I've always thought the menfolk had a touch of it too."

Birdie looked crestfallen.

"What can the male magickers do?" Tad asked.

Pondleweed pursed his lips and tugged at his chin. "I always thought my old grandda may have had a touch of the Talent," he said. "The way that man could catch fat minners—just whistle them out of the water, he could, like calling buzzflies to honey. And old Newtfoot at Water-oak Pond—*he* used to say that *his* grandda could turn frogs blue."

Birdie giggled.

Tad felt disappointed. Whistling minners and turning frogs blue didn't sound like the sorts of things a magicker should do.

"But it's the rare boy is born with so much as a finger-pinch of the Talent," Pondleweed said, "so I wouldn't close my nose flaps waiting." He poured himself a mug of mint tea and took a deep drink. "Not that a magicker with special powers wouldn't be welcome. Especially if this dry spell keeps up much longer. If things keep on the way they are, it could become a Drying Time."

Tad paused with his slice of rootbread partway to his mouth.

"What's a . . . Drying Time?" he asked.

"Times have come when the world dries," Pondleweed answered. His face was suddenly very serious in the yellow light of the beeswax candles, and the worry lines across his forehead grew deeper. "The weather changes. No one knows why. Some say it happens when the winds blow from the wrong direction. Others say it happens when Great Rune goes off on a journey and leaves the world for a time with no god to watch over it. In a Drying Time, no rain falls. The trees die and the grass turns brown and the ground turns to dust. Slowly, one by one, the ponds dry up and disappear. The small ponds vanish first, then the larger ponds, and finally even the biggest ponds of all."

Tad had a sudden awful vision of the pond, an empty bowl of caked and cracking mud, the lily pads brown and withered, the frogs and the turtles dead or gone. It didn't seem possible.

"*All* the ponds?" he asked incredulously. "Even Deep Pond?"

Deep Pond was a half day's journey to the south. Plumrose and Wallow lived there, in a tunnel-house in the pond bank, with their twin sons, Pickerel and Sticklepod. Deep Pond was said to be so deep that it had no bottom at all but instead went all the way through the earth and came out on the other side. "Even Deep Pond?" Tad repeated.

Birdie interrupted him. "The *trees* die?" she said in a horrified voice. "Our tree could *die*?"

Tad and Birdie and their father lived in the hollow base of the old willow tree that grew near the edge of the pond, a tree so gnarled and massive that it seemed to be as old as the world itself. Its broad yellow trunk soared so high that it almost touched the blue skin of the sky, and its yellow branches, thick with narrow green leaves, cascaded downward like a green-and-golden waterfall.

Tad looked around him in dismay. The little house had always seemed so safe and so secure. His eyes took in the solid mud-and-pebble fireplace with its bread oven and drying racks; the family beds with their moss-stuffed mattresses, built into cavelike hollows in the willow-trunk walls; the open door to the storeroom with its comforting stock of jam and honey pots, barrels of acorn and lilyroot flour, crocks of wild radish pickles, baskets of nuts, and strings of dried crab-apple slices and cloudberries.

"But where would we live?" Birdie's voice was a frightened wail. "Where would we go?"

"Now, Birdie," Pondleweed said, "the Drying Time hasn't happened yet. No sense in worrying about tomorrow's problems before we finish with today's. You and Tad wash up the supper dishes. Then, if you can stay awake, we'll have a story when you're in bed."

He crossed the room and lifted his spear—a longer, heavier spear than Tad's, with a worn wooden handgrip— from its brackets above the fireplace. "I'm going out for one last look around," he said. He was frowning.

He's still worried, Tad thought, with a prickle of alarm. *He thinks there's still something wrong at the pond.*

Tad squeezed his eyes shut for a moment, picturing the pond: the cattail thicket heavy with fuzzy brown-velvet flower heads, the bright patches of bellflowers and fairy-slippers, the water lilies with their flat floating leaves and rosy-pink blossoms. And the clear green water. The water level *was* lower, Tad realized suddenly. A lot lower. He turned and padded across the room to where Birdie, dripping soapy water on the floor, was scrubbing the clay mugs and acorn-shell bowls with a handful of scourweed.

"You can dry," Birdie said.

Tad took a linenleaf towel and reached for a wet bowl.

"Birdie? Those flat rocks that we were fishing from yesterday . . . didn't they used to be underwater?"

Birdie nodded.

"We used to be able to swim right over them," she said. "And the stream's drying too, Tad. It's gotten so quiet that you can't hear it anymore. I keep thinking every day that it will come back and be the way it was, but it hasn't."

Tad's prickle of alarm grew sharper. Now that he thought of it, he had known that something was wrong with the stream. The stream entered the pond at its northern end, a place half hidden by a tumbled fall of rock and a green curtain of leafy vines. Ordinarily the stream bubbled and chattered, tumbling frothily downhill to feed the pond. But now the stream's music was silenced. *How long has it been?* Tad wondered. *I haven't been paying attention. All this has been happening, and I've been fooling around with that stupid spear.*

By the time Pondleweed returned, Birdie, a motionless mound under her silkgrass comforter, was already asleep, making a rhythmic purring noise into her pillow. Tad, from the bed above her, lifted his head at the sound of the opening door and peered down past the twig ladder at his father on the floor below. It was always strange seeing him from this angle, looking down at the top of his head.

"Is everything all right?" he whispered.

"The water's still dropping," Pondleweed said, carefully replacing his spear on its wooden brackets. "It's falling faster than ever. I set out a marker stick at the water's edge this morning and already the water level is down a full frog's leap. I can't understand it. And the stream is running slower and slower. If it continues to dry at this rate . . ."

The last words were lost in a grating sound as Pondle- weed dragged the heavy wooden bar across the door, shutting the family safely inside for the night.

". . . be gone for a few days," Pondleweed was saying. "I'll take the boat out tomorrow and see if I can find any- thing blocking the flow upstream. Maybe there's been a cave-in somewhere along the banks. Or a tree that came down in just the wrong place."

"You're taking the boat?" Tad said. He sat up in bed. "Can I go too?"

He had always wanted to travel, to see what the world was like beyond the homely green circle of the pond. The farthest he had ever gone was to the yearly Gathering, when all the Fishers left their ponds and traveled to the Wide Clearing in the Piney Forest. Even Pondleweed, who always seemed to know everything, was vague about what lay beyond the forest. There were more forests beyond their forest, Pondleweed thought, filled with strange trees and animals—and with strange people too, people who belonged to none of the Tribes. The Hunters went there sometimes—or at least they said they did, but then Hunters would say anything, and you were lucky if even half of it were true. Then there were mountains somewhere, a vast distance away. The Diggers lived there, but not even the Hunters claimed to have been that far. Mountains were huge heaps of rock and stone piled up higher than a hawk could fly, and in places the water poured down off of them in great roaring falls, louder than the bellow of an angry black bear.

"Can I go too?" Tad repeated.

Pondleweed tilted back his head and looked up at him quizzically. "We'll see," he said. "We'll talk about it in the morning. Safe night, son. Bright dreams."

"Safe night," Tad said. There was a sleepy mumble from Birdie.

Tad closed his eyes. He could hear the shifting creak as Pondleweed settled himself in the rocking chair beside the fireplace. The chair had a seat of woven pea vines that stretched complainingly whenever someone sat down on it. Pondleweed was humming softly, an old lullaby that their mother used to sing, a song about the silver moon-fish who come out to swim at night when all the children are fast asleep. Tad sank deeper into his pillow. Nothing could really be very wrong, he thought, with his bed so warm and comfortable and his father near.

Sleep closed over his head like pond water, and he fell into a confusing dream full of silver moonfish, sunken stone palaces, and big blue frogs.

4

UP THE STREAM

The birchbark boat slid smoothly across the glassy surface of the pond. Sunlight flashed and glittered on the water like a flickering host of bright-tailed golden fish. Tad and Pondleweed, on moss-padded seats in the bow and stern, bent rhythmically, dipping their carved wooden paddles in the water. Birdie sat in the middle with the blanket bundles and the luncheon basket. She was clutching her paddle, but she hadn't started paddling yet.

Birdie had insisted on coming along, and Tad was cross about it. He was also ashamed of himself for being cross. After all, Birdie had saved him from a watery death just yesterday. If it weren't for Birdie, Tad knew, he would be lying there right now, all cold and pale in a coffin-basket, with his family weeping over him and saying what a fine young man he would have grown up to be. He dwelt pleasurably for a while on all the nice things they would have said about him while he lay there, heroic, tragic, and dead.

"Grak!"

Pippit, the small green watchfrog squatting on the bottom of the boat just behind Birdie, gave a sharp warning croak.

"Tad!" It was Pondleweed. *"Rocks to the right!"*

Tad came to with a start, quickly wielding his paddle to shift the boat out of harm's way. He took a peek back over his shoulder. Birdie still wasn't paddling. *And when she finally starts,* Tad thought resentfully, *in next to no time she'll be saying that her arms are tired and can't we stop to rest and how long before we get there. I wish that she had just stayed home. Like Fisher girls are supposed to.*

Pippit croaked excitedly.

"We're nearing the entrance to the stream!" Pondleweed called. "Everybody get ready to paddle together!"

They maneuvered the boat through the thicket of reeds and furry cattails at the end of the pond that masked the mouth of the stream.

"Now!" shouted Pondleweed.

All together they bent to their paddles. The boat shot forward, slithered between two towering boulders, and leaped from the pond into the flowing stream. Even though the stream was low, the paddling was much harder here. Tad dragged his paddle painfully through the water, arms straining, forcing the boat forward.

"The current is against us paddling upstream," Pondleweed called. "It's a little difficult going in this direction, but it will be easier coming home."

He was trying, Tad supposed, to be encouraging, but it was hard to be encouraged when your arms felt like they were about to fall off. *I'm not sure we're going to be able to do it even now,* Tad thought grimly, paddling. He felt as if they had been paddling uphill forever. His arms ached all the way up to the back of his neck and sweat dripped off the end of his nose. Behind him, at each dip of the paddle, Birdie was making a little moaning noise. *Pull,* Tad thought to himself with each stroke. *Pull. Harder. Pull.*

"I'm tired," Birdie said. *Right on cue,* Tad thought. "My arms hurt."

"There's not much more of this steep stretch," Pondleweed called again. He was paddling steadily, and he sounded infuriatingly calm and cheerful. "Don't stop now, Birdie, or we'll start going backward. The stream will flatten out soon and then we can rest a bit."

He was right. Soon the streambed grew level, the current slowed, and the paddling became easier. Tad found that he could straighten up and look around. A dismal sight met his eyes. The stream, like the pond at home, was dwindling. Drying stripes across the rocks showed clearly where the water level had been: higher—much higher—than it was today. The towering wildflowers and grasses along the banks looked limp and faded, and every once in a while Tad saw ugly patches of dead brown.

Brown.

Suddenly—without warning—he was thrust into a Remember.

He was standing beneath a dead and withered tree. His tongue was thick with the taste of dust and the parched gritty ground burned beneath his bare feet. Someone behind him was crying—a dry, painful sobbing—and he knew it was a child crying, a child dying of thirst. The forest all around him was the color of sand and ash, and the ground was littered with the brittle husks of dead leaves. The child's cries grew weaker and finally faded away.

"No!" he tried to shout. *"No!"* But the words stuck in his throat, scratchy as dead brambles.

"What?" said Birdie. "What did you say?"

The ruined forest vanished. Tad blinked and shook his head.

"Nothing," he said. *It's nothing,* he told himself firmly. *It's hot. It's just that I'm worried about what Father said last night. I'm daytime-dreaming.*

They paddled on and on, gliding along the shallow stream channel, maneuvering between still rock pools and bumping through little runs of rapids. At highsun, when the sun stood directly overhead in the sky, they stopped for lunch, pulling the boat out of the water and laying a picnic out on a wide, flat sun-warmed rock: rootbread sandwiches stuffed with radishes and peppergrass, a jar of lilyroot pickles, honeycakes, and a bladderpod filled with mint tea. Pippit stepped on the sandwiches and was scolded; ribbeting sulkily, he lolloped off to hunt for flies.

Tad was so hungry that he didn't care that his sandwich was damp and slightly squashed. They ate and drank hungrily. Pondleweed lay back in a hollow of the smooth stone, rested his head on a folded arm, and pulled his wide-brimmed woven-grass hat over his eyes.

Tad, still hungry, reached eagerly for the honeycakes. The Drying, for the moment, was pushed to the back of his mind. It was strange to be so far from home, but it was fun too, and exciting. Everything was new, different— and anything could lie in store for them up ahead.

"What do you think we're going to find?" he asked. He took an enormous bite of honeycake, chewed hastily, and swallowed. "Up at the top of the stream?"

From under the hat, Pondleweed shook his head. "I don't know, son," he said. "There are a hundred things that could block the water of a stream. A fall of stones. A tree trunk. A mudslide. I don't know what we'll find. Or what we can do about it once we find it. We'll just have to wait and see."

He yawned hugely, making the hat brim wobble, and fell into a doze. Tad silently finished his honeycake, licked the crumbs off his fingers, and reached for another. Birdie—leaving the uneaten crusts of her rootbread sandwich cunningly hidden under its leaf wrapping— slid down from the rock to wade in the shallow water of the stream, cooling her webbed toes in the wet sand. Suddenly there was a loud splash, a startled squeal, and a derisive blatting. Pippit leaped by, heading downstream, pursued by a shrieking Birdie. They vanished around a corner, then reappeared, both very wet, Birdie pursued by a squawking Pippit.

Tad, munching his third honeycake, wandered lazily down to the water's edge. The water, kicked into muddy froth by Birdie and Pippit, was slowly settling down again, returning to its clear glassy green. Tad crouched in the shallows, digging his toes into the mud, and bent forward, studying the reflections in the water. The stream, in this sheltered inlet, was as still and smooth as polished glass. In it, the world was upside-down. Behind his solemn brown face—topped by a shaggy tangle of greenish-brown hair—the images of trees seemed to plunge to astonishing depths, reaching toward a distant underwater sky. A sunken sun, blindingly golden, glittered up at him from the water. Tad blinked, squeezing his eyes tight shut against the glare.

When he opened them again, a strange face stared up at him from the silent stream. There, in his place, was an older face, square-chinned and defiant. This new face looked tired and troubled—its lips were compressed in a tight line, the eyebrows drawn together—but for all that, it was a kindly face. There were laugh crinkles at the corners of the eyes. Then the eyes shifted—green-brown eyes, Fisher eyes—and gazed right into Tad's. Tad gasped in surprise and jerked backward. The strange Fisher's lips were moving now, saying something, but Tad couldn't understand what it was.

Who are you? He thought the words as hard as he could, wrinkling his forehead with effort. The face looked surprised—and then Tad's foot slipped in the mud, and the reflection dissolved in a flurry of shimmering ripples. When he peeped into the water again, he saw nothing but his own face, its astonished mouth rimmed with honey-cake crumbs. Had it been real? He couldn't have imagined it. He would recognize the strange Fisher again anywhere. He tried to conjure up the vanished face and, probing, found only a fading whisper in his mind. *Sagamore. Beware of Ohd.*

Sagamore. Tad repeated the strange word to himself, tasting it on his tongue. The word was elusively familiar, like something he'd heard before, long ago, in one of Pondleweed's stories, or maybe in a dream. *And who or what was Ohd?*

On the rock above him, Pondleweed sat up, pushed his hat back, and began to pack the remains of the picnic back into the basket.

"We'd better move on," Pondleweed said. "We want to make as much headway as possible before dark. Come on, Birdie! Pippit! Back in the boat!"

They clambered into the birchbark boat, Birdie and Pippit dripping squelchily onto the blanket bundles, which luckily were wrapped in waterproof bags of oiled leaves. With renewed energy, they paddled on. The farther they traveled, the grimmer Pondleweed's face became. Something was terribly wrong, Tad knew. There could be no doubt now. The stream was drying. In places it was so shallow that their paddles scratched and scraped against pebbles on the bottom, and several times they had to get out to carry the boat over a stretch of streambed where there was almost no water at all.

When the sun was low in the western sky, just nudging the tops of the distant hills, they stopped and made camp for the night under a sweet-smelling honeysuckle bush. Birdie untied the braided grass cords fastening the blanket bundles and spread out the sleeping mats, while Tad dug a shallow fire pit at the edge of the stream, surrounded it with stones, and collected a heap of kindlesticks and dry wood. Pondleweed, spear in hand, prowled slowly back and forth in the water at the edge of the stream, searching for fish for dinner. Pippit excitedly hopped back and forth, stepping on things he wasn't supposed to and getting in everyone's way.

Tad added another dry twig to the bundle of kindlesticks already in his arms. It seemed strange to be doing all these homely chores so far from home — exciting, but a little lonesome too. Home-wishing, that's what Pondleweed called it. Fishers have pond water in their blood, Pondleweed said.

"Get too far from home and your pond tugs at you, calling you back again, reminding you where you belong. All youngers get an urge for traveling, but sooner or later . . . well, you'll see," Pondleweed had said, "as you get older. You're a Fisher. You'll settle."

Tad had never thought he would, but now he wasn't so sure. For a moment he felt a terrible wave of longing for the home pond. From the look on Birdie's face, she was feeling the same way. *At least all of us are together,* Tad thought. He was suddenly glad that Birdie had come along.

"I'm hungry, Birdie, aren't you?" he said. "Let's start the fire and make a pot of tea."

By the time Pondleweed returned with three minners, cleaned and scaled and wrapped in a wet maple leaf, Tad had the cooking fire blazing and Birdie had brewed a pot of mint tea. They sprinkled the fish with snippets of peppergrass, set them to roast on pointed sticks over the fire, and buried wild onion bulbs to bake in the hot coals. Soon the minners began to sizzle and give off a delicious smell. The smell made Tad's mouth water. He crouched down on his heels next to the fire, happily sniffing. He was so intent on the slowly crisping fish that he didn't hear a sound behind him until a voice spoke suddenly out of the underbrush.

It said, "Fishers!"

5

HUNTERS

Birdie and Pippit squawked in alarm, and Tad almost lost his balance and tumbled into the fire. Peering out at them through the honeysuckle leaves was a dark walnut-brown face. Tad recognized it immediately.

It was a Hunter.

The Hunter's teeth flashed at them in a broad white grin. His hair was tied back in a thick braided tail, and he wore a scarlet head-scarf, a pair of leather trousers, and a short fur vest that was open in the front, leaving his chest bare. A wooden bow and a leather quiver filled with red-feathered arrows were slung across his back. There were leather bracelets incised with red-and-black diamond patterns on his upper arms. Across each cheek was painted a horizontal stripe of bright blue.

Tad felt a pang of nervousness. Though Hunters and Fishers were not enemies, there was a coolness between the two Tribes. Hunters were said to be tricky and untrustworthy—and sometimes outright thieves, stealing vegetables out of gardens, laundry off of drying lines, even babies out of cradles. "Never turn your back on a Hunter" was one of Granny Thimbleberry's sayings. Hunters were dirty, they had no proper family feeling, and they ate odd things too, things that no self-respecting Fisher would ever put in his or her mouth. Tad wasn't sure what the odd things were, but they sounded horrible. Whatever the Hunter in the honeysuckles ate, though, he looked just as clean as Tad did—though his smell was different: a pleasant leafy bonfire smell of forest floor and wood smoke. He took a step forward and raised his right hand, palm open and outward.

"Nobono of the Hunter Tribe," he said. "Peace and plenty."

"Pondleweed of the Fisher Tribe," Pondleweed said, raising his right hand in turn. "And my son and daughter, Tadpole and Redbird. Peace and plenty."

"Well met," the Hunter said. "Shall we join our camps to share food and fire?"

"You are welcome," Pondleweed said with equal formality. It was the accepted code of Tribal behavior: upon first meeting, you introduced yourself and offered to share your food, even if you had nothing more than a crust of rootbread or a single berry, even if you suspected that your new acquaintances were going to pinch your bladderpods and blankets in the night.

The Hunter flashed his teeth again. "A strong boy you have," he said to Pondleweed. "And a fine girl. I, too, have sons and daughters. They follow behind in caravan."

Tad threw a worried glance at the three fish.

The Hunter laughed. "It will be enough," he said. "We will have food to share."

He turned and winked broadly at Birdie.

"A fine girl," he repeated. "Near old enough for trading. Perhaps we speak to your father, eh?"

Then he said, "I fetch my family." There was a rustle of leaves as he slipped back into the bushes and disappeared.

Birdie glared after him indignantly.

"What did he mean, 'old enough for trading'?" she demanded.

Pondleweed pursed his lips disapprovingly.

"It is what Hunters do when their youngers grow old enough to marry," he said. "They bargain, one family with another, to find the best mates for their sons and daughters. It seems to work well enough for the Hunter Tribe, but Fishers do not treat their children that way."

"Listen!" said Tad suddenly.

From some distance away, there came a rhythmic creak and jingle and the lumbering noise of something heavy, rolling.

"The caravan," Pondleweed said, answering the children's unspoken question. "You know that Hunters have no permanent homes like Fishers and Diggers have. They're travelers, never settling, always moving from place to place, searching for game." He sounded disapproving.

The creaking was louder now, and soon the leafy branches pushed apart to let the caravan pass through. Or rather caravans. There were two of them—both little houses on wheels. Nobono's family lived in a wooden wagon with a tentlike cover of stitched animal skins fastened to a frame over the wagon bed. The frame was decorated with colored ribbons of dyed and twisted grasses, and hung with strings of hollow seedpods and baked-clay bells that clattered and tinkled musically as the wagon moved. Bundles of pelts were strapped to the wagon's sides, and an earth-filled box fastened to the back was planted with herbs: onion grass, elf parsley, and tea mint.

Nobono and a woman with dark braids that hung to her waist walked before the wagon, pulling it along by a pair of wooden handles. Three children scampered beside them, and a fourth peeped shyly out from between the flaps of the skin tent. The children's faces were deep nut-brown like their parents', and their cheeks were also painted with stripes of blue.

The second wagon was smaller, its wheels gaudily striped in yellow, red, and green. It was pulled by a plumpish elderly Hunter whose long braid was almost pure white. He had a thick white mustache that curled up jauntily on the ends, and bushy eyebrows that looked like fat white caterpillars. When he grinned at Tad and Birdie, they saw that he was missing two teeth in the front.

"This is Branica, my *mari,*" Nobono said. "The mother of my children." He gestured expansively. "And these are my sons, Bodo and Griffi, and my daughters, Ditani and Kelti. Our Ditani, she is now of the Hunt, having brought home First Blood."

The Hunter boys were dressed like their father, in leather trousers and fur vests, while the girls, like their mother, wore bright full-skirted dresses dyed scarlet with berry juice. There were ropes of agate and amber beads around their necks; and carved bone bracelets on their wrists and ankles clacked and clattered as they walked. Even Kelti, the baby of the family, wore necklaces of blue and yellow wooden beads, and there were goldfinch feathers tied in her pigtails. Birdie, stricken with shyness, edged closer to Tad, tugging nervously at the hem of her fringed tunic.

"They look like flowers," she whispered.

Tad could hardly stop staring at Ditani. She was the prettiest girl he had ever seen. Her dark braids were threaded with red-dyed grasses and twisted into thick coils over her ears, and her eyes tilted up at the corners, which made her look as if she were laughing at some secret joke. With her black hair and scarlet skirt, she did look like a flower: a brilliant wild poppy or a slim stalk of flameweed. Beside her, Tad felt stodgy, clumsy, flapfooted, and dull.

"And this"—Nobono gestured again, teeth flashing—"is Uncle Czabo, my father's cousin, who travels with us."

The white-haired Hunter gave a loud bellow of laughter. Tad thought he sounded like a bullfrog.

"Well met, Fishers!" he shouted. Something glittered when he turned his head. Tad saw, astonished, that he wore a silver ring in his nose.

"We will eat, eh? And drink!" He dropped the shafts of his wagon, clapped his hands together, and pointed a long finger at Tad and Birdie.

"And you, Fisher cublings, I will show *you* my magic tricks!"

He winked at Tad and waggled his bushy eyebrows up and down at Birdie, who giggled.

The children were shy at first, but soon they were chattering together as Branica rummaged in the wagon, pulling out food. Hunter food. Tad peered at it suspiciously. It looked like perfectly ordinary food, though it smelled strongly of onion grass and wild garlic. Even more interesting than the food, though, was the neatly packed wagon, with its piles of tightly rolled sleeping furs, its red- and blue-painted wooden chests, and its rows of lidded storage baskets. Birdie was entranced.

"It's perfect," she said wistfully. "I wish we had a wagon like this."

"Eh, and so you should," Branica said, nodding approvingly. She was cutting thick slices of pungent sausage with a curved knife. "You Fishers stay too close to roof and doorstep. We Hunters, now — we live in all the world at once and sleep beneath new stars each night. It keeps the mind easy and the spirit free. To stay in one place, then that place comes to own you, no? When you find a place you can no longer leave behind, that is not to be whole."

She handed Tad a wooden plate piled high with sliced sausage, and laughed at his puzzled expression.

"You do not understand me, little pond-dweller, no? You Fishers are like the rocks, who sit-sit-sit, and let the

world pass by them"—she made a little crouching movement, then froze, rocklike, flashing dark eyes at Tad—
"but we Hunters are like the wind in the grasses, touching
all, seeing all. You should spend a summer with us in caravan. Then you see how it is to live."

Tad wanted to protest that that wasn't what Fishers
were like at all—even though, secretly, he had sometimes
thought so himself. *We don't just sit like a lot of stickmud
turtles,* he thought resentfully. He opened his mouth to
argue, but before he could speak, Ditani interrupted with
a question.

"Is that your frog?" Ditani asked curiously—and
then, when Tad nodded—"I've never seen anyone keep a
frog as a pet before."

Pippit, hovering at the edge of the campsite, croaked
and rolled his eyes at her, which was his way of looking
endearing. Ditani leaned closer to Tad.

"They're really good to eat," she whispered.

Pippit gave an outraged croak and vanished into the
shrubbery.

"To *eat*?" Tad repeated incredulously. *"Frogs?"*

Ditani nodded. "Their legs," she said.

Tad stared at her in horror.

"Nobono!" Branica shouted over his shoulder. "Talk
later, man! We need meat for the supper!"

Nobono, shaking his head, broke away from his conversation with Uncle Czabo and Pondleweed and walked
toward her, soft-footed, unslinging his bow. He smacked

Branica on the bottom. "No need to screech like a hunter-cat, woman," he said. He grinned at Tad, teeth flashing white in his dark face.

"Have you been on the hunt before, young Fisher?" At the shake of Tad's head, Nobono crooked a finger and jerked his head toward the dimness of the forest. "Time that you were then. Follow me and try not to set those webby feet to break twigs."

Tad looked anxiously toward his father for permission; Pondleweed shrugged resignedly and gave a little nod. Torn between anticipation and resentment, Tad hurried behind as Nobono slipped into the underbrush.

Tad had never seen anything like the Hunter's skill in the forest. Nobono was as swift and silent as a brown shadow, sliding from tree root to tree root, slithering through dead weeds and bracken, light as a dried leaf. Motionless, he became invisible, and Tad felt his heart give a nervous beat at the thought of losing him, of being abandoned in the forest all alone. A hand gripped his shoulder and Tad jerked with alarm.

"Softly." It was Nobono, speaking in a breath of a whisper. He crouched, pulling Tad down beside him, and pointed. "There. Can't you smell it? Blood."

Tad squinted in the direction of the pointing finger, sniffing the evening air. He couldn't smell anything. At least not anything different. Just leaf mold. And he couldn't see anything either. He turned to ask Nobono a question, but the Hunger impatiently jerked his head, gesturing for silence. Tad looked again. Was that something moving—there, beneath that shaggy clump of ferns? He couldn't be sure. Then he heard a faint rustle and a sound of scrabbling claws, and caught, just for an instant, a glint of beady eyes.

"Deermouse," Nobono murmured. He barely moved his lips.

Moving slowly, the Hunter reached behind his back, slipped an arrow from his quiver, and nocked it to the string of his bow. In one silent, fluid motion, he drew the bowstring back, took aim, and let fly. There was a whispered rush of air and a sharp cry. Tad winced.

Nobono stood up, nocking a second arrow. "Be wary yet. Deermice are dangerous, wounded," he said. "Behind me now."

He moved forward, soundlessly, and Tad followed. No matter how carefully he set his feet, they still made tiny crackling sounds. He wondered how Nobono did it.

The deermouse was dying. It lay on its side, Nobono's arrow buried deep in its chest. Its muzzle was dark with blood. As Tad watched, it twitched once, convulsively, and went limp. Its bright eyes glazed over and turned dull. Tad felt sick. Nobono reached down and gripped the haft of the arrow, then pulled it sharply out of the deermouse's flesh. He bent to clean the stone point on a withered blade of grass.

"Never leave your arrows," he said. "A good arrow"—he reached back to pat his quiver affectionately—"a good arrow, he is a friend. Faithful like your greeny frogs, eh?"

His teeth flashed at Tad, bright in the dimness. Then he pulled a knife from the leather sheath at his belt, knelt, and with a sharp downward slash cut off the deermouse's front paw. Blood dripped sluggishly onto the dead leaves.

Tad gasped.

"It is the way of the Hunters," Nobono said. He was scooping a shallow hole in the dusty forest floor. "It is the Honor of the Hunt. To prepare the weapons, to stalk, to take blood. And then, always a part of the kill to Great Rona. To show our gratitude."

He placed the bloody paw in the hole, covered it with earth, and tamped it down. Reverently, he drew a circle around the spot with the point of his knife, muttering soft words under his breath.

Then he sprang to his feet, flashing his white grin again at the gaping Tad.

"Now we skin the kill and prepare the meat."

In the following quarter hour, as he struggled to help Nobono, Tad became convinced that he could never be a Hunter. Nobono, with quick skillful cuts, skinned the mouse, sliced the meat of its haunches into slabs, and directed Tad to stack them on a fallen birch leaf.

"We drag the meat home, eh? Easier than carrying it," he explained. "Though this mouse, he has not much meat on his bones. It is the Dry. The eating is poor."

His arms were red to the elbows. Tad felt sicker than ever. It must have showed in his face, because Nobono paused in his cutting and slicing and sat back on his heels.

"You do not like the Hunt, eh?"

Tad felt guilty and awkward. He averted his eyes from the stripped remains of the mouse carcass.

"It's just different," he said haltingly. "It's not . . . I'm just not used to it, I guess."

"To eat is to kill," Nobono said. "To survive is to spill blood, little Fisher. It is the way of the world. The fox kills the squirrel; the hawk kills the sparrow; the owl kills the mouse. Even you, you hunt your watery fish."

"But . . ." Tad stopped, confused. It wasn't the same, he wanted to say. Fish were different. Not warm and furry like the deermouse. What Fishers did was *different*. More natural.

Nobono bundled the mouse pelt into a tight roll and fastened a loop of twisted ropegrass to the stem of the meat-loaded leaf.

"You see how you like the kill when it is roasted, eh?" He seized the ropegrass loop in both hands and jerked his chin back over his shoulder. "That way toward camp, little Fisher. You'll feel better for some supper. And me, my stomach is beating against my backbone."

Roasted deermouse, Tad had to admit, was awfully good. They sat in a circle around the campfire, passing wooden plates and bowls from hand to hand. The Hunters ate with their fingers, piling slices of meat and fish with shredded swamp cabbage and scooping it into their mouths, while Pondleweed, Tad, and Birdie used carved forks and spoons. Tad and Birdie had never tasted anything like the Hunters' food. The sausage, smelling more strongly than ever of onion grass and wild mustard, made their noses tingle and their tongues burn. Tad bit into a tiny round red berry and gasped. His mouth was suddenly on fire. His eyes filled with tears. He reached, panting, for his mug of mint tea, and found Ditani laughing at him.

"It's a firepepper," she said. "You're not supposed to eat them, silly. They're just for flavoring."

Uncle Czabo, squatting on the opposite side of the fire, gave his bullfrog bellow of laughter. "Give the boy some drink or we see smoke coming out ears!"

Flavoring! Tad thought furiously, gulping cold tea and reaching out his mug for more. The things were hot enough to melt your teeth. He tried surreptitiously to cool his tongue by breathing through his mouth.

"I've eaten hotter peppers," he said defiantly. "Back home we eat them all the time."

Birdie, caught by surprise, snorted. Ditani looked impressed.

"It's been many moons since we have seen Hunters in these parts," Pondleweed said. His plate was empty. He reached for another helping of Branica's sausage. Tad noticed that he avoided the firepeppers.

"It is a bad year for Hunting," Nobono said briefly.

"The forest is dry and the feed poor," Branica said. "The animals grow few and thin. Like this skinny mouse, eh? In a fine year, our wagon now would be heavy with pelts, but we have only these small bundles. You, too, have seen it, no? The Dry?"

"It is the Drying Time then?" Pondleweed said.

Nobono threw a fish bone into the fire, where it flared and sparked.

"A Dry and perhaps more," he said. "We Hunters in our travels hear many stories, and the tales these days are dark and feary."

Branica nodded, pursing her lips and glancing quickly at the children. Kelti had her head in her mother's lap and seemed to have fallen asleep. Birdie and the Hunter boys, giggling, had scraped a smooth spot on the ground and begun a game of pebblehop. Tad stared down at his webbed toes and tried hard to make himself invisible. The olders always seemed to have something important to talk about that the youngers weren't supposed to hear. Well, he'd had enough of that. He was going to stay right where he was. Now that he'd been given his first spear, it seemed to him that he was old enough to be told what was going on.

Uncle Czabo spoke with lowered voice.

"Weasels," he rumbled. "A whole warren, by the paw marks. They fell upon a Hunter camp seven sunrises ago at the north side of the Piney Forest. When the camp was discovered, naught was left but toppled wagons and chewed bones."

Ditani, her eyes enormous in the firelight, edged closer to Tad. She really was the prettiest girl he had ever seen. For a moment Tad almost forgot to pay attention to the conversation.

"My cousin Vico came upon a stone circle," Nobono said, "and in the center of it were charred marks as of a great fire and an altar stone smeared with dried blood."

Tad's heart gave a huge lurch in his chest. *A stone circle* . . .

He heard Ditani, startled, say his name. He turned to answer, but before the words could pass his lips, the scene before his eyes shifted and changed.

He felt as if he were falling backward, whirling down and away through a long dark tunnel. His head spun dizzily and his vision blurred. He squeezed his eyes tight shut. What was happening? The Remembers hadn't felt like this before. Or maybe this wasn't a Remember. This felt . . . more real. The very air felt different—cooler, sharper, redolent with pine. When he opened his eyes again, he was in darkness. Pondleweed and the Hunters, the campsite by the honeysuckle bush, were gone. A voice—a familiar, somehow furry-sounding voice—spoke softly in his ear.

"There, just ahead. I can smell them. Go easy now."

His bare feet stepped cautiously on dry evergreen needles. Far ahead, a pinpoint of yellow shone in the darkness, then flared and blossomed. Someone had lit a fire. He and his companion moved forward together, setting their feet down carefully, barely daring to breathe. The stone circle rose above them—twelve great rough-cut rectangular stones, set on end, and in the center, lying flat, the thirteenth. The altar stone. Hooded figures moved around it, their shadows leaping, black and gigantic in the yellow firelight. The ground beneath Tad's feet felt suddenly cold.

Is this real? Tad thought. *Where am I?*

He looked back over his shoulder at his companion and saw, with a shock, a narrow humorous bright-eyed face covered in short red fur. The creature wore a tight leather cap with earflaps and a leather jerkin stitched all over with tiny rings of bronze. In one hand it carried a polished longbow, a yellow-feathered arrow notched in the string.

"We can take them, Burris," he heard his own voice—gone deeper—say. "We're a match for her lackeys, you and I."

A strong hand gripped his shoulder briefly, then withdrew.

"I am ever with you, Sagamore," the fur-soft voice said.

Sagamore . . .

"Are you all right?" Ditani was saying. "Are you all right, Tad? You were making the funniest faces."

Tad grinned at her weakly. "Sure," he said. "I'm fine."

Inside, his thoughts were in turmoil. *Whose lackeys? What's happening to me? And who is Sagamore?*

On the other side of the fire, Pondleweed and the Hunters talked on.

"This is more than a Dry," Branica said. "Some evil is afoot. Danger is to all of us, and all should meet it together. It is time for a Gathering of the Tribes."

"What of the Diggers then?" Pondleweed asked.

Tad pricked up his ears in curiosity. He had never seen a Digger. The Digger Tribe had left the forests long ago—long before he was born—to live like moles in burrows beneath the far mountains. There were all kinds of strange stories about them, none of which agreed. "Wise as a Digger" was a common saying among the pond folk, but even commoner was "mad as a Digger," which meant really crazy, and "twisty as a Digger," which meant clever but not to be trusted.

Branica shrugged.

"Who knows what they think under yon stony mountain?" Uncle Czabo put in. He shook his head, making his silver nose-ring flash and glitter. "Perhaps with all their cleverness they make water out of rocks."

"Best to leave Diggers alone," Nobono said repressively. "They do not know the Honor of the Hunt."

"The Hunters, we have sent out word," Branica continued, "calling all to meet for council at the Wide Clearing in the Piney Forest on the ninth day of the Shrinking Moon. Perhaps the Tribes together can discover why this strange Dry has come and decide then what to do."

Pondleweed nodded slowly.

There was a whoop of delight from Birdie as she hopped Bodo's last two pebbles, winning the game. Bodo clapped a hand to his head and moaned.

"Another match!" Griffi shouted.

Nobono laughed. "I see the luck is with the Fishers tonight," he said.

"It is too late for more playing." It was Branica, summoning her children. "Bodo and Griffi! When you are ready for sleeping, then we will have some music. Go and wash your faces, all. And unroll your sleeping furs."

It was clear that there would be no more talk of menacing weasels or terrible stone circles that night—or at least not until every child was fast asleep. Tad snuggled into his silkgrass blankets next to Birdie, his head toward the fire, resolving to stay awake, just in case.

"Now I show you my magic, eh?"

It was Uncle Czabo. He wiped sausage grease off his mustache and stepped forward into the firelight. Then he bowed deeply to the right and the left, flexed his fingers once or twice, and held out his hands, empty, palms up. He showed them all that there was nothing behind his back, nothing hidden up his sleeves. Then suddenly, out of nowhere, there was an orange bittersweet-berry ball—then two, then four. He juggled them expertly, throwing them high into the air. First they circled in front of his face, then behind his back. Around and around they went, faster and faster, until—the children gasped—they were gone again, all in an instant, and his hands were empty. Then he produced a shiny pearlstone from behind Tad's ear; and then, stepping back, Uncle Czabo pulled a scarlet bandanna out of his mouth that grew longer and longer until it was impossibly long, and then—*whap!*—he clapped his hands together and the bandanna somehow knotted itself up and turned into a butterfly. Tad and Birdie stared in amazement. Uncle Czabo bowed again, chuckling, and sat down.

"Enough tricks for now, eh?" he said. Tad didn't think he'd seen nearly enough tricks. He could have watched all night.

Then Pondleweed told stories, pointing out all the people and places in the clear night sky overhead: the thick hazy band of stars that was called Rune's River (the Hunters called it Rona's Path), the long-handled Fishing Net, and the enormous Swimming Frog. Then the music began. Nobono played a wooden flute and Uncle Czabo strummed the strings of a painted lutegourd while Branica and Pondleweed sang. They sang a song that Tad had often heard his father sing around the family campfire at home.

> *Keep the floating stars alight*
> *In the River of the Skies.*
> *Make the midnight moon shine bright,*
> *Make the morning sun arise.*
> *Make the rain around us fall,*
> *Nurture lake and pond and stream,*
> *Keep the forest proud and tall,*
> *Keep the world forever green.*

Tad had always thought of it as a happy song, but tonight somehow it sounded heartbreakingly sad. He tried his best to stay awake, to listen longer, but he just couldn't. Before he knew it he had fallen asleep.

He awoke sometime far into the night with a pointy rock digging into his left shoulder blade. The campfire had burned down to ashes. He could see the dark heaps that were the sleeping bodies of his family and the Hunters—Uncle Czabo was snoring—and, glittering in the moonlight, the bulging eyes of Pippit the watchfrog, hunched beside them. A little wind rustled dry leaves and chimed the hanging bells on the frame of the Hunters' caravan.

Tad lay awake. He was thinking about what Branica had said, sounding so superior and amused: "To stay in one place, then that place comes to own you, no? When you find a place you can no longer leave behind, that is not to be whole." To travel, free as the wind. It sounded gloriously exciting. *But it would be lonely if I had no place to come home to,* Tad thought. It's not that a place owns you—it's that the water smells sweeter there and the wind blows gentler and your feet know the feel of the grass. *You need to have roots,* Tad thought.

From somewhere far away, deep in the forest, came the hooting cry of a hunting owl. *Hoo-oh! To-hoo-oh!*

A last thought flickered before Tad fell asleep again. *Who is Ohd?*

6

THE BLACK LAKE

The morning dawned clear, cloudless, and sunny with a light breeze blowing out of the west. They crawled out of their blankets with much yawning and rubbing of eyes. Branica was already bustling about, directing the packing of the caravan and shouting at Bodo and Griffi. After a cold breakfast of sweet rootbread with blackberry butter, the families prepared to go their separate ways.

Bodo shouted saucily to Birdie, "We'll play another pebblehop at the Gathering! We'll see who wins then!"

Kelti, peeking between the wagon's skin flaps, waved a fat fist.

Ditani, scarlet skirts swirling, called to Tad, "I'll see you at the Gathering!"

"Until the Gathering!" Uncle Czabo bellowed, sounding more than ever like a bullfrog. He pointed a long finger at Tad. "I teach you my tricks," he shouted, and winked.

"Until the Gathering!" Pondleweed echoed, raising his hand in farewell. "On the ninth day of the Shrinking Moon!"

Nobono and Branica lifted the wooden handles of the caravan and bent forward, straining to start the wagon rolling. Uncle Czabo followed. Slowly they trundled away through the underbrush. Pondleweed, Tad, and Birdie stood on the stream bank, waving until the last scraps of scarlet, yellow, and green had vanished from sight and the sound of the wagon's creak and jingle had faded away.

"They were *nice*," Birdie said, still looking after them.

"Best to be cautious with Hunters," Pondleweed said. It was his teacher voice, the same voice he used for pointing out the dangers of diving off lily pads in the dark, running across open ground, and interfering with wasps. "Their ways are not our ways, and too much togetherness leads to trouble. Birds don't live with beavers."

"Well, I liked them, anyway," Birdie said.

She paused.

"But I'm not going to let that Bodo win at pebble-hop," she added.

"We should be on our way too," Pondleweed said after a moment. "We still have a long way to travel."

They launched the little boat again and paddled determinedly onward. Birdie chattered excitedly about Bodo and Griffi and the Hunters: "How many days is it until the ninth day of the Shrinking Moon? Will we really go to the Gathering? All of us? Can we camp near Bodo's family?"

Tad dipped his paddle in silence. He had a lot to think about. *What would it be like to live like the Hunters, traveling from place to place all the time? Do Hunters ever want to settle down? What would it feel like to be traded? Did Ditani like me?*

Nobono want to trade for me—that is, if I ever get better
e spear? Or do Hunters think that Fishers are never good
enough? Did I look really stupid trying to eat that firepepper?

Hours passed. The sun rose higher in the sky. The
streambed gradually widened and then merged with a
broader stream—once, Pondleweed said, it must have
been a river. The river now was shallow and drying, a
mere thread of water among tumbled stones. Many of the
rocks that had once lined its bottom were exposed, bare
and whitened in the sun. On either side of them the banks
rose up higher and higher, until soon it seemed that they
were paddling along the bottom of a deep canyon. The
rocky walls cut off the sun.

Goosebumps formed on Tad's arms, even though the
day was warm, and he shivered. Something was wrong
here. There was something hateful up ahead. He could
feel it. Even the water smelled different here. *Wrong.* Tad
glanced worriedly over his shoulder at his father, but
Pondleweed was staring over his head, studying the sides
of the canyon walls.

As they rounded the next rocky curve, Pondleweed
gave a startled exclamation, then thrust his paddle sharply
into the water, driving the boat to the side of the shallow
stream. Its birchbark hull scraped along the ground. Pippit, jolted awake, croaked in alarm.

"Why are you stopping?" Birdie asked crossly. Her
nose was pink with sunburn and she was thirsty. "What's
the matter?"

"Look," Tad said in a stricken voice. "That's what happened to our water, Birdie."

"What is it?" Birdie finally asked in an awed whisper.

Pondleweed answered, "It's a dam."

"A . . . beaver dam?" asked Birdie uncertainly.

Pondleweed silently shook his head.

"Beavers don't build dams like that, puddlehead," Tad said. "They build dams out of sticks."

The dam stretched solidly across the mouth of the stream. It was massive, wide and tall, built from layer after layer of roughly shaped and chiseled stones. The cracks between the stones were wedged with twigs, leaves, and muddy clay, creating a watertight seal. Across the top of the dam, a row of sharply pointed stones had been set on end. The stones loomed ominously above them, black against the sky, looking like jagged teeth. A Remember jolted Tad. *I've seen stones like this before,* he thought. *Stone towers. Where were they?*

"What could have built it?" Birdie asked, craning her neck to gaze upward.

"I don't know," Pondleweed said slowly. He pulled off his broad-brimmed hat and ran his fingers through his hair. "I don't know."

Tad was feeling more jumpy by the minute. He felt as if something were watching him, holding its breath, waiting to pounce. Even the air felt different here. It was heavy, menacing. But wherever he looked, all was empty and silent. Nothing stirred, not so much as a beetlebug or a riffle of wind. Birdie's eyes were wide and dark and she was biting her lip.

"I'm scared," Birdie said in a small voice.

Pondleweed laid down his paddle and stepped out of the boat, splashing into the shallow water. He seized the boat by its bow and shoved it firmly out of the stream, up onto the dry rocks of the shore. Then he stepped back and looked up consideringly at the stream bank high above his head.

"I'm going to climb up there," he said. "I want to see what's on the other side of the dam. You youngers wait here. You'll be perfectly safe, Birdie. I'll try not to take too long."

"I want to go with you," Tad said quickly. He *didn't* want to see what was on the other side of the dam. But he didn't want to stay behind either, not with this creepy feeling of eyes on the back of his neck.

"Me too," said Birdie. "I don't like it here. I don't want to stay and wait all by myself."

Pippit rolled his eyes back and forth, looking from one to the other, and bleated piteously.

"He wants to go too," Tad said. "Look at him begging."

Pondleweed sighed in resignation. "All right," he said. "All of you follow me. But be very careful. Once we get up near the top, it's a long way to fall down."

He dug his webbed toes into a narrow ledge in the side of the bank and grabbed an overhanging root with both hands. He pulled himself up, then fumbled with his toes for another foothold. Tad and Birdie followed close behind him, Pippit clinging clammily to Tad's back. Fishers were quick and agile climbers. Their webbed toes could grip the tiniest cracks and crevices. They climbed like tree frogs scrambling up the rough bark of trees. Hand over hand and foot over foot they went, clinging to rocks and roots and tufts of dried grass. Finally they heaved themselves, one by one, over the top of the bank. Pondleweed and Tad bent to help Birdie, who was last. Then they turned and stared. Pippit gave one horrified croak, closed his eyes, and huddled behind Tad's back.

On the far side of the dam was a broad lake—but a lake like nothing Tad had ever seen before. The water was utterly still, thick, motionless, and black. Nothing green grew near it. The grass beside it was brown and brittle; the bushes bare and leafless. Shriveled blossoms and berries dangled from blackened vines. At the lake's edge, shattered stumps of dead trees and twisted branches poked above the water. There was a withered thicket of dead reeds and cattails, their stems cracked and brown. Broken fish bones and dead dried fish with flat staring eyes were washed up along the shore. A dead sparrow, its beak wide open, was half buried in black mud. Birdie gave a frightened gasp. There was the skeleton of a squirrel, its bones bleached white, its eye sockets gaping empty, and beyond it the curled white fingers of what looked horribly like a Fisher hand.

"What a terrible place," Birdie said in a trembling voice.

"An evil place," Pondleweed said. His face looked pinched and angry—and frightened, Tad realized with a shock. He had never seen his father frightened before.

Tad's mouth was dry, and his knees felt weak and strange. Something awful lived in that lake. And it was watching them. He knew it. *Who's there?* he shouted in his mind, but nothing answered.

He turned to tell his father about the feeling—*could Birdie and Pondleweed feel it too?* he wondered—but Pondleweed was no longer standing beside him. He was heading toward the dam.

"Where are you going?" Tad called. His voice sounded high and thin. He cleared his throat and tried again. "What are you going to do?"

"This dam is trapping our water," Pondleweed said tightly, without slowing his stride. "And I am going to pull it down."

Tad and Birdie hurried to catch up with him. Tad tripped awkwardly over Pippit, who, in an effort to keep Tad between himself and the black lake, was hopping nervously and closely underfoot. Pippit squawked.

Birdie tugged at Pondleweed's tunic sleeve. "But how can you pull it down?" she protested. "It's so enormous."

Pondleweed paused for a moment. "We don't have to pull the whole dam down," he said gently. "I'm just going to try to make a hole in it. Just enough for the water to come through." He put a hand on the top of Birdie's head and ruffled her hair. "Like the story of the Busy Muskrat, remember?"

The Busy Muskrat had been a favorite of Birdie's when she was little. She nodded. "There was a flood that filled the muskrat hole with mud, and all the little muskrats were trapped inside," she said. She sounded brighter and more like herself. "But the Busy Muskrat chipped and chipped away at the mud, and dug and dug, and pretty soon there was a hole, and the little muskrats all swam out into the big pond. . . ."

"Exactly," Pondleweed said. He took a deep breath and squared his shoulders. "And that's just what we're going to do. We're going to chip."

He continued determinedly toward the dam, with Birdie close at his heels. Tad trailed behind them, still entangled with an agitated Pippit. He had never liked the Busy Muskrat. It was a dull stickmud story. All that chipping until *one* little muskrat swam free, then more chipping and *another* little muskrat, and on and on. Chip. Dumb little muskrat. Chip. Dumb little muskrat.

Tad paused, gulping nervously. *Muskrats* . . . He shook the thought away. There was real danger here. What was the matter with Pondleweed and Birdie? Couldn't they feel it?

Pondleweed and Birdie had clambered onto the top of the dam. Tad followed reluctantly, threading his way cautiously between the black fanglike stones. Now that he was closer, he could see that the stones were carved, each with the image of a swimming fish. At least they might have been fish. Monster fish. They all had round bulgy eyes and big grinning mouths full of wickedly pointed teeth. The teeth were inlaid with little pieces of silvery mica that made them glitter.

Tad edged away from the hideous fish-monsters and gingerly peered down over the edge of the dam. On one side was the lake with its frightening black water; on the other, a steep drop to the rocky bed of the drying river. If I had to jump, Tad decided grimly, I'd jump off on the river side. I'd rather smash onto those rocks than dive into that black water. The very thought of touching the lake water was somehow horrible.

Pondleweed and Birdie, in Busy Muskrat fashion, were scrabbling determinedly at the packing between the stones of the dam wall, scraping away at the mud, tugging out twigs, flattened brush, and crumbled leaves. A handful of pebbles, yanked free, bounced and clattered, then vanished with a scattering of dull plops into the dark water. Pondleweed gave a grunt and a great heaving shove and managed to dislodge a stone. It tottered, toppled slowly, then splashed heavily into the black lake and sank from sight. Birdie waved her arms in the air and gave a piping cheer.

Tad winced. *She shouldn't,* he thought. *We should be really quiet. We shouldn't make any more noise than we have to.*

He poked Birdie in the back. "*Hush,*" he whispered. "Don't be so loud."

Birdie turned to stare at him in outraged surprise. "I don't see what difference it makes," she said. "There's nobody here. And that *hurt*. You don't have to poke at a person like that."

Pondleweed began to chip away at another stone. Tad stared at the heaving black spot where the first stone had fallen. The lake below him roiled and bubbled. It looked like an oily black cauldron, a dark and evil-smelling witch's brew. The feeling of being watched was almost overpowering. *There is something here,* Tad thought in a panic. *And it's coming closer. It heard Birdie yelling.*

And then the scene before his eyes changed. He felt as if an enormous wave had washed over him, tumbling his mind around and around like a pebble caught in the current of a stream. He floundered, blinded and gasping. When he opened his eyes, he was standing on a polished tile floor. He was in the middle of a great room—a throne room—and he was underwater, in the dark depths, far beyond the reach of the warming sun. Three doorways led out of the room, each hung with bead curtains of glimmering black pearls. He strode forward, naked sword in hand, moving slowly through the water.

At the far end of the room was a square stone chair, its back and arms richly studded with amethysts and aquamarines. On its seat lay a glimmering white crystal, shining softly with an inner light. There was no one else in the room. Then someone spoke to him, mind touching mind, in a clear silver voice edged with anger and fear.

You shall not have it, Sagamore!

In two more steps he reached the throne and bent to pick the crystal up. Tad watched as his hand, looking strangely disembodied and distorted through the dark water, closed around it. And then the voice began to sing. The song was infinitely sweet and seductive, a heavy drugging music like enchanted honey or poisoned strawberry wine. He looked down at the gleaming crystal clutched in his hand and struggled to remember: *Why did I want this? What is it? What am I doing here?* Slowly he raised his sword. . . .

Somewhere, far in the distance, someone was shouting his name.

"Tad!" the new voice shouted. "Tad! Tad! *Tad!*"

An urgent hand tugged at his arm. The throne room vanished.

Birdie, her face pale, was yanking on his elbow and pointing desperately toward a thick tangle of dead brush and withered cattails that stood in the black lake's shallows. Something was moving about inside it. There was a slithering sound and ripples began to fan out through the dark water. Several of the innermost cattail stalks began to thrash wildly back and forth. Pippit, on the shore, croaked frantically.

"There's something wrong with Father!" Birdie shouted.

Pondleweed was gazing blankly out across the black lake, his eyes round and wide. His face wore a strange expression, an intent *listening* expression, as if he were straining to hear someone calling to him from very far away. His ears tilted slowly forward, then back.

Pippit croaked furiously.

"Father?" said Tad uncertainly.

"Do you hear it?" Pondleweed said. His voice was slow and blurred. "Do you hear the music? The pearl-shell harps and coral pipes? And the singing? Can't you hear her singing?"

And Tad could hear it. It was the same song he had heard in the blue-lit throne room, but fainter now and less compelling. *She's no longer singing to me,* he realized.

The Witch can catch but one fish at a time.

The phrase leaped into his brain as if he had known it all along.

Else she would not need servants.

Pondleweed began to walk rapidly across the top of the dam, moving back toward the shore. He brushed by the children as if they were invisible.

"Father! Where are you *going*?" cried Birdie in alarm.

Pondleweed never paused. He strode past, unhearing, climbed off the dam, and skirted the cattail thicket, heading blindly toward the black water. He walked stiff-legged, as if he were a puppet pulled on strings. He splashed right into the dark lake. Black ripples sloshed over his feet.

Pippit's croaking rose to a wail.

"Father! What are you doing!" screamed Birdie.

"Father! *Stop!*" shrieked Tad. "Come back! Don't go in there!"

Pondleweed never faltered. Steadily he continued to walk into the black lake, his face slack and empty of expression, his eyes staring. The black water reached his ankles, his knees, his waist. In the cattail thicket, something rustled slyly. A thick black bubble rose to the water's surface and broke.

Tad, dragging Birdie by one arm, flung himself off the dam and raced across the black shore. Bones and dead branches snapped under his feet. He was shouting his father's name. He threw himself forward, splashing madly into the inky water. Behind him, he heard Birdie sobbing.

"Tad! He's gone!"

Pondleweed had disappeared. Not even a ripple showed on the thick black surface of the water to show where he had been.

Tad took another step forward.

"I can save him!" he shouted, turning back to Birdie. "I'll swim out—"

Birdie screamed.

Her scream was echoed, long and louder, in the sky high above them. Plummeting toward them, lethal talons open wide, was the monstrous form of a hunting bird.

7

THE DRYAD

"Run!" Tad shouted. "Run! Birdie, *run!*"

There was, Tad knew, no escape from a stooping hawk, but anything was better than crouching frozen on the ground, waiting helplessly to be slaughtered. Birdie fled across the barren shore toward the too-distant forest, with Pippit pelting at her side. Tad sprang after them.

But he was too late. The hawk was upon him. The wind of its killing dive was so violent that Tad was thrown forward on his face, skidding painfully across the rough rock and sand. Behind him there was a thunderous impact that shook the ground and an earsplitting shriek of triumph. Tad, scrambling to his feet, gaped in astonishment at the hawk rising into the air. It clutched in its talons a great black snake with flaming red eyes. The snake writhed and hissed in its captor's grasp, immense fangs bared—and then suddenly went limp, dangling heavily from the hawk's claws like a thick black leather rope.

As Tad stood, staring, the hawk dropped the snake. Or rather flung it down, hard, to lie limply motionless on the lakeshore. The bird hung in the air above the snake's body, wings outspread, looking after it in what seemed to be disgust. Then it shrieked again, a lower-pitched cry, and swooped toward Tad, flaring its immense red-and-brown wings. Tad stumbled back. The bird retreated, then swooped once more, screaming angrily. The air thundered as it dived low over Tad's head. It turned and circled, preparing for another dive. *It's as if it's driving me away,* Tad thought, frightened and puzzled. *Why doesn't it just kill me? I've never seen a hawk behave like this before.*

The hawk screamed and rocketed toward him again. Tad turned and ran. He tore through tangles of leafless vines, stumbled over rocks, and shoved his way through withered grass clumps. Thorns scratched and caught at his hair. He ran until he reached the sheltering safety of the forest, where he found Birdie and Pippit huddled together on the ground at the foot of a gigantic oak tree. He dropped down heavily beside them, his heart hammering in his chest and his breath coming in painful gasps.

Birdie had been crying. Her eyes were red and puffy and her voice was choked with tears.

"I thought the hawk had caught you," she said.

Tad shook his head. He still couldn't understand what had happened. "It saved us," he said. He had to stop to pant between words. "The hawk saved us, Birdie. That thing thrashing around in the cattails—it was a snake. An enormous snake, like nothing I ever saw before. The hawk just fell on it and killed it. It must have broken its back."

"Maybe it didn't even see us," Birdie said. "Hawks kill people. They're one of the Four Great Dangers." Her voice trembled as she counted on her fingers. "One: hunting birds. Two: weasels. Three: watersnakes. And four: foxes."

"It saw us, all right," Tad said. "At least, it saw me. It chased me. It could have grabbed me, but it didn't. It just chased me, as though it were trying to make me run into the woods. Away from the water."

The water. His eyes stung with sudden tears. He had never imagined anything so terrible as his father walking past him, vanishing into that black lake. Being left to drown.

What will we do now? he thought. *How can we live without Pondleweed?* And then, *How will we get home?*

Suddenly there was a sound of running feet. A pair of gray squirrels came streaking across the forest floor, chasing each other through the leaves, leaping up tree trunks and springing back down again. Their tails bobbed up and down behind them like huge fluffy plumes. They skidded to a halt beside the children. Then, in unison, they sat up on their hind legs, peering down at Tad and Birdie with blinking bright eyes. They looked almost like twins, though one had a reddish cast to its fur and the other — the grayer of the two — had bigger ears. Together they tipped their heads back and forth, first one way and then the other. Then, in a flash of fur, they turned and swarmed up the trunk of the mammoth oak. Tad could hear them overhead, thrashing about in the branches. There was a loud thumping noise, followed by an outraged screech.

Tad and Birdie exchanged startled glances.

The screech resolved itself into words. Someone high above them sounded angry.

"What do you want *now*?" shrieked the voice. "Get out of my flower pots, you great stump-thumpers! How many times have I told you—"

The voice abruptly grew less strident. "Oh. Oh, I see. On the ground? Right now?"

More rustling. Tad and Birdie, squinting, looked upward. Leaves parted and a face, wearing a definitely cross expression, appeared. The face—brown and wrinkled as a dried-apple doll—belonged to a little woman in a full-skirted dress pieced together from tiny scraps and patches in many shades of green. The dress seemed to change color as she moved, shifting imperceptibly from yellow-green to leaf-green to olive, and then to a rich dark color that was almost brown. Her hair was as tangled and wild as a bird's nest and her eyes were a startlingly brilliant robin's-egg blue.

"Well?" she demanded. "What do you want? Who are *you*?"

"I'm Tad," Tad said. He hastily remembered his manners. "I mean, Tadpole of the Fisher Tribe. This is my sister, Redbird. Birdie. And the frog is Pippit. We live at Willow-tree Pond at the bottom of the stream. The northernmost of the Ponds."

He started to point in the proper direction and then stopped, confused.

"I'm not sure where it is anymore," he confessed. "We were running. . . ."

A furry squirrel face poked out, one on either side of the little green lady. Both wore eager expressions of bright curiosity.

"Don't mind them," the woman said. "They don't like to miss anything that's going on." She looked sternly from one squirrel to the other. "Nosy parkers," she said. "Snoops. Pair of peeping Toms." The grayer squirrel chittered at her.

She turned back to Tad. "Go on," she said. "You were running . . ."

"There was a hawk," Birdie said. She stopped and turned to Tad. "You tell it," she said. "Begin at the beginning. With the pond."

"Yes," the green woman said. "Do." She sat down on the branch, folded her hands in her lap, and crossed her ankles. One foot began to wiggle back and forth impatiently. "Well?"

"Our pond is drying," Tad began, hesitantly. "The water level just keeps dropping and dropping. It fell so much that our father was worried, so he decided to take our boat upstream to see if he could find anything wrong. He let us go with him. Me and Birdie and Pippit."

The reddish squirrel, never taking its eyes off Tad, began to gnaw busily on an acorn. Its teeth made a loud grating sound. Tad raised his voice.

"It was a long trip," he said. "We had to camp overnight along the way, and we met some Hunters. They had seen the Drying too. Only they just call it the Dry. The hunting was poor, they said, and the animals thin and few."

The grayer squirrel chittered angrily. The green woman poked it.

"Then"—to Tad's dismay he felt his eyes begin to sting and his throat tighten—"then we found what we were looking for. Something—someone—had built a dam up at the top of the stream, where all the water comes from. Behind the dam, the lake . . ."

Birdie started to cry again. "The lake was horrible. The water was black and all filled with bones," she sobbed. "And our father just walked into it. He said he heard someone singing, and he walked right into the water and disappeared."

The green woman's face filled with sympathy and sorrow, then with misgiving, and finally with something that looked like shock.

"Singing? What did it sound like?"

Birdie opened her mouth and then closed it, looking puzzled. "Like harps, Father said, and . . . coral pipes." She looked blankly at Tad. "But I couldn't hear it. I didn't hear anything at all."

"The Witch can only catch one fish at a time," Tad said without thinking.

There was a sudden pause. The green woman went silent and still, staring at Tad. The squirrels looked up, startled, beside her, and the reddish squirrel stopped chewing.

"No more she can," the green woman said slowly. She studied Tad, frowning, her brilliant blue eyes narrowed. Then she seemed to reach some decision.

"Wait right there," she said. She pushed the crowding squirrels aside and vanished backward into the leaves.

Birdie tugged at Tad's tunic sleeve.

"*What* Witch?" she demanded.

Tad shook his head helplessly. Nothing made sense.

With a rapid whickering sound, a rope ladder came down, unrolling itself dizzily until it reached the children's feet. The rope was made of twisted vines, braided, knotted, and then braided again.

"Climb up!" the voice screeched from overhead. "Bring your frog!"

Birdie, with a nervous look over her shoulder at Tad, set one bare foot on the lowest rung and cautiously began to climb. Tad followed, with Pippit clinging tightly to his back. It was a long and tiring climb, high into the very heart of the great tree. About halfway up, Pippit, who didn't like heights, began to make nervous wheepling noises. At last—just as it seemed that they were going to have to go on climbing forever—they scrambled out onto a broad branch and found themselves at the door of a house.

The house, invisible from the ground, was firmly anchored in a crotch where two broad branches met the oak's immense trunk. It was built of notched sticks, tightly fitted together, the crevices between them packed with clay. It had a steeply pointed thatched roof, windows hung with green curtains, a window box planted with pale blue forget-me-nots, and a braided grass doormat. As they stared, the door flew open with a bang, and a voice screeched from inside. "Come in!"

Tad pried the clinging Pippit off his back, which was difficult because Pippit had his eyes squeezed tightly shut and was refusing to let go. They wiped their feet carefully on the doormat—Pippit, protesting, was made to wipe twice—and stepped over the threshold. The green woman—Tad realized that she had never told them her name—was busying herself at a small wooden table, pouring out mugs of maple water from a baked-clay pitcher and cutting generous slices from a frosted cake on a round bark platter. The cake had a whole half of a cherry on the top and looked delicious.

"Sit down and eat," she snapped. "Things always look better on a full stomach."

She handed the children laden plates.

"And when you've finished, we will talk. And then we will decide what to do next. Clean your plates!"

Tad's stomach rumbled embarrassingly, and he suddenly realized that he was starving. He hadn't had anything to eat since breakfast, and that had only been a half slice of rootbread. He took an enormous bite of cherry cake. There were no sounds for several minutes but those of chewing and swallowing. When the plates were empty, the green woman helped them to some more. At last they laid down their forks and sat back. Birdie, looking guilty, began to lick her fingers. Pondleweed was strict about finger licking. Their mother, he said, would never have approved of it.

Tad was puzzled. The Fishers lived on the shores of streams and ponds; the Hunters never stayed long in any one place; and the Diggers—at least so everyone said— lived in burrows in the ground. He'd never known that any of the Tribes lived high in the branches of the trees. "Which Tribe do you belong to?" Tad asked.

The green woman shook her head slowly and gave him a pitying look. Tad felt at once that he'd said something irreparably stupid. "My kind came long before the Tribes," she said. "I am a Dryad."

"A Dryad?" Birdie repeated blankly.

The green woman's voice sharpened. "Yes," she snapped. "A Dryad. *Dry-ad*. A Tree Witch."

The woman's name, the children learned, was Treeglyn. She also told them the names of the squirrels, Flicktail and Scooter, and of her tree, the giant oak, a long complicated word filled with bird whistles and wind sounds. Birdie gaped at her.

"Trees have *names*?" she asked. She sounded as if she didn't believe it. "Real names?"

"Of course they have real names," Treeglyn squawked irritably. Her normal speaking voice, Tad thought, sounded like an outraged crow. "What else would a tree have? You can't just call them all *Tree,* can you, as if one were just the same as another? How would you like it if people just called you *Girl* or *Boy?*"

Birdie shook her head. "I wouldn't," she said.

"A tree learns its name on the day it first opens its leaves to the wind," Treeglyn explained. Her crow voice dropped lower and softened; her words took on a rhythm as if she were reciting a familiar poem. "Forever after when the wind rustles its leaves and branches, the tree repeats its name. The forest is full of the names of trees. Some names are so old that your great-great-grandfather must have heard them spoken. Some are so new that they were heard for the first time just yesterday."

Birdie's eyes were round. "Our willow must have a name, Tad," she whispered.

"The old willow by the northernmost pond?" Tree-glyn demanded. "Of course." She spoke another word in the strange windlike language, a name with quick little lilts in it that reminded Tad of the thin green points of willow leaves. The wind words were oddly familiar some-how, as if he had heard them sometime long ago, perhaps when he was a baby. He felt as if any minute he would begin to understand them.

"Lawillawissowellowellomore."

"I wish I had a tree name," Birdie said wistfully.

"You do," Treeglyn said. "Redbird. *Roossoollaweralliss.*" It sounded like flute notes and whispers. "You have a feel for trees, you do, girl. Now and again the New People are born with a touch of green blood."

"Roossoo . . . ," said Birdie.

"The old willow," Treeglyn said at the same time. "Remember to give her my best wishes when you return home again. Is she doing well?"

"I don't know," Tad said. All their terrible troubles suddenly returned to him, like a great black flood. He ached to have Pondleweed back again. Pondleweed would have known what to do next, how to make everything right again. "If this is a Drying Time, like my father said—"

"Father said our tree could die," Birdie said. "He said that the pond could vanish and the whole world turn to dust."

Pippit gave a dismal croak. Treeglyn was silent for a moment.

"The forest is also drying," she said finally. "The trees grow brown and the saplings are dying. The squirrels have brought stories, but I have failed to heed them. I have been a fool not to understand."

"Understand?" Tad asked.

Treeglyn's face for a moment looked old and tired, and her piercing blue eyes were dim.

Then she said, "The Nixies are awake."

8

TREEGLYN'S STORY

It was morning. Treeglyn had refused to explain more on the previous night, saying that it was too long a story to begin when they were all so tired. Instead she had made them a bed on the tree-house floor and left them alone in the deepening dusk.

Tad had thought that he would never be able to sleep, perched up in the air as he was with so much *nothing* underneath him, but instead, worn out by fear and grief, he had slept deep and dreamlessly. He would have slept even more if he had not been wakened by Treeglyn, shrieking out the window at the squirrels.

Treeglyn laid down her spoon—they were having acorn porridge for breakfast—and ran her fingers through her bird's-nest hair, making its tangles stand even more on end.

"So you've never heard of the Nixies?" she said.

"We know a little about the Witches," Tad said tentatively. "In the Very Beginning, before the coming of the Tribes, there were Witches. The Old Folk."

Every Fisher child was taught how Great Rune had shaped the world, scooping out the ponds and streams with his giant Digging Stick and filling them with water from his starry river in the sky. He had made all the people and animals, too, putting them together from pond mud and then breathing on them with his warm green breath to make them come alive. He had made the Witches first, and then the animals, and finally the Tribes. But the Witches had vanished long ago—though every once in a while, Pondleweed said, if you were very lucky, you might come upon one still, and if you were luckier yet, they might give you a magic gift, like a spider-web tunic that made you invisible or mouse-fur boots that let you cross a whole forest in a single stride. But you should never eat the Witches' food or enter their houses, because when you came out again, it could be hundreds of years later and all your family and friends would be gone. . . .

Tad looked up guiltily.

"Father used to tell us a story about the Witches," Birdie was saying. "They lived in the skunk-cabbage patch and gave people wishes."

Treeglyn glared at her so fiercely that Pippit gave a nervous croak. Tad hastily pretended that his mouth was full of porridge.

"Skunk-cabbage patch indeed," Treeglyn said huffily.

"It was just a story," Birdie said.

"Malignant misrepresentation," Treeglyn snapped. She rapped her porridge spoon sharply on the table. "There were three races of Witches," she continued, very slowly and deliberately as if speaking, Tad thought, to persons who were very stupid. "The Dryads, the Witches of the

Trees. The Kobolds, the Witches of the Mountains. And the Nixies, the Witches of the Waters. Does this sound familiar?"

"I don't think so," Tad said uncomfortably. "Father just said Witches."

Treeglyn sighed. Her shoulders slumped, and her wild hair seemed to wilt.

"No, of course not," she muttered, almost to herself. "It's only to be expected. It was so long ago. I forget how old I am."

"How old are you?" asked Birdie.

Tad nudged her. It was a question Pondleweed said they were never supposed to ask. At least not of olders. But Treeglyn didn't seem to mind.

"So old," she said. "I remember the forest that grew here before this one, and the forest before that. I remember the sprouting of the first trees. I was here when the world was young, when the mountains were building, when the singing in the water was joyful and sweet as the song of new birds."

She gazed out the little window for a moment, looking over the children's heads. Her eyes sparkled with tears, and the room was suddenly swept with a smell of wet leaves and rain. Then, in her tree voice—a voice as gentle as spring wind in the branches—she began to speak.

"This is how it all began," Treeglyn said. "Long ago in the Very Beginning, so the story goes, Great Rune, the Sun-and-Rain God, was lonesome, so he decided to make a world. From the pouch he carried on his starry belt, he took a handful of magic Stones. He spread the Stones out on his great green hand and saw that he held the Earthstones. The Earthstones were brown crystals striped with red and black, and from within them came the sound of rumbling earthquakes and crackling flames. When Great Rune threw them in the air, they grew larger and larger and they crashed and smashed and fused themselves together. They formed the round ball of the Earth itself, with all its mountains and valleys and rocks of the ground."

Birdie slipped off her chair to lie on her stomach on the floor, webbed feet waving in the air, gazing up at Treeglyn. Tad pushed his plate aside and leaned forward, resting his chin on his hands.

"Then," Treeglyn continued, "Great Rune drew out the Waterstones. These were pure white crystals threaded with veins of silver, and when you held them to your ear, you could hear the sound of running water. When Great Rune threw them in the air, they burst apart in a great spray of white-and-silver fragments and formed all the lakes and rivers, the streams and brooks, the ponds and waterfalls.

"And finally from his pouch, Great Rune took out the Lifestones. These crystals were as green as grass, and from within them came the sound of rustling leaves. Great Rune crumbled the Lifestones to powder in his green hands and scattered the powder all over the new Earth.

And everywhere that powder fell, living things were born. The animals came into being, and the plants grew up: the trees and the bushes, the thickets and the grasses, the wildflowers and the climbing vines.

"But there were three Stones left over."

Treeglyn paused and Tad held his breath. Suddenly he knew somehow that this story was very important.

"What happened to the three?" he whispered.

"Great Rune gave them to the First Peoples," Treeglyn said. "The Earthstone he gave to the Kobolds, the Gray Men, the Witches of the Mountains, that the rock of the Earth would stand ever firm beneath us. The Lifestone he gave to the Dryads, the Witches of the Trees, that the world would grow green and fruitful. And the Waterstone he gave to the silver-eyed Nixies, that the lakes and streams would fill to brimming and the rains would fall. And the Witches promised that they would guard the Stones faithfully and use them well."

"And the ponds," added Birdie anxiously. "The Waterstone would keep the ponds full too."

"And the ponds," agreed Treeglyn.

Her voice grew deeper and darker. Tad felt a shadow fall over the story, like the shadow cast by a great fish swimming above him in bright water.

"All was well for many hundreds of sun turns. The trees grew tall under the hands of the Dryads; the animals ate well and prospered. The New People, the people of the three Tribes, appeared and built dwellings and raised families. For a time all flourished and lived together in peace. Then slowly, slowly, over the long centuries the Witches grew old and tired. The Kobolds, one by one, fell into a doze in the depths of their mountains; the Dryads sank into sleep in the hearts of their great trees. Finally only the Nixies remained, and they, left too long to themselves, forgot their promise. They grew greedy. Why, they asked, should they share their water? And they began to use the powers of the Waterstone to capture all the world's water for themselves. The ponds and streams and rivers emptied; the forests and meadows withered and turned brown; the Earth grew burned and dusty; and the people began to die of thirst."

Tad sat up straighter.

"So then what happened?" Birdie asked. "Where were you? What did you do? Couldn't you take the Stone away from them?"

Treeglyn shook her head.

"When a Stone is in its proper place," she said, "only its proper keepers may touch it. There's a sort of protection mechanism, to keep the Stones from being stolen. And besides"—a defensive note crept into her voice—"I was asleep. Everything was going so well. It seemed a good time to catch a bit of a nap—"

A chittering of squirrels sounded outside. Treeglyn raised her voice.

"Everybody makes mistakes!" she shouted.

She turned back to Tad and Birdie.

"Even Witches have their human side," she said. Her tone of voice indicated that a human side was a great cross to bear. "Which is why Great Rune sent the Sagamore."

Tad's heart gave a lurch. "The Sagamore?"

"The Sagamore is a sort of balance wheel," Treeglyn said. "When things get out of joint, when *some* Witches cease to do their duty"—she gave an outraged sniff—"the Sagamore has the power to set things right. He or she—or it, for that matter—can confiscate the Stones. Take them from the wrongdoers and set them to do their proper work again. And the Witches can't do a thing about it. They can't harm him (or her or it). Not directly, anyway."

"Which is it?" asked Birdie. "What do you mean, 'him or her or it'? What kind of *it*? Doesn't it have to be one or the other?"

"It doesn't," Treeglyn said sharply. "Because it's neither. The Sagamore is a Mind. It passes from bearer to bearer, always watching, waiting to be needed. Many have carried it, some knowing, some not."

She drew a deep breath. "It's not called out by everyday troubles, you understand. You're expected to deal with *those* on your own." She gave the children an accusing look, and Tad tried to look apologetic, even though he didn't think he'd done anything wrong. "The Sagamore only wakes when the peril is great, when the old powers meet and battle, when"—her voice dropped to a portentous whisper—"when all is nearly lost."

"You mean the Mind just crawls into your head?" Birdie asked, horrified. "Like a bloodworm? It could be there inside you and you wouldn't even feel it?"

"It's a gift!" Treeglyn snapped. "An *honor*!"

"So what happened all that time ago?" Tad asked quickly before Birdie could say anything else. "Did the Sagamore come and get the Stone?"

"So they *said*," Treeglyn screeched. "But by the time anyone thought to wake me, it was all long over. My sisters were gone; the Kobolds were gone; and the Nixies were gone, too, or wherever they were, they weren't talking. *Not*," she added sharply, "that I would have tried to speak to them anyway, seeing how they had behaved."

She ran her fingers through her wild hair, making it stand up in a tangle around her face. She had long, curiously bent fingers, Tad noticed, like twigs.

"The folk of the forest spoke of a great hero, but no one — you creatures are so short-lived — quite remembered who or what he was. By the time anyone thought to tell *me* anything, the Nixies had gone dormant, like apple trees, and the Waterstone was nowhere to be found."

Her wild hair crackled and her voice grew more annoyed.

"One slips off for a refreshing nap . . . a matter of a few centuries or so. . . ."

"A few *centuries*?" Tad repeated.

"It doesn't do to sleep too long," Treeglyn said reprovingly. "Too long and you sleep deep and deeper until you forget about waking altogether. You *change*. The tree rings wrap around and around you, layer upon layer; the bark grows over you and covers your eyes. . . ."

"So why didn't the Nixies just stay asleep?" Tad demanded. "Don't *they* change?"

"They fight it," said Treeglyn shortly. "Fight it, claw and scale. You don't catch *them* settling for sleep when they could be up and about and making mischief. Grab-snatchers, every one of them, hunkering down at the bottom of their water, waiting for their next chance."

"So they must have gotten their Stone back again," Birdie said, "if they're awake now and taking all the water."

Treeglyn gave a wild pig–like snort.

"It was never *their* Stone," she snapped. "It was a sacred trust. *They* tried to make it *their* Stone, which was where all the trouble began. Some things are not meant to be owned."

Birdie began to bite her lip, which meant, Tad knew, that she was thinking.

"So if the Nixies have *the* Stone back," she said carefully, "what happens next? What can we do?"

Treeglyn studied Tad, then Birdie, then Tad again, frowning.

"There's a reason that you're here, you two," she said. "A reason you came to the black lake and then here to my tree. You'll see. It will all become clearer to you as you go along."

"I think," she said finally, "that next you should go see Witherwood."

"Who's Witherwood?" Birdie asked.

Treeglyn ran her fingers through her hair again, which sprang up like bird straw, wilder than ever.

"They say his mother was a Dryad," she said, "and if that's true, he's half a Witch, which may explain why he is as he is. He's wise, Witherwood is; I'll say that for him. There's not much he doesn't know. Though"—Treeglyn's voice spiraled upward suddenly in a squawk—"what he chooses to tell may be another story. Still, Rune willing, you'll get good advice from him."

She hesitated for a moment, gazing at the children with a worried frown. "I wish I could go with you," she said, "but of course I can't."

"Why can't you?" Birdie asked.

"Dryads," Treeglyn said impatiently, "cannot leave their trees. If we try, we die. It's like taking a fish out of water, though it takes longer. First we grow breathless and irritable." Tad had a sudden terrible desire to giggle. *How would anyone notice?* he wondered. "Then there are headaches and digestive upsets. Then lethargy. And then we just fade away altogether. But you'll be fine on your own. You look a capable pair."

She eyed Tad and Birdie up and down.

"Stop slouching!" she snapped suddenly.

Hastily Tad and Birdie straightened their backs, and Pippit, croaking nervously, did his best to straighten his.

"Now that you've decided what to do," Treeglyn said briskly, "best to be on your way. The sooner you take the first step, the sooner you'll reach the last; that's what I always say."

Birdie's eyes widened in surprise. It was one of Pondleweed's sayings.

Treeglyn sprang to her feet and stamped across the floor toward the door. "Wait there!" she snapped.

The door banged shut behind her.

"What do you think she's doing?" Birdie whispered. "Chasing away the squirrels?"

The door slammed open—*Pondleweed would never approve of the way Treeglyn handles doors,* Tad thought— and the Dryad reappeared. She was limping and her face was tight with pain. In her hand, she carried a short stick of rich brown wood.

"Oak," she said briefly. She thrust it into Tad's hand. It was warm and smelled sweetly of saps and resins. Faint patterns were traced on it. They looked, when he looked closely, like ripples of wild hair and the almost invisible features of a face. Tad looked up at Treeglyn, startled.

"Keep it safe," she snapped. "And keep it with you. You may need it."

"You've hurt yourself!" Birdie cried. "What happened?"

Treeglyn pressed her lips tight and shook her head. It was clear that whatever had happened, she wasn't going to talk about it. She hobbled painfully across the room

to an alcove that held a little wooden bed made of art-
fully bent and woven branches. The bed was covered with
a green-and-brown patchwork quilt. Treeglyn reached
beneath it and pulled out a small basket. "I'll pack some
food for your journey!" she screeched.

With Treeglyn's last shrieked admonishments — "Pick
up your feet! Don't slouch! No loitering now!" — still
ringing in their ears, they walked in single file along a
dusty little forest path heading east. First came Tad, then
Birdie, and finally Pippit, hopping excitedly and treading
much too close to Birdie's heels. Every few minutes he
hopped into the backs of Birdie's legs, which made her
stumble and say "Stay *back,* Pippit!" and Pippit would
look sulky.

"Is she always like that, do you suppose?" Birdie
asked. "*Stop it,* Pippit! Treeglyn, I mean. So . . . bossy and
snappy?"

A Remember flickered in Tad's head. A wisp of a
conversation shared. What had they been talking about?
A voice heavy with resignation. *"Dryads!"* it said. "It's
always hurry up, stay in line, shoulders back, and stand up
straighter! I can't think where they get it! It must come
of living among tree trunks." Someone else — was it his
voice? — laughed.

"I guess she is," Tad said. "But she was nice too. I
liked her."

"I did too," Birdie said. "I wish she would teach me
how to speak her language. The tree language."

Lamallalanga. The word popped unbidden into Tad's head.

"You could ask her," he said. "If we see her again."

He picked up his pace. "We should try to walk faster, Birdie. Treeglyn said it was a long way, and we want to get there before dark."

9

THE STONE CIRCLE

It soon became clear that they would never reach Witherwood's house before dark. Traveling became increasingly
difficult. The path before Tad, Birdie, and Pippit was
clogged with fallen branches and thickly overgrown with
brambles and blackberry vines studded with knife-sized
thorns. They struggled along, pushing their way through
twisted masses of tendrils and snarls of twining branches.
Now it was not so much a matter of walking as of crawling to wiggle under things, climbing to scramble over
things, and sometimes squirming desperately to squeeze
in between. Thorns tore at their fringed tunics. Birdie
tripped over a twist of creeping woodbine and went
sprawling, skinning both her knees. Tad's hands were
striped with bloody scratches. Pippit, who had stamped
on a particularly nasty bramble, was limping. Tad desperately missed Pondleweed. If only his father were here to
tell them what to do. He had never felt so alone.

By the time the path grew clear again, the light was
growing dimmer and long shadows stretched across the
forest floor.

"How much farther is it?" Birdie wanted to know. Her
knees stung with every step.

Tad shook his head. What had Treeglyn said? A three-hour walk, she'd thought, with time for rests. It seemed as if they'd been walking much longer than that.

Then suddenly, from behind them, Pippit set up an anxious croaking. It was the last thing Tad needed to hear. He was hot, tired, and scratched all over, and there was no sign of their destination in sight. And now a fussing frog.

"Shut up, Pippit!" Tad snapped.

Pippit croaked louder.

"Tad!" Birdie tugged at his elbow. "Don't yell at him. Listen! It's his warning cry!"

The watchfrog was right, Tad realized. Something was coming. He felt a faint tremble of the dry ground beneath his feet, the vibration of something large advancing toward them, moving in the direction of the forest path. Birdie felt it too. She and Tad exchanged worried glances.

"We don't know that it's an enemy," Tad said, talking lower. "It could be a big Hunter caravan, lots of wagons all traveling together. Father says they do that sometimes."

Pippit croaked agitatedly and began to jump up and down.

"We don't know that it's a friend, either," Birdie said. "Quick, Tad! Whatever it is, it's getting closer. Let's hide!"

Hastily they plunged into the brown underbrush off the side of the little beaten path and burrowed under a heap of dried leaves. Tad crawled forward on his elbows and raised his head, peering cautiously through a clump of concealing grasses. The light had dwindled further. It was true twilight now, and the forest was gray and dim, slowly fading toward night. Then, moving toward them from out of the forest, Tad saw glimmers of yellow light.

The lights were burning torches. The company that carried them marched in silence except for the heavy thump of many feet on the dry ground. There were dozens of marchers. The first ranks wore long black robes with deep hoods and wide belts of black leather. Their faces, even in the torch light, were hidden and invisible. Next came a phalanx of foot soldiers wearing leather boots, round leather caps, and quilted leather vests, and carrying long metal-pointed spears. Then bowmen, in curving helmets made from hawks' beaks, with polished longbows and quivers filled with black-fletched arrows. The rhythmic tramp of their feet sounded threatening and ominous, like the slow rolling grumble of distant thunder before a summer storm. Tad caught his breath.

Birdie wriggled steathily forward and peered out under the leaves at Tad's side.

"Who are they?" she whispered.

"Grellers," Tad whispered. "They're Grellers."

The Remembers came so easily now that sometimes it seemed as if they truly were his own. He had heard the story around a campfire. They had camped on the floor of a sheltered canyon, he and Burris and Vondo, and had talked far into the night. He could see Burris as if he were sitting beside him now—his bright brown eyes, round and shiny as new horse chestnuts, glinting orange with reflected firelight—and could hear his voice as he told the tale:

"They left the Digger Tribe long ago. There was a quarrel, and the Grellers left to make new diggings of their own. Some say they lived aboveground for a time"—the voice became mocking—"foolish as the Fishers and the Hunter folk, which is where the name comes from: Greller, ground-dweller. Or they might have had a leader named Greller. Nobody knows. We became enemies. The Grellers turned from the Tribe."

There was a silence, while all absorbed the enormity of the Grellers' deed. Then:

"Eh, that's Diggers for you!" Vondo, taunting, gold earrings and white teeth flashing in a dark brown face. "*Scritch . . . scritch . . . scritch . . .* Always the heads in the ground; no care for anything outside their own tunnels—"

Burris's broad hand, covered in short red fur, shoving him over, both of them laughing.

"Better that than behaving like the Hunters, care-for-nothings, eating pillbugs—"

"I could do with a juicy pillbug right now! Better than your earthworms, furface!"

Scuffles. Laughter.

Unexpected pain lanced through Tad. *I saw them die.*

He tore himself away from the Remember, thrusting it behind him, wincing away from it.

"Look," Birdie whispered fearfully.

Behind the armed marchers came a row of larger shapes, small eyes glittering and long necks swaying snakelike in the light cast by the torches.

"Weasels!" Tad whispered.

There were eight of the great black weasels. Each wore a harness of gleaming oiled leather set with nuggets of raw gold and rough-cut chunks of turquoise. Grim-faced riders perched on their shoulders, each armed with a metal-tipped leather whip.

The company took no notice of Tad, Birdie, and Pippit crouching silently in the underbrush. One by one, legs and arms swinging in unison, eyes resolutely forward, they turned onto the path and proceeded in the direction the children had been going, swiftly marching east. Tad uttered a long relieved sigh.

"We'll have to follow them," he said. "They're going in the same direction we are. We'll stay far enough behind so that they won't see us. We'll just have to be careful that we don't fall over them suddenly in the dark."

Birdie nodded.

"And try to be quiet," Tad added. "You too, Pippit."

Cautiously they set off along the path. Around them the evening deepened steadily into darkness. Soon they could barely make out the pale track of the path before them.

"I can hardly see anything anymore," Birdie complained. "And I'm hungry. Can't we stop, Tad? We'll never be able to find Witherwood's house like this."

She was right, Tad realized. It was getting darker by the minute. Then, in the distance in front of them, he saw a wavering beam of light.

"There's something up ahead," he whispered over his shoulder.

"Witherwood?" Birdie whispered back hopefully.

"I don't think so," Tad said.

The light seemed to be coming from a clearing to the left of the path, a short distance into the forest. Tad and Birdie, with Pippit hopping anxiously behind them, moved softly toward it, setting their bare feet down carefully, trying not to make any sound. Then they heard a high wailing voice, chanting. It seemed to be repeating one word over and over. *"La-dy! La-dy! La-dy!"* Tad's heart began to pound uncomfortably in his chest. His skin felt cold. Behind him, he heard Pippit croak once, to be promptly hushed by Birdie.

Other voices took up the chant.

"La-dy! La-dy! La-dy!"

Booted feet began to stamp in rhythm.

"La-dy! La-dy! La-dy!"

"Let's get away from here, Tad!" Birdie was tugging at his tunic, urging him backward.

Tad stubbornly shook his head. "I need to see what's happening," he said.

He crept closer, Birdie reluctantly following, Pippit even more reluctantly bringing up the rear. At the edge of the clearing, they hid at the foot of a massive oak tree and cautiously raised their heads to see over the top of one long twisted root.

In the center of the clearing was a stone circle. The stones were roughly hewn upright slabs, black in the flickering torch light, towering high over Tad's and Birdie's heads. There were twelve of the slabs, set in a wide ring, with a thirteenth laid down flat like an immense table at the circle's center. Within the stone ring the Grellers stood in rows around the flat central stone. They were silent now, all faces turned toward a single Greller in a long black robe, who stood on top of it. The hood of his robe was thrown back, and beneath it the Greller wore a mask made of fish scales, with round holes cut out for eyes. The flat white mask and the black eyeholes made the Greller's face look like a bony skull. Tad heard Birdie, at his elbow, give a little gasp. The Greller had his arms stretched high over his head, and he was shouting.

"La-dy! La-dy! Come to us! La-dy!"

"What lady?" Birdie whispered.

Tad shook his head. He didn't know either.

Then the Greller's arms dropped to his sides. For a long moment he stood perfectly still. No one in the stone circle made a sound. When he spoke next, it was in a new voice. A cold silver voice, as clear and cruel as winter ice.

"I am come," it said.

An awed murmur arose from the waiting Grellers.

"The Lady!"

"The Lady comes to us!"

"The Lady speaks!"

Tad's fingers clenched on the rough woody surface of the tree root. *It's not possible,* he thought. *It can't be . . .*

Within the circle, the Grellers had all fallen to their knees. A few in the very front rows had toppled forward, put their foreheads to the ground, and wrapped their arms around their heads.

"All shall be as I have promised," the silvery voice continued. A thin strain of music crept into it, a high sweet whine like the very highest notes coaxed from a lutegourd with a willow-twig bow. Tad could feel it in his teeth. *"All the burrows of the Stone Mountains will be yours once more. We will defeat the False Diggers and drive them forth. You will have wealth and slaves and power beyond all your greatest dreams. But first you must find the boy."*

"What boy?" a bass voice shouted.

"A brown boy," the voice belled coldly. *"A brown boy of twelve sun turns, who swims through the water like an eel. I have told you of him, children. Why have you not found the boy?"*

"We do send out searchers," someone else cried, "but we have heard no rumors of a boy such as you have described."

"Perhaps there be no such boy!" shouted a third.

The voice shot out in a silvery hiss, so angry and menacing that the Grellers in the front row shrank back. *"There is a boy."* The music began again, faintly at first, then louder. *"There is a boy,"* the voice caroled enticingly. *"There is a boy. And he is near. He is . . ."*

The face in the fish-scale mask lifted and turned from one side to the other, seeming to peer out between the tall black stones. Then the Greller lifted an arm and pointed across the circle, directly toward the tree root where Tad and Birdie crouched.

"He is there!" the voice cried. *"He is there!"*

The Grellers, moving as one, all turned in the direction of the black pointing finger.

10

THE SAGAMORE

Tad and Birdie, staring at each other in horror, ducked behind the concealing tree root.

"They can't possibly see us," Birdie said incredulously. "All the way out here. It's too dark."

Tad, with a sinking feeling in his stomach, thought that they probably could. Or at least one of them could.

"We've got to get away from here, Birdie," he whispered urgently. "I don't know how they know we're here, but they do. At least they know *I'm* here. That voice . . . the Greller that was doing all the talking? That was the same voice I heard in the pond. It's the Nixie talking— talking through him. And she can feel me somehow. She knows where I am."

"How?" Birdie asked. Then, before Tad had a chance to answer, "Are you sure?"

Tad nodded. "But she doesn't know about *you*. Or Pippit. If they find me . . ." He gulped and went on. "If they find me, all you have to do is hide and keep very still. They're not looking for you, so they won't even know you're here. Just stay hidden until it's safe, and then go for help. Go back to Treeglyn's tree."

He paused, thinking. "We should split up right now. If you and Pippit go in one direction and I go in another—"

Birdie stuck out her lower lip and stubbornly shook her head. "We're not going to leave you here," she said. "With those *weasels*."

Pippit gave an equally stubborn-sounding croak.

Tad sighed. It was just as Pondleweed always said: Birdie, when she made up her mind about something, was as stubborn as a snapping turtle.

"All right," he said after a moment. "We'll all stick together. Go very carefully now. Let's crawl back around to the other side of the tree. Don't let them catch so much as a hint of anything moving. That means you, too, Pippit. No hopping. Stay down!"

Behind them a babble of voices rose from the stone circle, growing louder and finally joining in a single rallying roar.

Bent low, Tad and Birdie stumbled over the uneven ground, clambering over the wall-like roots extending from the great tree.

"Faster!" Tad said. "They're coming!"

He risked a quick look behind them.

The Grellers were running toward them, pouring out of the stone circle in a dark tide. Some held flaming torches aloft. The flames threw glimmering gold reflections across the bristling points of spears, the blades of upraised swords, the polished tips of long black-feathered arrows.

Tad, Birdie, and Pippit threw themselves over the last obstructing root, landing in a confused tangle on the ground. Tad leaped up, dragging Birdie to her feet.

"Faster!" he said again. "Once we get deeper into the woods, they'll never find us. Not at nighttime like this."

Unless they bring their fish-faced friend along to help, he thought.

Then Birdie screamed.

A massive dark shadow had reared up before them, looming higher and higher. Its long front paws reached out, and its neck stretched upward and arched like some ancient monster—like the dragons Pondleweed said had once walked the Earth. It opened its mouth and hissed at the children, showing a double row of pointed yellow teeth.

It was a black weasel.

Tad and Birdie cowered back, while Pippit, croaking frantically, tried to hide behind their legs. The weasel lowered itself once more, front paws dropping to the ground, so that the children could see the rider on its back: a Greller armored in leather and bronze, with a black feather thrust in his silver-banded cap. He held a black leather whip in one gloved hand. The tips of the whip thongs were capped with wicked little metal points.

When Tad whirled to look about him, he found that all avenues of escape were cut off. A ring of spearmen had silently closed in behind them, their weapons leveled and poised. For a moment no one spoke.

Then one of the spear carriers lowered his weapon to point curiously at Tad's webbed toes. "Be this the boy, Captain? The swimming boy the Lady do be seeking?"

"Mayhap, Ulrid," the weasel-rider said. "We will take him to Hagguld and he will tell us." He raised his whip and gestured toward the circle of dark stones. "Bring him into the circle. Bring these others with him."

A spearman stepped forward and prodded Tad between his shoulder blades. Another poked threateningly at Birdie. Tad stood his ground. He felt as if his stomach were boiling hot. He felt tingly all over, as if he had come instantly and intensely awake and alive. He seemed to have extra senses popping out everywhere. He could see and hear more acutely than ever before. It was as if he had extra nerves in his skin. The hot feeling rose higher and higher, boiling up into his chest. Tad realized in astonishment that he was furiously angry.

You are the Sagamore!

It was as if a voice had spoken sharply in his ear.

Me? Tad tried to thrust the Remember—was it a Remember?—away. But the voice came again, angrily now, a voice sounding not quite, but almost, familiar.

You are the Sagamore! Stand, Fisher, and show them what you're made of!

Tad folded his arms across his chest. Something strange was happening. The hot feeling kept growing, spreading into his toe- and fingertips, crackling across his skin. Something was waking inside him, struggling to break free. He felt like a butterfly straining to wriggle out of its cocoon.

"You have no right to take us prisoner here in the Open Forest," he said. "The paths here are free to all. It is against the Law."

Is this me? he wondered. *Did I know this?*

Birdie, trembling beside him, gave a start of surprise.

The black weasel pulled against its leather harness, and the rider tightened his grip on the reins.

"I don't know of no law," he said. "All I know is that High Priest Hagguld—and the Lady, worshipful her name—do be wanting you. A boy who swims, she said, and if my eyes do not fail me, you do be a Fisher boy."

The weasel bucked and tugged, and the captain slashed at it with his whip, struggling to bring it under control.

"Take them into the circle!" he shouted. "Right up to the altar stone! We will show the Lady who her faithful servants are! Go! Swiftly now!"

The weasel pawed the air and danced, then plunged off into the forest. Tad and Birdie followed it, driven by the jabbing spears. They were thrust between the dark stone slabs into the very center of the circle and forced to halt before the tablelike altar stone.

The soldier named Ulrid stepped up beside them and tugged off his round leather cap. "We do bring him, Hagguld," he said. "There do be three of them."

"I can count, Ulrid," the fish-scale-masked figure said. It was a different voice now, Tad noted, a deep irascible elderly voice. The awful mask with its empty-seeming eyeholes turned toward Tad.

"What be your name?" the High Priest said. Then he drew himself up taller and spread his black-draped arms out wide. The fish-scale mask glittered silver in the torch light. *"What is your name?"*

Behind the children, the gathered Grellers gave a long low moan.

"The Lady," voices muttered.

"It be the Lady."

"The Lady comes again."

And Tad suddenly felt something change.

It was as if something tiny and tight inside him sud-denly opened and changed shape—as if a flower had suddenly burst into blossom or a butterfly had torn free of its wrappings and spread its glorious new wings. It felt incredibly, wonderfully different—but natural, too, and infinitely comfortable, like wearing an old, soft, and much-loved suit of clothes.

This is the way I'm supposed to be, Tad thought.

"What is your name?" The silver voice rose to a shriek.

Before Ulrid could stop him, Tad sprang to stand beside the High Priest on the altar stone.

"I am the one you seek, Witch!" he shouted. "I am Tadpole of the Fisher Tribe!"

The Grellers were staring at him in astonishment, as if they'd set out to catch a docile minner but had hooked an angry rockbiter by mistake. Tad clenched his hands into fists.

"I am Tadpole of the Fisher Tribe! I am the Sagamore!"

The black-robed High Priest lunged toward him, his furred fingers curled like claws.

"Kill the boy!" The cold voice echoed off the tall stones, bouncing from one to the other until it seemed that there were hundreds of voices singing in chorus, each louder than the one before. *"Kill the boy! Kill the boy! Kill the boy!"*

The Grellers, moving as one, lifted their spears.

A terrible calm came over Tad. Time, for an endless moment, seemed to stand still. He felt a power gathering inside him, swelling, filling him up. And then, astonishingly, the night was full of voices. Some were no more than distant whispers, too faint and muddled to understand; some were clear as crystal, as if the speakers' lips were pressed close to Tad's ears.

". . . slaves and power, she said we'd have, and riches, too, red gold, mayhap, and fire opals big as huggleberries . . ."

". . . high time and more I were captain in his place, and now I do have the Lady's promise of help . . ."

". . . Lady, guide my aim, as I be your faithful servant . . ."

It wasn't voices, Tad realized. He was listening to people's minds. No, not just people. From the edge of the clearing, just beyond the towering stones, came a high inhuman jabber of mind voices that twisted slyly around one another, coiling together like snakes in a nest. The voices rose and fell and overlapped, filled with anger, fear, pain, and despair. Slaves now, they were slaves, the voices mourned, taken from the kinship circles in the warm earth-smelling warrens, dragged with chains and bands of leather, forced to carry the Masters who held the stinging whips. One mind was black with misery; another, a red ember of fury and hatred; a third, a confused jumble of cravings for escape, to run and run, back to the deep of the forest, where the only blood spilled was in honest kill, where family waited, welcoming, curled together in the narrow tunnels. But that could never be, never, because one must obey the Masters. There was no other way. Slaves, they were slaves; obey, they must obey . . .

It was the weasels. They clustered together in the shadows, tethered to polished stakes driven deeply into the ground. Tad cautiously reached toward them. *No. Not slaves. Pull free.*

The sinuous coil of minds fell silent, alertly listening. *Simple minds really,* Tad thought, moving gently among them—little earth-soft minds filled with thoughts of hunger and hunt, home and kindred, field and forest and deep long sleep.

Slaves. Obey. The weasels' minds murmured, but Tad, prodding, could feel them beginning to question.

No, he thought, squeezing his eyes shut with the effort to make himself heard. *No. Not slaves. Pull free.*

One weasel mind — the angry red one — joined him. He could feel the weasel bracing its front paws, tugging wildly at its leather rope.

Home. Free. Hate Masters hate.

Another weasel joined in. One tremendous heave, and a tethering stake yanked out of the ground.

Slaves? Obey?

No! Pull free!

Another weasel followed, and another. A Greller on the outskirts of the circle shouted an alarm. Another weasel tore itself loose, and then another and another. They sprang forward, hissing, pointed teeth bared.

Hate Masters hate! Hate Masters hate!

Those Grellers nearest the weasel rush were flung violently off their feet. Some managed to stagger up again, to be dragged away by terrified companions; others lay where they fell. Hagguld the High Priest took a horrified step backward, tottered, and crumpled to his knees. In the center of the scattering crowd of Grellers, a weasel reared up on its hind legs, screamed, and struck. Tad saw it raise its head, its eyes glaring, blood on its muzzle. It screamed and struck again. Grellers, shrieking, fled in all directions, stumbling and shoving in their rush to escape, forcing their way past one another, out of the stone circle, away into the forest. Birdie and Pippit scrambled up to stand beside Tad on the altar stone. Around them, weasels darted and pounced, their minds bright with astonishment and joy.

Not slaves! Pull free!

The stone circle now held only a leaping confusion of weasels and the limp fallen forms of savaged Grellers. One of them, Tad saw, still clutched his metal-pointed whip.

Not slaves! Home!

The weasels turned, all together, and streaked like swift black arrows into the enveloping night.

Home! Free!

Tad, suddenly remembering the High Priest, looked down, but there was no sign of Hagguld to be seen.

"What happened to the High Priest?" he asked.

Birdie shook her head. "I didn't see," she said. "He must have run off with the others. You did it somehow, didn't you? The weasels?"

Tad nodded.

"How?" asked Birdie in a small voice. "You were yelling and then you scrunched your eyes up and then the weasels were free. I don't understand, Tad. How can you be the Sagamore?"

"I don't know yet," Tad said. He could still feel the power inside him, damped down now, but ready to grow again.

Not this time, Azabel, he thought into the quivering dark.

"It's getting lighter," Birdie said. "It must be nearly morning." Suddenly she leaned forward and pointed over Tad's shoulder. "Look, Tad, it's one of the weasels. It must not have been able to pull itself loose."

One black weasel still remained. As the children drew nearer, they saw that it was tied by its leather harness to a young sapling. The bark of the tree was rubbed raw where the creature had tried to tear itself free. Now it huddled against the ground, trembling slightly, its head between its paws.

Anger. Fear.

Tad put out a cautionary hand.

"Don't go too close, Birdie," he said.

"It doesn't look dangerous," Birdie said. "It's just a young one, Tad. It looks scared."

She moved toward the weasel, one hand held out.

Comfort. Friend. Tad thought.

The weasel stopped trembling. It lifted its head and looked directly at Birdie. Then it scrambled to its feet. Standing on four paws, it was not all that much taller than the children themselves, though it was much longer. *It would make three or four of me,* Tad thought, *if I were lying down.* It still wore its elaborate harness: straps and belts of leather that passed across its chest and over its narrow shoulders, each strap inset with oddly shaped gold nuggets and chunks of blue turquoise.

The weasel stretched out its long snakelike neck until

it just reached Birdie. Then it gently nuzzled her shoulder. Birdie stroked its head, and it nuzzled some more. She turned to Tad in delight.

"It *likes* me!" she said. "It's *tame*!"

Birdie was petting the weasel again, rubbing the top of its sleek head and its small rounded ears. The weasel had its eyes closed and looked ecstatic.

"I don't think anybody was ever nice to it before," Birdie said. "I'll bet those Grellers were horrible to it. Look." She prodded with her toe in the dust. A discarded whip lay there, three knotted leather thongs fastened to a wooden handle. "I don't see how they ever managed to tame it in the first place."

"They didn't," Tad said. "They didn't tame any of them. They captured them."

"And then hit them," Birdie said bitterly. She seemed to have forgotten all about number two (weasels) of the Four Great Dangers.

She kicked at the whip on the ground, tossing it as far away from the weasel as she could.

"No one will ever hurt you again," she said to the weasel, scratching the fur under its chin. The weasel butted its head against her and made a sound that was almost a purr.

Birdie was unfastening the straps that tied the weasel to the tree. "We could ride him," she said. "Let's, Tad. I'm awfully tired."

So, Tad realized suddenly, was he. His legs were shaking with exhaustion. He could have lain right down on the ground, limp as a piece of boiled grassroot, and gone to sleep. He looked doubtfully at the weasel, remembering the look of those sharp pointed teeth, but the weasel mind radiated nothing but gratitude and contentment.

"Bend down a little," Birdie was saying. The weasel crouched lower to the ground. Birdie braced one bare foot against its leather harness and scrambled onto its back, reaching for the dangling reins.

"Hand me Pippit," Birdie said.

Tad passed up the struggling Pippit—frogs, it seemed, did not like weasels—and then clambered reluctantly onto the weasel's back himself, while Birdie stroked its neck and murmured soothing words. The weasel's back was warm and beautifully soft. Its black fur was shiny and smooth, touched with blue in the early morning light. It was just the color of a crow's feather.

"Which way do we go?" Birdie asked. "To Witherwood's house?"

Tad pointed silently. He felt worn out.

I could fall asleep right here, he thought. *If I could just do it without falling off.*

Silent as a shadow the weasel with the three passengers on its back slipped away through the forest.

"I think I'll call him Blackberry," Birdie said.

11

WITHERWOOD

The weasel paused at the edge of a clearing in the forest, and Tad, Birdie, and Pippit slid from its back to the ground. The sun was almost directly above them through the opening in the trees, warm on the tops of their heads. Almost highsun. *Half-day eating time,* Tad thought wistfully. Meals had been few and far between lately, and he was hungry. He wondered if Witherwood—if they ever managed to find him—would offer them something to eat.

The clearing must have been beautiful in the days before the Drying. Now its thick carpet of velvet grass was brittle and brown, and the bluebells and daisies that edged its borders were limp and withered on their stalks. The only sound was a worried humming of black-and-yellow bees, searching vainly among the drooping flower heads for nectar. The quiet was so heavy that it almost felt solid, like a crystal blanket. No one wanted to disturb it. One exclamation, one loud noise, Tad felt, and the whole clearing might shimmer into nothing and disappear like a burst bubble. The weasel was as still and silent as a black stone, and even Pippit was quiet, goggly eyes shifting back and forth hungrily following the bees.

Finally Birdie spoke. "Is this the right place?" she whispered. "Is this where Witherwood lives?"

"Shh," Tad whispered back. He tugged her arm gently and pointed toward the far end of the clearing. "Look."

There, almost hidden by the dappled patterns of shade and sunlight, stood a little stone cottage covered with greenbrier vines. A mortared stone chimney poked up through its bark-shingled roof, and wooden shutters were pulled wide, leaving windows open to the warm summer air. The cottage door was open, too, and in the doorway, on a wooden bench in the sun, sat an old man.

Tad and Birdie advanced toward him, moving quietly across the dry grass. Pippit—distracted by hovering bees—hopped reluctantly behind. Birdie led the weasel by the reins. As they drew nearer, they saw that the old man was asleep. One eye was closed. The other was covered by a leaf patch, secured and tied around his forehead with a band of braided grass. His face was deeply lined, and his shoulder-length hair was pure white. He wore a tunic of soft gray feathers. A wooden crutch leaned against the wall by his side. A dreadful puckered scar ran down one side of the old man's face and slashed across his throat.

"He's been terribly hurt," Birdie whispered.

At the sound of her whisper, the old man opened his single eye. Birdie gave a start of alarm. The eye was yellow, as bright and fierce as the eye of a hunting bird.

Tad gasped.

The yellow eye turned and fixed itself on Tad, studying him with sharp interest.

Birdie started to ask a question, but Tad didn't hear her finish. Again, the world slipped and shifted. He felt as if he were falling, spiraling down and downward, into the yellow depths of that strange eye. Then the old man and the stone cottage vanished, and Tad saw only a great circle, glowing gold. The circle flickered and went dark. Suddenly it became a doorway, a gaping hole in a great dead tree. The bare twisted branches of the tree were hung with bones—bones in clacking bundles dangling from strings of dried skin, and, here and there, whole skeletons topped with grinning ivory-colored skulls. The bones shivered and chittered in the wind, and cold tendrils of night mist rose and wrapped around them, draping them in ghostly cloaks. Tad stepped forward, and his feet crunched on piled bones, the broken remains of many midnight feasts. He was in an owl's lair. The hollow stank of fear and blood. Then something huge moved in the darkness. Great moon-round eyes blazed far above his head, and an immense claw—a talon as long as his arm and sharper than the Grellers' spears—slashed at his face. He cried out and flinched back.

"Who-oo are you?" A deep hollow voice, heavy with menace. "Who-oo are you, who comes to brave the Owl?"

There was a rustle and a scraping sound as something enormous moved toward him.

"Wait . . . I see . . ."

It was an immense snow-white owl. Around its neck it wore a heavy silver chain from which hung a silver medallion as big as Tad's head, studded with polished moonstones. Its hooked beak and huge gnarled talons looked black in the dim light. It stared, unblinking, at Tad. Tad staggered backward, raising his right hand to make a circle—Great Rune's sign—in the air before his face.

The Owl laughed.

"His sign will not help you here," it said. "Those who come to me leave Rune behind. Rune cannot give them what they seek."

"What do they seek?" Tad whispered.

"They come to me for wisdom," the Owl answered. "Though wisdom is not always the gift that it appears. Still, those that would have it must pay the price, in blood and sacrifice and pain."

It took a shuffling step closer.

"What would you give for wisdom, boy?"

Tad took another step backward and found himself against the wall of the lair.

"Who are you?" he rasped.

"You know me," the Owl said. "All know me. I am the Destroyer. I am Death. I am fear and pain; I am rot and wither and despair. I am winter and midnight; I am the empty black behind the stars, and I am the dark of the moon. You know me, you little fool."

The talon slashed out again and Tad screamed.

The Owl said, *"I am Ohd."*

There was blood in Tad's mouth, and he was shaking. He had bitten his tongue. Birdie was clinging to his arm, and on his other side, Pippit, croaking in distress, was clinging clammily to his leg.

A bell was ringing. Witherwood had reached over his head and was pulling on a length of greenbrier vine from which hung a hammered-metal bell. It rang with a high chiming sound that echoed through the clearing. Moments later there was a thrashing in the bushes and a tall gangly boy—really a young man—appeared, running. He was dressed in a short belted tunic over silkgrass breeches, and his hair—in a single bright orange braid—hung down the middle of his back. Beneath the flaming hair, the young man's face was peppered with orange freckles. He looked hot and harassed.

"I regret that I was not here to greet you," he panted. He pulled a wisp of mullein leaf out of a tunic pocket and mopped his hot forehead with it. "We were not expecting guests."

He stopped in mid-mop and gaped nervously at Blackberry, the weasel, crouched watchfully behind Birdie on the grass.

"It's all right," Birdie said reassuringly. "He's quite tame."

"I do hope so," the young man said in disbelieving tones. "Perhaps . . . if he could just move back a bit and stop staring at me—"

"There's nothing to worry about," Birdie said firmly. "You're perfectly safe." She patted the weasel soothingly on the nose. "He's a friend, Blackberry. Stop staring at him."

The weasel and the young man exchanged identically suspicious glances. Finally the young man sighed, shrugged, and stuffed the crumpled scrap of mullein leaf back in his pocket. At the same time, Blackberry stopped staring, nuzzled Birdie's shoulder, then rolled over onto his side, curled up into a tight furry ball, and fell asleep.

"Weasels," the young man said unhappily.

"I think he's cute," Birdie said. "Look at him, with his paw over his nose."

"'Cute,'" the young man repeated. "I'm sure many would agree with you, of course. Briefly. In their last moments."

He cleared his throat and edged gingerly away from Blackberry. "And how may we help you?" he asked.

"We came—" Tad began.

"Treeglyn sent us—" Birdie said.

They both stopped and started again.

"Treeglyn said—"

"We came—"

The young man flapped his hands helplessly.

"Perhaps one at a time," he suggested.

"Are *you* Witherwood?" Birdie asked. "Because we came to see—"

"Oh, no," the young man said. He gestured toward the old man, who sat silently watching them from his wooden bench in the sun. "That is Witherwood. And I am Witherwood's Voice."

Tad and Birdie looked at each other in puzzlement.

"Witherwood's *voice?*" Tad repeated. "How can you be Witherwood's *voice?*"

The old man moved his hand, gesturing toward the terrible scar across his throat.

"My master cannot speak like other people do," Voice said. "Instead he uses a language made of signs. He speaks with his hands. Every movement of his hands is a word or a name." He made a fluid rippling motion with one palm. "That means *water*. And this"—he put both hands together, raised them high over his head, and let them fall open—"means *tree*. My master—"

Witherwood's hands were moving, weaving rapid patterns in the air.

"He wants to know who you are," the young man said.

"I'm Tad," Tad answered. "Tadpole of the Fisher Tribe. And this is my sister, Birdie." He paused, waiting.

"He can hear you," the young man said patiently. "He understands everything you say. It is only his voice that is lost."

Witherwood regarded Tad with his single yellow eye, a long measuring look. His hands moved, tracing invisible figures.

"Why have you come to me?" the young man murmured softly.

Tad didn't take his eyes from Witherwood's face.

"We need your help," he said.

Carefully Tad began to tell his tale once more. He told about the pond and the Drying, the trip up the dwindling stream and the meeting with the Hunters, the stone dam, the strange and terrible singing, the loss of Pondleweed. At this last, his voice quavered and broke, and Witherwood reached out and touched his shoulder with one wrinkled hand. At a signal, the young man vanished into the cottage. Soon he reappeared carrying a wooden tray heavily laden with acorn cups of cold mint tea, a towering pile of seed cakes, bowls of pea tomatoes and wild onions, a sliced yellow mallow-cheese.

"My master says you are to eat and drink," the young man said. "You are hungry, thirsty, and tired."

Tad and Birdie ate and drank, then ate and drank some more. Food and drink had never tasted so delicious. Blackberry woke up, ate three helpings of seed cakes, and lapped down two brimming bowls of tea. Then he curled up and fell asleep again, purring contentedly, with his paws folded over his nose. Birdie looked at him fondly.

"Do you think I'll be able to keep him?" she asked wistfully. "I mean, after we get back home again?"

"Certainly," said Voice, too quickly. "And the sooner you take him there, the better, wherever your home is, of course . . ."

Pippit gave a protesting croak, and Tad almost grinned in spite of himself. Then the grin faded.

"I don't know, Birdie," he said unhappily. "I don't even know when we're going to *get* back home. Or how." *Or if,* he added silently to himself. *And anyway, how can there be a home without Pondleweed?*

The red-haired young man had cleared away the empty cups and bowls. Now he returned and settled himself on the ground beside them. Witherwood's hands were asking a question.

"Please go on," Voice said.

Tad resumed his story. He talked on and on into the afternoon. He told about Treeglyn the Dryad and what she had told them of the Nixies, about his mysterious visions and Remembers, about his first hearing of the name Sagamore. At the sound of the name, Witherwood went even stiller than still, and his yellow eye gleamed. But his hands said nothing.

"Go on," Voice said, as Witherwood closed his eye.

Tad told about the Grellers and their dark stone circle, about the sudden change inside his head, about the mind voices and the weasels. At last—taking a deep breath—he described what had happened when they first arrived at Witherwood's cottage: the frightening meeting with the Owl in his dead tree hung with bones.

"Oh, Tad!" Birdie cried in a horrified voice. "How *awful*. How did you get away?"

"I don't know," Tad said. "It's one of the things I don't understand. I was just back here all of a sudden. It happens that way. It's like waking up out of a dream, but each time the dream is realer and longer, until I can't tell which is real and which is just the dream." His voice wavered uncertainly. "It was a dream, wasn't it?" he asked Witherwood.

He paused, frightened all over again. It *must* have been a dream. The Owl had clawed him and nothing had happened; he was still here, unclawed, and all in one piece.

"Who is the Owl?" he whispered. "Witherwood, who is Ohd?"

12

THE OLD TURTLE

Witherwood had sat with his single eye closed through-
out most of Tad's recital, leaning against the stone wall,
looking as if he were asleep. Now the yellow eye opened,
and the old man's hands began to move.

"Ohd," Voice said slowly. He made the name sound
low and long and eerie, like a hunting owl's hoot. "Ohd is
the other half of Rune."

Witherwood leaned forward on his wooden bench,
and his old hands flashed and flickered, weaving patterns
in the air.

"Nothing exists without its other half," Voice said, his
eyes fixed on Witherwood's moving fingers. "There can
be no light without dark, no truth without lies, no life
without death. No creation without destruction. Everything"—he paused as Witherwood spread his hands out,
palms flat, and moved one up and the other down—
"balances," Voice said. "It's the way the universe is made.
Rune and Ohd, Life and Death, Making and Unmaking,
Being and Nonbeing."

"But"—Tad frowned, puzzled—"everyone knows
about Rune." Birdie and Voice together raised their right

hands and drew a circle in the air. "I never even heard of Ohd."

Witherwood's fingers flickered.

"You have," Voice said. "The gods have many names and faces. But it is Ohd all the same, though the Diggers have a tale of a Checkered Snake; the Hunters, of a Ghost Weasel, the Fishers—"

"The Winter Fox," Tad said suddenly. "He's the Winter Fox, Birdie. Don't you remember?" It was one of Pondle-weed's stories.

"A long, long time ago, our father said, back when the world was young, it was always summertime and nobody ever grew old or died. But then one day a strange animal came to the Ponds, a huge white fox with eyes the color of ice. The Fox called all the Fishers together and said, 'I will make a bargain with you. Each moon bring me one of your kind to eat so that I will not be hungry, and I will leave the rest of you alone.'

"But the Fishers wouldn't do it. 'How can we choose someone to be eaten?' they said. 'If we did that, no one would feel safe. Friends would no longer trust friends, neighbors would be afraid of neighbors, and even families would turn against each other. We must make another bargain.'

"'So you shall,' the Fox said, 'but you will all be sorry for it. From this day on, then, you will grow old and die, just as the year will die each autumn with the falling of the leaves. You think that you have saved yourselves, but you have chosen a path of heartache and despair. Now,' said the Fox, 'sooner or later I will eat you all.' And with that he turned into mist and vanished.

"So from that day on, our father said, people grew old and died, just as every sun turn, the year died, too, and became winter. But the Fishers were never sorry for the bargain they had chosen, because all through the Ponds, friends and neighbors trusted one another, and inside each home tree, love of family was always strong and warm."

He stopped, out of breath.

"I remember now," said Birdie. "The Winter Fox lost and the Fishers won."

"I don't think anybody *won*," said Tad. "I don't think the story's supposed to be about winning."

"They faced the Fox," said Voice, watching Witherwood's hands. "They learned what they valued, and chose death rather than lose what they cherished. That is what it is to grow."

So it was with the Owl.

Tad glanced up quickly and found Witherwood's yellow eye upon him. Witherwood's hands moved again, a quick cupping gesture, and then pointed toward the cottage doorway. Voice scrambled to his feet and disappeared inside. He returned carrying in both hands a flat bundle the size of a big dinner plate, carefully wrapped in a silk-grass cloth. He laid the bundle reverently in Witherwood's lap. Slowly the old man undid the wrappings, folding the cloth back to reveal a thick gnarled brown slab, roughly four-sided. It looked like a chip of old bark or an odd slice of stone.

Birdie drew in a startled breath. "It's a piece of a turtle's shell," she said. "A really old turtle. Why . . . ?"

Witherwood held the fragment of shell toward Tad, gesturing for him to take it.

"Take it," Voice said softly beside him. "You have seen the Owl. Now take this, Fisher boy, and tell me what you see."

Tad stretched out his hand. His fingers closed around the fragment of shell. It felt warm to the touch, warm and heavy and ringed and creased with little ridges. Tad ran his hand across its surface, puzzled. "I don't understand," he said. "What am I supposed to see?"

Witherwood held out a hand, palm up, and then touched his index finger to his eye.

Wait. See.

And Tad saw.

He stood beside a pond—but a pond like none he had ever seen before. Wide white stones formed a ledge all around it, and white stone cliffs towered high above him on all sides. It was as if the pond lay at the bottom of a huge white bowl. There was a scattered litter of fallen white pebbles and toppled boulders. The water of the pond was clear turquoise-blue.

Everything was utterly silent. Nothing moved, not so much as a waterskater or a dragonfly. Tad had never seen a place so bare, so scoured clean, so empty.

Then a voice spoke, a deep hoarse whisper of a voice that seemed to come out of the white stones themselves.

I have been waiting for you, Sagamore.

Tad turned his head. A huge gray boulder—at least at first it looked like a boulder—had opened its eyes and moved its head. It was an ancient turtle. Its shell was thick and worn as weathered stone; its heavy legs and feet ended in heavy cracked claws; and its mouth was a fierce bony beak. Tad had never seen a creature so massive, so silent, so old. The turtle looked as old as the very world itself. Tad moved closer. The turtle's hooded eyes were filmed over, milky pale. Tad realized with a shock that it was blind.

Who are you? he whispered. *Do I know you?*

The old turtle made a breathy sound that might have been reptilian laughter.

You do, young one, it murmured. *We have met before. I wear many faces. But that is not what you need to learn here. Better to ask me "Who am I?"*

Tad sank down at the old turtle's feet.

Who am I, then? he asked. *What's happening to me?* His thoughts stumbled over themselves in his eagerness to know. *I have these Remembers. They come in bits and pieces. Sometimes they're like pictures in my mind, and sometimes it's as if I'm someone else, somewhere else, in some other time. And the Remembers are all scrambled up somehow, so they're hard to understand. It's like knowing just the middle of a story, with no beginning and no end. It's as if I'm not me anymore. Or only partly me.*

The old turtle shifted its claws, scraping restlessly against the warm rocks.

Time passes, it said. *Time passes, but the Mind and the Magic only rest, waiting to wake again. And this time they awake in you.*

In me? Tad asked.

You were born here, the old turtle said.

It paused for a minute, breathing in and out with a sound like wind in leafy branches.

He came long ago and drank from my pool. He was the first. You have much yet to learn, but even now you are growing. You are only at the beginning.

The beginning? Tad echoed.

The turtle nodded its heavy head.

Think, Sagamore, and remember.

Tad racked his brains.

He was kneeling at the edge of the pond. He could feel the slabs of rock beneath him, hot against his knees. He bent over, farther, farther, dipping his hands in the turquoise water. He drank and felt the blue liquid, cool and sweet, slide down his throat. Then something happened. An explosion of stars within his mind. He looked up, astonished. . . .

Yes, said the turtle. *Yes. That was the beginning. The birth of the power. And the power, once awakened, does not die; it merely rests, waiting for the next to bear the Gift. Now, as you reach manhood, the Mind opens. It is a Gift, young one. A great Gift and a terrible burden.*

Burden?

Burden, the old turtle said. *For in this great world of ours, your lot is to watch and worry, to battle the wrongs, comfort the sorrows, and right the ills. And more than that—to do it all unknown, for the Great Conflicts are not for the little folk of pond and wood. Their concerns must be for their own time and place, and for happenings close at hand. They will forget you, Sagamore, time out of mind, and your name will fade away.*

It was too much to take in. Tad felt ready to burst with questions.

But what will happen to me? He struggled to understand. *What am I supposed to do? Set things to rights, Treeglyn said, but I don't know what to do. Or how.*

Almost imperceptibly the old turtle shook its heavy head.

You will, it murmured. *It will come. You will grow.*

But who am I? Tad thought to himself, frightened and dismayed. *Am I me anymore? With this Mind inside me, swallowing me up?*

You and more than you, the turtle said. *You are you and more than you.*

It had closed its eyes. Its face was wrinkled and gray, like a weathered piece of driftwood.

You are the Sagamore, it whispered. *Use the Gift wisely, Tadpole of the Fisher Tribe.*

The turquoise pond was gone. Tad was sitting on dry grass again, still clutching in his hands the fragment of

ancient turtle shell. How long had it been? The others—
Witherwood, Voice, and Birdie—were staring at him.
Birdie's mouth was open. When she did that at home,
Pondleweed always asked her if she was waiting to catch
buzzflies.

"There was an old turtle," he began, but Voice put
a quieting hand on his arm. Witherwood's hands were
spelling a message.

The old man rose painfully from the bench, reaching
for his wooden crutch. Voice sprang to help him, but
Witherwood waved him away. He grasped the crutch,
thrust it under his arm, and, leaning upon it, turned to
face the little group on the grass. Then he bowed his head
toward Tad.

"My master says," said Voice—he paused and cleared
his throat. "My master says that you are indeed he who is
called the Sagamore."

13

THE RED BOOK

Perhaps the help they were seeking, Voice told them, could be found in Witherwood's Books.

"What books?" asked Birdie.

"*The* Books," said Voice, trying to sound impressive. He tripped over the cottage threshold as he said it, which spoiled the effect.

The Books, he explained, rubbing his toe, were the history of the Tribes, a long record reaching back for hundreds of sun turns. The earliest books were difficult to read, since they were written in strange alphabets and archaic languages. Some of the books had been damaged. Several had been burned in a long-ago fire; nothing was left of them but blackened spines and the crumbling remains of illegible pages, but they were still faithfully preserved. *The* Books, Voice said in shocked tones when Birdie asked, were never discarded, *never.*

"Are we in them?" Birdie asked. "The Fishers?"

"All the Tribes," Voice said, "and a lot more too. But even when you can read them, the books can be hard to understand. Some of the book keepers must have been muddle-headed. Or maybe they just couldn't write very well. Come in and I'll show you."

Inside, the walls of the stone cottage were covered with books. The books were arranged in order, Voice explained, from the very oldest to the newest, the book that Witherwood himself was writing in now. The oldest books were rolled scrolls of birch bark. Next came books with carved wooden covers tied with brittle ribbons of ancient silkgrass, and finally rows of thick volumes bound in snakeskin or mouseleather. Some of them were held together with blackened metal clasps. The latest book lay on a wooden table next to an open window. A square clay bottle of walnut-hull ink stood beside it, carefully corked, and a neat row of goldfinch-quill pens.

Tad and Birdie gaped at the shelves in awe. They had never seen so many books before. Books were rare among the Fishers, and few of the woodland Tribes could read. Tad had always cherished a secret hope that someday he could learn.

Voice helped his master to his chair and placed a wooden footstool under his feet. Then he ran his finger along the shelves until, at a nod from Witherwood, he pulled out one volume, carried it across the room, and laid it gently in the old man's lap. The book was bound in red-dyed leather with an incised border of black and gold. The pages—brown at the edges and crumbling, fragile as dry leaves—were covered with cramped slanted handwriting. It looked to Tad like the twisted patterns engraver beetles sometimes made under the bark of trees.

Witherwood turned page after page, running his fingers along the lines, searching. Then, halfway through the book, the handwriting on the pages changed. It became bigger and bolder, punctuated with loops and sweeping swirls, and the ink was now a deep cranberry-red.

"A new writer," Voice murmured. "Many have kept the Books, and this volume is very old."

Witherwood's hands hovered over the page.

"This is the place," Voice said. He cleared his throat importantly and began to read.

"A time came when the Nixies, the Witches of the Waters, turned against the Tribes and used their power to take all water for their own. And so the world dried. And these were the names of the faithless ones: Adrielle and Umbellene, Graella and Damia, Cedra and Selena, and foremost of them all, Azabel."

"*Azabel,*" Tad said. "She told me her name was Azabel. That first time in the pond."

Voice stopped reading and looked pointedly at Tad. Birdie poked Tad with her foot.

"Go on," she said to Voice. "Please keep reading."

"In the third year of the Drying," Voice continued, louder, "the streams and ponds were empty and the forest burned. The Fishers were driven from their homes and the Hunters from their hunting grounds. The Diggers in the mountains starved as the land above them turned to dust. And so there was called a Gathering of the Tribes."

Tad's nostrils tingled suddenly with the smell of burning.

There before him was a clearing, brown with dead leaves. A cluster of grimy caravans, their bright ribbons tattered and their skin covers black with soot and smoke. Cooking fires. A row of furred faces, solemn, leather boots and jerkins dusty and travel-stained. Thin barefoot children.

A Gathering with no dancing!

It was a rueful voice, touched with bitter laughter. A young woman's voice.

"Who are you?" Tad whispered. "Did I know you?"

There was no answer.

Voice spoke past him. "And to the Gathering came Waterleaf of the Fisher Tribe, the Sagamore. It was he who told us of the Waterstone, the source of all the Witches' magic, and then he swore that he would find and steal away the Stone and hide it for safekeeping, so that the Witches' power would be broken and the water would return to the Earth. And with him also swore his boon companions, Burris, of the Diggers, and Vondo, of the Hunter Tribe."

Tad caught his breath. They stood before the crowd, the three of them together, upraised hands clasped. A mass of faces, friends and strangers, cheering, shouting. *Two of them would not come back.* Vondo, the gambler, the joker, the teller of too-tall tales, drowned, pulled by the singing beneath the black water. Burris—*Burris*—felled on the shore by a Greller spear.

Tad doubled over suddenly and clutched his stomach. They hurt, these Remembers, hurt terribly, even though he, Tad, had not been there, had never met that dark Hunter or that bright-eyed Digger with his love of loud tuneless singing, his clever fingers, his unshakable loyalty, his reckless bravery in battle.

"What's the matter, Tad?" Birdie had her arms around his shoulders. "Are you sick?"

"I'm all right," Tad said. "It's all right."

"But first," Voice continued, worriedly watching Tad, "the three journeyed to the Kobolds of Stone Mountain, who gave them—"

He stopped. Witherwood had turned the page. The old hands froze. Voice, Birdie, and Tad craned anxiously forward. The page beneath Witherwood's fingers was empty. Or rather not empty, but washed away, the words blurred to a crimson smear as if a great splash of water had fallen on the paper and dissolved the ink.

They were outside in the sun. Witherwood sat again on his wooden bench, his eye closed. Voice and the two children sat cross-legged beside him on the ground, Voice as far away from Blackberry, the weasel, as he could possibly get.

Birdie was chattering cheerfully, but Tad had seldom felt more dismal and downcast.

"So now we understand," Birdie said brightly. She began to check things off on her fingers. "The voice in the stone circle that the Grellers called the Lady—it's Azabel, the greatest of the Nixies. She's awake again after all this time, and the Nixies must have gotten the Waterstone back somehow, because they're taking all the water. But the Sagamore and his two friends beat her, all that long time ago. They got the Waterstone away from her. . . ."

She paused, looking puzzled.

"Why hasn't anybody ever heard of the Sagamore?" she asked. "Why isn't there a Sagamore in any of the stories? There are all kinds of tales about heroes. Like Bog and Frostwort and Ula the Diggermaid who showed her Tribe how to defeat the Firefoxes. Why don't people tell about the Sagamore?"

"Perhaps," Voice translated, "perhaps the Sagamore did not wish to be remembered."

"That doesn't make sense," Tad said. *Who could be a hero and not want anyone to talk about it?*

"Well, he was remembered in the Book, anyway," said Birdie practically. "Just not very well. What did he *do*? And how did he do it? All the important parts were on the next page, the page that was all washed away."

Voice stirred restlessly. "There's something wrong with that," he said. "How could water wash just one page—*one page*—without touching anything else, before or after?

I think it's the Nixies at work, doing their wickedness. Throwing brambles in your path."

"Well," Birdie said, "even with the brambles, we did learn *something*. We found out where to go next. To the Kobolds of Stone Mountain. Whatever they gave him must have helped, mustn't it? I mean, the Sagamore won, all that time ago. Maybe it was a weapon. Or a secret potion." Her voice grew more excited. "Or a great magic spell."

"It would take us months to get to the mountains, Birdie," Tad said. "And then we'd have to find the Kobolds once we got there." He sighed dejectedly. "And even if we managed to do that, how do we know they can still help us? Or that they'd be willing to?"

"We could take the weasel," Birdie said. Her lower lip stuck out. "He could get us to the mountains, couldn't you, Blackberry?"

Stubborn as a snapping turtle, Tad thought.

"I wish," he said, "I *wish* the book had told us what happened next."

"I don't see that it matters all that much," Birdie said, scratching Blackberry's ears. "How do you know that things will happen the same way twice? 'Every day is new and different.' That's what Father always says."

Tad couldn't help himself. He made a rude snorting sound. New and different! *I've had enough new and different,* Tad thought crossly to himself, *to last a lifetime.*

"She's right," Voice said, turning toward him. "No one ever knows what's going to happen next. The last Sagamore—*he* didn't know how things were going to turn out, even though he must have had Remembers, too, just like you do. This Sagamore thing is more like a tool—the same tool for everyone who has it, maybe, but each has to use it in his own way."

Suddenly a huge dark shadow swept across the bright clearing. Alarmed, they all looked up. It was a hawk, just skimming the highest branches of the treetops. It was hunting, rapidly flying in ever-tightening circles, spiraling closer and closer to the ground. Around it passed, and the shadow swept over them again. Pippit bleated in alarm. The hackles rose along the back of the weasel's long neck, and he began to growl deep in his throat. Again the shadow passed, blocking out the sun.

"Can it *see* us?" Birdie asked tremulously.

"Yes," said Tad shortly.

From the time they had barely learned to paddle, all Fisher children were taught to beware of hunting birds. There was a prayer about hunting birds that Pondleweed had taught them when they were little, but Tad could only remember the first two lines:

> *From owl by night and hawk by day,*
> *Great Rune deliver us.*

•　•　•

He wished he could remember more of it.

"Don't move," Voice said urgently. "We could never get away from it, anyway. And it may not bother with us if we don't move."

Witherwood remained leaning against the sun-warmed wall, his eye closed and his hands resting gently in his lap, seemingly unaware.

Or perhaps nothing matters to him anymore, Tad thought. *Perhaps death doesn't frighten those who have already seen it once.*

A shocking thought struck him. *I have seen death, too,* he realized suddenly. *And not just once—not just Father— but many times. How many Sagamores? They died, whoever they were, all that time ago. I died. But what happened? Father says that when we die we go to live in Great Rune's garden at the end of the rainbow. But I can't remember. Maybe some things we're not supposed to remember....*

Birdie crouched closer to the ground and gave a little whimper. Blackberry buried his face in his paws. Pippit tried to hide behind Tad. He felt cold, clammy, and nervous against Tad's back.

The hawk's shadow swept over them again, growing larger and darker, plunging lower. Wind whistled past their ears. With an earthshaking thud, the hawk landed in the middle of Witherwood's clearing.

The bird was enormous. It towered hugely above the frozen group in the grass. Then it folded its vast wings across its back, cocked its head fiercely, and stared at them with one hot amber-colored eye.

Why doesn't it just grab one of us? Tad wondered. *Why is it just standing there, watching us?*

The hawk's head swiveled as it scanned the silent circle, resting at last on Tad. It opened its beak and let out a long, low, hoarse cry. There were words in the cry that Tad could understand.

14

BROTHER HAWK

The hawk's voice was like wind in high mountains. It was a strange wild voice with an edge of cruelty to it, an uncompromising voice full of valor and pride. No one having such a voice would ever give up or give in, no matter what. *It was,* Tad thought, *a warrior's voice.*

"I know you, Sagamore," the great bird said.

Tad opened his mouth but no sound came. Shakily he got to his feet. His knees felt as wobbly as crab-apple jelly. He had never been this close to a hunting bird before. The hawk loomed over him, terrifyingly huge.

"H-how . . . ?" He tried again. "How do you know me? I don't understand."

"By your marking," the bird said.

"Marking?" Tad repeated blankly. *What marking?* He was sure he didn't have any special marking. He was just ordinary. Not like Witherwood with his terrible scar, or like Voice with all that red hair.

"Each Family has its own marking. It is how we tell one from another," the bird said. "The goshawks by their striped faces; the marsh hawks by their gray wings; the rufous hawks by their red shoulders." He bent forward slightly and flared his fiery tail. "The red-tails as you see." His amber eye, unblinking, regarded Tad.

"You are marked," the bird said, "by your shine."

Tad held a hand out in front of his face and looked at it, puzzled. He looked down at his bare webbed feet. *Shine?* He couldn't see so much as a glimmer. All he saw was brown skin—somewhat grubby—and a dusty brown tunic that was now much the worse for wear.

The bird blinked rapidly and cocked his head at a different angle. "There is a glittering rim around you, right at the edges," he said helpfully. "It's quite plain." The hawk gestured with his beak toward Witherwood, still seemingly dozing on his sunlit bench. "The Old One can see it too."

Witherwood turned his head, and he and the hawk studied each other solemnly for a long moment. An understanding seemed to pass between them. Witherwood made a gesture with his hands, the first fingers linking tightly together.

"Brother," said Voice. He sounded as if something large were caught in his throat. "That means 'brother.'"

The bird's eye gleamed brighter for an instant, then clouded with sorrow.

"I am Kral of the Red-tails," the hawk said. "I have come to seek your aid. The times are ill and the Families are fearful. The winds beneath our wings are dry and thick with dust. My mate has been taken by the black water. My nestlings are weak with thirst."

"It's what my father calls a Drying Time," Tad said. "We think that it's caused by the Nixies, the Water Witches. They have a magic token called the Waterstone that they're using to capture all the water."

The bird nodded. His feathers glowed in the sunlight, gold-brown tinged with red, the color of leaves on bright afternoons in the Moon of First Frosts. Tad had never realized that a hawk was so beautiful.

"There is an old tale among the Families," the hawk said. "It tells that in time of great trouble a groundling will appear called the Sagamore, the Shining One. I had thought this was a story for nestlings. But then, beside the black lake, I saw your shine."

"So it was you who killed the snake," Tad said.

"It was an evil creature," the hawk said. "It was bitter with poison." He made a gesture of wiping his beak, as if to rid himself of a bad taste. *"Pthah!"* he said with disgust.

"You saved our lives," Tad said.

The bird shook his head dismissively.

"I saw your shine," the hawk said. "I have come to speed your quest."

"But why?" Tad swallowed nervously. "Since the Very Beginning, the hawks have always been our enemies."

He suddenly remembered, with awful clarity, Pondle-weed's tale about Great-aunt Thistleseed, who was snatched by a hawk one autumn day while gathering beechnuts. Nothing was left behind but a half-filled basket and one mouseleather boot. Nobody had liked Great-aunt

Thistleseed much — she had a wart on her nose the size of a blueberry, and a nasty temper — but that, as Pondleweed was always quick to add, was hardly the point. Even if you carped and complained and generally behaved like a ferret with a sore paw, you didn't deserve to get eaten in one gulp by a monstrous murdering bird the size of a house.

The hawk blinked his amber eye. When he spoke again, he sounded regretful. "It is a harsh world, little brother," he said, "and one must eat. To us, who live in the air, one groundling has always been much like another, whether it runs on two legs or four. But one can listen and learn, Shining One, and the old ways can change."

"What is it talking about?" Birdie, still crouching on the grass, sounded small and frightened. Tad realized that she and Voice could only understand one side of the conversation. If that. Had he, too, been speaking in that strange harsh language of the hunting birds?

"His name is Kral," he said. "He says he wants to help us. That he came looking for me. 'To speed my quest,' he said."

"To tear your head off, more like," said Voice. He shot a suspicious glance at the hawk. The bird had pulled himself majestically erect and was seemingly absorbed in something interesting in the far distance. He appeared to be paying no attention to the little group on the ground.

Giving us a chance to talk things over, Tad thought.

"It might not be able to help itself," Voice continued. "It's the hunting instinct, you know. They see something that's small like a mouse and runs like a mouse, and they eat it. I'm not saying there's ill will there, nothing like that. No *feelings* are involved. It's just the way they're made." He gave a little shiver. *"Predators,"* he said.

"'The heron will never be friends with the frog,'" Birdie said. She glanced nervously out of the corners of her eyes at the silent hawk, without turning her head. "That's what Father always says."

"And quite right too," said Voice. "Food is food. You may make conversation with it and appreciate its finer qualities, but sooner or later, when one feels nibbly—"

Pippit squawked.

"He saved our lives at the black lake," Tad said stubbornly.

He took a deep breath. *Sometimes,* he reflected, *you just have to trust in what you feel.* And no matter what Voice and Birdie said, this felt right. He felt sure somehow that the hawk was an ally. A friend. And hadn't Witherwood said "brother"?

Tad glanced toward Witherwood, but the old man was leaning back against the wall again, silently shut in upon himself, his eye closed. Then Witherwood's hands moved.

"He speaks to you, Tad," Voice said. "He tells you to listen with your Mind."

Listen with my Mind? *How?* Tad squinched his eyes shut, trying to concentrate. How could he listen with his mind? And then, as it had happened in the stone circle, something—*stretched*—inside him and he could hear. Though it wasn't hearing exactly—and not quite seeing or touching, either, but a strange combination of the three. *Maybe it's my Third Eye,* Tad thought. That's what Pondleweed always said when he knew all about something that the children thought he couldn't possibly have discovered. "I saw you two with my Third Eye," Pondleweed would say.

This Third Eye, though, not only saw, it saw *beyond.* Tad looked at Birdie and saw not just Birdie's small greenish-brown face and dandelion-cotton hair but the Birdie *beyond* Birdie, a warm essence that spoke in a thought language all its own. The real Birdie. He could see—or hear or feel—what Birdie was feeling and thinking. On the surface, she was afraid, but deeper down, there was a hard core to Birdie like the heartwood of a tree, fiercely protective of the people she loved, determinedly courageous, indestructibly loyal and loving. Tad felt a surge of love for his little sister. Quicker than thought, his Eye flicked away. It passed over Pippit, a small moist green mind filled with thoughts about swimming and buzzflies; and over Blackberry, a velvety half-wild mind filled with a passionate devotion to the small female who had saved him from the dark ones. The Eye was growing more skillful now. Tad shifted it deliberately toward Witherwood and encountered something different: a tawny golden glow with a dark center. He reached toward it curiously, and it spoke.

Most will never know that you can see them, Witherwood's Mind said. *It is a Talent of the Old Folk. The Witches spoke mind to mind among themselves and could touch the minds of others. That, too, is your Talent, Sagamore. It is what lets you know the languages of the forest; now the tongue of the hunting birds, but soon—soon—the tongues of all creatures, from the smallest to the greatest, that of the lowliest creepers to that of the Wild Wulvs, and even of the Mogs, which your people call the bears.*

Tad took a deep breath.

Can the hawk be trusted? he asked the old man silently. *Will he truly do as he says?*

Look and see, Witherwood answered in the same way.

Tad moved his Eye, searching for the hawk's mind. There. A strange ripple of being. It felt, as he drew closer, like blue wind. Clean and clear, threaded with a black vein of sorrow—a mate, lost—but no deceit there, no falsehood. *Honest and honorable,* Tad thought.

He had his answer.

He moved closer to the great bird, reached up, and laid his hand on the tip of the longest wing feather.

"Could you take us to Stone Mountain?" he asked.

"In three hours, as the hawk soars," the harsh voice answered. "If you can cling to my back, little brother, I shall take you to the Burrowers and bring you safely home again."

"He can take us to the mountains," Tad explained to the others. He found it hard to remember they could not understand the hawk's words. "To the Burrowers, he said."

"The Burrowers . . . ," Voice said. "He must mean the Diggers. They've built whole towns there, underground, in huge rooms whittled out of rock." He paused, looking worried.

"Diggers are strange," Voice said.

Birdie came to stand beside Tad.

"If you're going to the Mountains," she said in a determined voice, "I'm going with you."

She was wearing her snapping-turtle look. Tad's heart sank. He couldn't let Birdie go along. Who knows what he might find at Stone Mountain? It might be dangerous. If anything happened to Birdie, he would never forgive himself.

"No, you're not," he said. "You stay here, Birdie, where it's safe. And take care of Blackberry and Pippit."

Birdie ignored him.

"Voice can look after Blackberry," she said.

"No, I can't," said Voice. "Weasels give me crawly feelings."

"And Pippit can stay with them," Birdie continued.

Pippit gave a horrified squawk that seemed to say that weasels gave him crawly feelings too.

Birdie stuck out her lower lip and looked more obstinate than ever.

"You'll all be fine," she said loudly. "The Sagamore before, the one in Witherwood's book—*he* didn't go to the Mountains alone. He took friends with him. You wouldn't want Tad to go all by himself, would you?"

"Yes," said Tad.

"No, of course not," said Voice at the same time.

The hawk broke in, its harsh voice tinged with amusement. "This shouting one is your mate?"

Tad shook his head vigorously. "She's my sister," he said. "My younger sister, Birdie. She's only nine. She wants to go with us."

"Your nest-mate," the hawk said. He nodded approvingly. "A female as valiant as the males. It is a trait much prized among the Families." His voice dropped and saddened. "Such was my mate, Kakaara, Lady of the High Air, Wind of my Heart." The hawk fell silent for a moment. Then he stretched his neck and flexed his broad wings. Banded feathers rippled. "I can easily carry two," he said. "Or three or four. You groundlings are as small as the veriest mice."

It was an unfortunate comparison. Tad decided not to repeat it.

"All right," he said ungraciously to Birdie. "He says he can take both of us. But if you go, you can't change your mind in the middle, you know. You'll have to go all the way. We're not going to turn around halfway there to bring you back."

"As if I'd want you to," Birdie snapped, glaring.

The hawk gave a hoarse caw that might have been a chuckle.

"Truly a young hawk," he said.

Hastily, preparations were made for the journey. Voice assembled a picnic-packet of food, wrapped in a fresh green leaf and pinned with bent thorns. Birdie explained (several times) to Blackberry that she would be back soon and that Voice would look after him in her absence. She made Voice scratch Blackberry behind the ears and persuaded the weasel to roll over on his back so that Voice could tickle his stomach. Blackberry soon became entranced with his new friend and developed a tendency to frisk and to poke Voice playfully in the stomach with his nose.

"Nice weasel," Voice said unenthusiastically. He was trying to maneuver a bench between himself and Birdie's pet. "Good Blackberry."

Pippit, however, refused to be left behind. He croaked piteously, clinging first to Birdie and then to Tad, and then flinging himself flat in the dry grass and kicking, a picture of froggish misery.

"We might as well take him," Birdie said. "Besides, we might need a watchfrog. Remember how he warned us about the Grellers."

Pippit stopped kicking and sat up, rolling his eyes hopefully.

"I suppose you're right," Tad said in an exasperated voice. He turned on the suddenly revived Pippit. "But you behave yourself, Pippit. Don't go wandering off. And don't *hop* on people all the time."

Pippit subsided into the grass, blinking rapidly, clearly trying to look like the model of a well-behaved frog.

They scrambled onto the hawk's back, with the help of a twig ladder thoughtfully produced by Voice, and perched, one behind the other, on the bird's broad shoulders, settling themselves between his folded wings.

Even now, Tad thought with a churning feeling in his stomach, they seemed awfully high above the ground. Sitting there, they were as high as Witherwood's stone chimney.

The hawk roused, flexing his wings. Beneath their bare legs, Tad and Birdie could feel the shifting ripple of powerful muscles.

"We fly, Sagamore," the great bird said.

"He's going, Birdie," Tad said over his shoulder. "Hang on. And hang on to Pippit."

He raised a hand in farewell to Voice and Witherwood. They were standing close together in the cottage dooryard, Witherwood leaning on his wooden crutch. As Tad watched, Witherwood's hands moved, spelling out a message. "Farewell!" Voice called up to them. "My master wishes you safe journey!

Good fortune, Sagamore, Witherwood spoke in Tad's mind.

"Take good care of Blackberry!" Birdie shouted.

At the sound of his name, the weasel pricked up his ears. Then he kicked up his hind legs delightedly and butted Voice in the stomach. Voice's lips formed the word *Oof,* and he sat down without meaning to, heavily.

There was a rustle of unfurling feathers, then a violent buffet of wind struck them as the hawk leaped into the air. Tad felt as if the bottom had dropped abruptly out of his stomach. The ground fell dizzily away. The children, peering over the hawk's shoulders, could see Witherwood and Voice waving beneath them, faces upturned to watch them go.

The wavers on the ground grew smaller and smaller. Soon they were only brown dots at the edge of a clearing the size of a dinner plate. Then they were gone altogether, lost in a great sweep of browns and faded greens. Tad caught his breath. He had dreamed all his life of the world beyond the pond, but he had never dreamed of anything as immense—as magnificent—as this. The world was far vaster than he had ever or could ever have imagined. From the air, the land spread out endlessly in all directions, rising and falling, fading bluely into distant horizons, farther than his eyes could see. He had never in his life felt so small and insignificant. He clutched the hawk's feathers tighter and felt Birdie's hands behind him, gripping his shoulders.

The world below was dry. Tad could see it, even at this great height. What should have been rich summer greens were sickly pale. The forest was striped and splotched with brown and yellow and ashy gray. Some trees thrust naked branches out of the forest canopy: skeletal, leafless, dead. Far away, in the distant east, an ominous column of smoke was rising. Tad remembered what the Dryad had said about forest fires.

The bird climbed higher and higher, wings beating strongly in a powerful rhythm. Then the hawk's flight leveled. Now he sped smoothly through the air, sometimes gliding, wings outstretched, like a paddler before a carrying current of water. Wind whipped through the children's hair. The red-brown feathers brushing their arms and legs were beautifully soft and smelled sweetly of dried grass and pine needles. Tad had never seen the sky so close, so brilliantly blue. He felt as if he could reach up and touch it and that if he did, it would be as smooth and cool as the inside of a shell or the surface of a rain-washed stone.

The hawk flung itself onto a rising updraft of air and soared. He let out a long keening cry. Tad realized that the bird was singing — or rather chanting — a battle song to the drumbeat rhythm of the wind.

> *I am the Harrier.*
> *I am the Hunter.*
> *Cloud-rider, Wind-rider,*
> *Lord of Air.*
> *I am the Death-dealer.*

I am the Blood-breaker.
Storm-rider, Rain-rider,
Lord of Air.

There was a lot more like that, all rather boastful, and somewhat monotonous after a while. The repetitive beat was soothing. *Bah*-bah-bah, *bah*-bah-bah, Lord of Air. Tad's eyelids drooped, and he began to feel sleepy. He must have even dozed a bit, for he jerked awake suddenly to find that the chant had ended. A long chain of mountains now lay before them in the distance. One loomed taller than the rest, its lofty peak silvered with unmelted snow.

"Stone Mountain," the hawk said.

15

THE DIGGERS

The mountain for which the hawk was heading was shaped like a swimming fish. It had a high humped back with a sheer rocky ridge running along the very top of it like a dorsal fin; then it trailed sinuously away to the south, curving gracefully like a fish's powerful tail. A bare white outcropping on the mountainside marked the fish's eye, and a pair of ragged hillocks looked a bit like tail fins.

"We could call it Fisher Mountain," Tad said over his shoulder. He had to shout to be heard over the rushing of the wind. "Maybe it's a good omen, Birdie."

Birdie shouted something back, but the wind whisked away her words.

The hawk was preparing to land. He slowed and began to lose altitude, braking dexterously with twists and tilts of its broad flight feathers. Gradually, as the children watched, objects on the ground came into focus. Shapes of trees emerged from the blurred sameness beneath them; then the outlines of branches and leaves. They dropped lower, moving in long lazy circles, down and down. Finally, with a sharp upward flip of his tail, the bird settled to the ground. His talons made a scraping sound on the rock-strewn surface.

"There." The hawk gestured with his beak, pointing out the direction. "That way can be found the Burrowers. They may be able to lead you to what you seek."

Tad and Birdie, clinging to feathers, slid cautiously down from the bird's back. It felt strange to be standing on solid ground again after the swift flight through the upper air. Pippit sprang incautiously after them, changed his mind in midair, gave a panic-stricken squawk, and landed with a thud next to Tad's feet.

"I will stay here at the edge of the trees and wait for you," the hawk said. "The Burrowers are no friends of the Families, and I have no wish to face their flying arrows. I will be here when you return. You have only to climb the path and circle behind the boulders, and you will reach the door to their dens."

The hawk shook his wings fussily and began to preen, smoothing and rearranging his feathers one by one with his beak.

"We'll be as quick as we can," Tad said.

The bird paused in his grooming. "A safe wind beneath you, Sagamore," he said. He motioned with his head toward Birdie. "Have a care for the young hawk."

The path was narrow and dusty, and rough with gravel, and once the children left the shelter of the trees, the stones were uncomfortably hot under their bare feet. Tad, glancing back over his shoulder, saw the hawk staring after them, motionless and almost invisible in the dappled sunlight at the edge of the forest. The bird nodded once, encouragingly, and blinked one amber eye. Then Tad, Birdie, and Pippit rounded an immense granite boulder, and Tad lost sight of him.

The path wove in and out through a field of huge stones that looked as if they had been dropped by giant children playing a giant game of pebblehop. There were so many turns and twists and backtrackings that Tad lost all sense of direction. It felt as if they were going around in circles. He was hot. And his feet were beginning to hurt. Then Pippit suddenly stopped dead in the middle of the path and began to croak unhappily.

"He's tired," Birdie said to Tad.

She prodded the frog with her toes. "We can't stop *now,* Pippit."

But Pippit refused to budge. He hunkered down stubbornly, blinking rapidly, and making agitated little wheezing noises.

"What's the matter?" asked Tad.

"He won't go," Birdie said. "Come *on,* Pippit. *Move.*"

Pippit hunched his head into his shoulders and pretended to be a rock.

"There's something wrong," Birdie said. "There's something he doesn't like up ahead."

Pippit whimpered.

"We *have* to go on," Tad said.

"It's all right, Pippit," Birdie said. "You've warned us. 'The most dangerous snake is the one you don't know is there.' That's what Father says, Pippit. If you're expecting danger, then you're prepared."

Pippit gave a long series of croaks, clearly indicating that if you were expecting danger, you ought to be going in the opposite direction.

They edged nervously forward, Birdie keeping watch to the right, Tad to the left. Pippit dragged between them, tugging at their tunics and making doomful sounds.

Birdie said doubtfully, "I don't see anyth—"

Before she finished her sentence, Pippit gave a terrified squawk and leaped violently backward, knocking both children off their feet. Just where they had been standing, a heavy bundle of rope thudded down onto the path. The bundle quivered, jerked, gave a hiccuping little heave, and then—with a gigantic tug—gathered itself into a bag, turned upside down, and shot up into the air. Tad and Birdie stood staring after it.

"It's a net," Tad said after a moment. "Like our fishing nets back home, only bigger."

"It's a trap," Birdie said. "If it weren't for Pippit, we'd have been caught in it."

Pippit made satisfied noises, indicating that he had done his job well and been proved right, while Tad and Birdie had behaved foolishly and been proved wrong.

"Look!" Tad said. "It's doing something. The net's moving all by itself. Look—it's running along a line, on a little wheel. Let's follow it."

They scampered along the ground beneath the net bag, which was zipping busily through the branches overhead. Then the net stopped abruptly with a jerk, released itself from the line, and dropped heavily onto a long wooden platform.

The platform was much higher than the tops of the children's heads. A thick strip of oiled cloth ran across the top of it and then around the bottom in a long unbroken loop. The cloth, Tad realized, was moving somehow, dragging the limp net along with it.

Whump!

The whole platform shook.

Whump!

"What's *that*?" said Birdie.

Tad stood on tiptoe and pointed.

"It's a *club*," he said. "Birdie, it's an enormous club! It's connected up over that platform somehow. This must be how the Diggers hunt. They must catch things in those nets, and then the club falls down on top of them and . . ."

"Squashes them," said Birdie, looking horrified.

Whump!

"That could have been us," Birdie said again in a small voice. "I don't think I like the Diggers much."

"We've come all this way," Tad said. "We can't stop now. Besides, we need their help."

Birdie nodded reluctantly. "Let's get away from here," she said. "Come on, Pippit. No, not *that* way. That's back the way we came. This way."

Pippit gave a distressed-sounding croak, clearly saying that backward was by far the best way to go.

They had been walking steadily for some time—Pippit grumbling unhappily behind them—when they heard, far up ahead, a babble of voices. Tad hushed Pippit, and they moved forward cautiously, their feet silent on the stony ground. As they drew nearer, the voices grew louder and more distinct, and the babble resolved itself into the sound of two people bickering.

"I tell you, I saw it," the first voice—a high excited tenor with a tendency to squeak—said.

The second answered in a suspicious growl. "And you saw the ferrets, too, not seven days ago, all lined up in the moonlight, you said, with their little eyes a-gleaming, and what did we find when we got out here?"

An unhappy mutter from the squeaker.

"I'll tell you what we found," the growly voice continued relentlessly. "Stones, nothing but stones, and all that hauling for no reason." There was a ringing clatter, followed by a protesting grating noise. *"Ferrets!"* the growly voice said in disgust.

"Anyone can make a mistake," the squeaker said defensively.

"And anyone does," the growler retorted. "Over and over and over again. And always on the days when I'm on duty. Pick another day, why don't you, and share your mistakes with another watchman?"

"It was right overhead, I tell you!" It was the first voice, shriller. "You'd have to be blind to miss it, big as it was, and nasty-looking, too, with its big hooky beak and little yellow eyes. . . ."

Birdie nudged Tad violently in the ribs. "It's the hawk," she whispered. "He's talking about our hawk. He must have seen us. But the other one doesn't believe him."

They edged forward cautiously and peered around the edge of a jagged granite ledge.

"What's *that*?" whispered Birdie, staring. "What are they *doing*?"

There was a wide archway cut in the stone of the mountainside before them. The archway could be closed off with a pair of heavy wooden doors, but now the doors were swung wide open to the afternoon sun. Just outside the doors, a pair of figures, their backs toward the children, struggled awkwardly with a complicated-looking device on metal-rimmed wooden wheels. The taller of the two suddenly stopped whatever he had been doing, straightened, and turned. He was a Digger. His face and body were covered in short reddish-brown fur, and his eyes were as round and dark as a pair of polished black beads. He wore a tight leather cap on his head, and a leather apron with a row of pockets across the front.

"It's gone now, anyway," the tall Digger said crossly. He was the squeaker. "By the time a chap can get any attention—" He stopped suddenly as he caught sight of Tad and Birdie. *"Who's there?"* The squeak, startled, became piercing. *"Who are you?"*

"That's quite enough for one day, Grummer," the growler said testily, straightening up in turn and clutching the small of his back. "We've all had quite enough of your confusions and commotions and false alarms—" He stopped in midsentence as Grummer tugged insistently at his arm. Then he, too, turned to look toward the children. His eyes widened and his mouth fell open.

"What did I tell you?" the squeaker said smugly.

"Fishers, as I live and breathe," the shorter Digger said. "And young ones, if I'm not mistaken. Come out, then, the both of you. We won't hurt you. Unless mayhap Grummer here falls on you by tripping over his own big feet. Where do you two come from? And what brings you to Stone Mountain?"

Tad and Birdie hesitantly moved out from behind the sheltering ledge and came forward.

"I'm Tadpole. Tad," Tad said. "And this is my sister, Birdie. We come from the northernmost of the Ponds."

"A goodly distance," said the shorter Digger drily. His name, he told the children, was Werfel, though Tad and Birdie would always think of him as the Growler. He was the day's watchman, charged with guarding the gate and keeping alert for strangers and enemies.

"We take it in turns," he told the children, "since it's a dull job most days, and none of us likes to be taken from our proper work. There's not much that comes to Stone Mountain, for all that Grummer here sees ferrets behind every rock and tree. We're well protected, mind, and the word gets around."

Grummer looked so downcast that Birdie felt sorry for him. "Well, 'you can't hide too often from the Owl,'" she said. "That's what our father always says. It means it's safer to hide even if the Owl isn't there than to *not* hide and find out that the Owl *is*."

"There's them that will wish they'd listened to me someday, when their bones are munched by a hungry ferret," Grummer said darkly.

Tad was peering curiously at the workings of the contraption on wheels. Now that he had a chance to study it more closely, he saw that it resembled an immense bow laid on its side. The bow could be raised or lowered with a crank and its heavy string could be pulled back by means of a hook and a winch. The bow was partially drawn now and loaded with a huge metal-pointed arrow that was longer than Tad himself. Werfel gave the device an affectionate pat on the wheel.

"What is it?" Tad asked.

"It's a ballista," Werfel said. "A mechanical crossbow. A very powerful weapon, this is. Properly set up, it can take a hunting bird out of the air—down before it knows what hit it, and a good thing too."

He squinted up measuringly at the empty sky. Tad and Birdie exchanged worried glances.

"But *not*," Werfel continued, with a telling look at Grummer, "*not* something to be hauled out at a moment's notice, heavy as it is, because *someone* sees a falling leaf and thinks that it's a dangerous flying menace."

As he spoke, he was tugging at the winch and loosening ropes and pulleys. The taut bowstring slowly relaxed. Werfel released the poised arrow.

"Next time," he advised the disgruntled Grummer, "next time you start seeing birds, you just come out here by yourself and throw rocks. Now make yourself useful and help me roll this thing back inside." He turned to Tad and Birdie. "And you two better come along with us. All strangers must report to the High Council, the rules say, and Furgo'll be wanting to know all about who you are and what's your business. Bring your frog."

He set his shoulder to a brace above a metal-rimmed wheel. "Come on, Grummer, shove! Put some effort into it! Don't mess about over there like a flitty-headed butterfly!"

The stone passage leading into the mountain was cool and dim, illuminated with lamps set at intervals high up in the walls. The lamps burned with a strange bright blue flame that made a hissing noise. As they walked past, their shadows swelled and shrank eerily in the blue light, first dwindling down to almost nothing, then shooting up very dark and tall against the rock walls.

Werfel and Grummer, trundling the crossbow, rumbled along in front, still bickering. Scraps of phrases, alternately tenor and bass, drifted backward.

". . . nonexistent birds . . ."

". . . proper attention to duty . . ."

Tad, trailing behind with Birdie, felt increasingly apprehensive. Werfel and Grummer seemed nice enough, but the Diggers were strange, Voice had said. *What if we wanted to get out of here,* Tad thought, *would they let us go?* He glanced up at the rough ceiling of the passage and suddenly thought of the entire mountain of rock over his head.

On the right, hollowed out of the solid rock, there was a small room, evidently a sitting room for the current watchman. A long metal tube stuck out of the wall next to the door. Werfel put his mouth near the end of the tube and began to speak into it. Then he shifted position, bringing the tube close to one ear. A message seemed to have been delivered and received.

"Right," Werfel said importantly. "Now, you younglings come with me, and we'll go find Furgo. The High Council is expecting you. *You* can go back to the gate and keep watch, Grummer. Just try not to spot any more of them stony ferrets or phantom birds."

Grummer, muttering sullenly, began to trudge back up the passage in the direction of the gate.

Tad and Birdie hurried after Werfel. They rounded a corner, passed through another stone archway—and stopped dead in astonishment. They were in an enormous cave, a cave so huge that its ceiling was lost in shadow. It seemed that the entire center of the mountain was hollow. Lining the rock walls on either side were rows of stone houses, buildings piled upon buildings, with flights of narrow stone stairs leading to their upper stories. Tad and Birdie had never seen so many dwellings clustered together.

"They just live like this? All of them crowded on top of each other?" Birdie asked unbelievingly. "Why, there must be hundreds of them, all in the same place. *Thousands.* All together, like a huge school of minners. How do they do it?"

Tad shook his head in amazement.

Werfel, now far ahead of them, paused and beckoned.

"Come along now!" he shouted. "This way!"

The cave was filled with a steady hum of activity. In the distance there was a steady pounding and clanging of hammers and picks, and repeated sounds of something heavy rolling, then stopping, then rolling again. In open-fronted workshops, Diggers in leather aprons hammered slabs of red-hot metal over roaring fires, or bent over wooden benches, piecing together peculiarly shaped objects that Tad didn't recognize. Everyone Tad, Birdie, and Pippit passed stopped whatever they were doing to stare at them. Probably most of the Diggers had never seen a Fisher before, Tad realized. Or a frog. *We must look funny to them, not having any fur.*

He was quite taken up with that thought, imagining how he would look with a sleek coat of reddish fur, when Birdie suddenly screamed and Pippit gave a squawk of terror. There before them was an immense silver-colored . . . something. It was moving frantically, its huge jointed arms pounding vigorously up and down, its eye-like red lights flashing brilliantly. Without warning, it gave off an earsplitting whistle and spat out a scalding cloud of steam. Birdie and Pippit leaped backward so fast that they almost knocked Tad down. A little group of Diggers, dwarfed by the massive whatever-it-was, were rapidly shoveling lumps of black rock into a fiery mouth in the object's side. The Diggers wore padded leather protectors over their ears, and the fur of their faces and arms was black with dust.

Werfel, his face filled with concern, was hurrying back toward them, waving his arms up and down.

"It's all right!" he panted. "It's all right. It won't hurt you." He panted for a moment, trying to catch his breath. "It's called a steam engine. The coal goes in there, see, to fuel the fire, and the fire heats up the water in the boiler. That's the big tank there."

Tad gaped at the engine. This was more than he could take in. "Those black rocks—they *burn*?"

Werfel nodded. "The fire boils the water, see? Then the steam from the boiling water goes through those pipes there and pushes those arms up and down"—he pointed—"which makes those wheels go round, which moves the mining cars." Tad followed the pointing finger to a row of little wheeled carts fastened to a cable. Each cart held a Digger carrying a shovel or a pickax. As Tad watched, the carts trundled off into a side tunnel and disappeared. At the same time, a second set of carts — these loaded to the brim with silvery-colored ore — emerged from the tunnel, moving in the opposite direction. More Diggers rushed forward to unload them.

Werfel was urging them forward.

"It's not much farther," he said. "Furgo and the other Council members live in the next cave. It's quieter there."

"What's that?" Birdie asked.

It was a great wooden wheel set in a broad stone trough. Above the wheel, shallow stone steps led upward as far as the children could see, toward the roof of the cave.

"It's the Waterwheel," Werfel explained. He rubbed his nose worriedly with the back of his hand. "Usually there's a waterfall comes down those steps there and falls on the Wheel and makes it turn. Then it runs off down that channel, see? It's a regular river. But something's gone wrong. It's mostly all dried up now. The engineer chaps have been having a look at it."

Tad and Birdie exchanged anxious glances.

"The Nixies?" Birdie whispered. "Even here?"

They passed through another archway, into a branching tunnel.

"Those are the bat stables," Werfel said, pointing to an open doorway. Tad and Birdie craned their heads to peer inside. The stable—a vast open area—looked empty.

"Where are they?" Birdie asked. "There's nothing here."

Werfel chuckled and pointed upward.

The roof of the cave was a mass of sleeping bats. There were hundreds of bats, hanging upside down in rows from their perches, leathery wings folded, eyes tightly closed.

"Those big fellows on the right are the transport bats," Werfel said, speaking softly. "The mothers and babies are over there, toward the middle, and these here, closest to the door, they're all trainees."

Tad stared up at the nearest bat. It was a middle-sized bat, velvety brown, with a pointed mouselike face and big ears. It was sound asleep, making a rhythmic purring sound.

Werfel tugged Tad's elbow. "The Council Chamber is over this way," he said.

This cave *was* quieter than the first. Its walls, too, were lined with stone houses, but these were richer and more elaborate, with intricately carved windowsills and doorways.

"There's the Council Chamber," Werfel said.

It was an imposing building at the end of the row of houses. Tall stone columns supported a portico across the front. Beneath the portico was a heavy wooden double door, studded with polished pebbles and inlaid in curly patterns with silver. One of the doors stood open.

"Go on in," Werfel said. "Furgo'll be waiting for you. Just stand up straight and talk respectful, and you won't have any trouble. Good luck, now, the both of you. I have to be getting back to the gate before that Grummer starts seeing more ferrets." He lowered his voice and tapped a finger against the side of his head. "Grummer's not a bad sort, you know. He had a close call with a ferret when he was a little chap, and he's been nervouslike ever since."

He strode away in the direction from which they had come, looking once behind him to give an encouraging wave. Tad and Birdie waved back. Then, together, they turned toward the entrance to the Council Chamber.

16

THE HIGH COUNCIL

The Councilors looked, Tad thought, like silver statues.

The eight members of the High Council sat at the far end of the Chamber in a row of high-backed stone chairs. Each wore a wide-sleeved gray robe thickly embroidered with silver thread and fastened at the throat with heavy square silver buttons. There were round silver-embroidered caps on their heads and silver-trimmed leather boots on their feet. In a middle chair, taller than all the rest, sat an elderly Digger with a knitted shawl draped over his shoulders. He was thin and bent, and his short fur was entirely gray except for faint black circles around his eyes. He held a polished metal rod in his right hand, which he rapped sharply three times on the arm of his chair as Tad and Birdie approached. All the Councilors, moving as one, turned their heads to look at them. Tad had never felt so small and so grubby. So . . . barefoot.

"Ah, the Fisher younglings," the gray Digger said. "Sit down, sit down, both of you. I am Furgo, Head of the High Council of the Diggers."

Tad and Birdie sat on a low stone bench.

"I am Tadpole of the Fisher Tribe," Tad said. "But mostly I'm called Tad." He remembered that Werfel had warned him to be respectful. "Sir," he added hastily. "And this is my sister, Redbird. Birdie."

Furgo introduced the Councilors. "There are seven," he explained, "one from each of the seven workers' guilds. This is Gerda of the Growers. She oversees our moss and mushroom farms, and directs the cultivation of the Outer Gardens." Gerda had brown-and-black striped fur and wore silver rings in her ears. She gave the children a small polite smile. "Bodric of the Leatherworkers. He tends our deermouse traps and tanning pits." Bodric, a short toast-colored Digger, bowed briefly in the children's direction. "Hadnar of the Stonecutters." A big burly Digger. "Sindri of the Metalworkers." An orange-furred female with a delicate white stripe across her nose. "Sidda of the Engineers. Our technological specialists." A small chocolate-brown female with a serious expression. "Edelbert of the Skalds. Our poets and scholars." Edelbert was a tall slender Digger with sleek black fur and elegant white patches under his ears. He had an exceptionally long pointed nose on which was perched a pair of silver-framed spectacles. He gave the children the barest of nods. "And Pegger of the Miners." A plumpish dusty-brown Digger with a friendly look. He winked. Tad and Birdie liked him at once.

"We have few visitors here," Furgo explained, "so we are most interested in the news of the outer world. And in what brings you younglings so far to Stone Mountain."

Tad took a deep breath. "It's a little complicated, sir," he said.

"Then take time to explain," said Furgo. "The Council is here to listen. Begin at the beginning."

But what was the beginning? Tad thought. And then he thought: *It began with the spear.* He almost smiled. It seemed so long ago that all he had had to worry about was learning how to throw the spear and getting guggled at by a bunch of mudflapping frogs. He was a whole different person now. Words and images tangled in his head. The voice in the water, the journey up the dying stream, the Hunters. The dreadful black lake and the terrible loss of Pondleweed. The Dryad and Witherwood. The Sagamore. How could he begin to explain?

He felt Birdie's touch on his arm.

"The first part was the water," Birdie said. "Back home our pond is drying. That was how we knew something was wrong. That was the beginning."

There was a rustle of movement and a murmur as the Council members turned and whispered to each other.

"The Drying," Furgo said. "We have seen it too."

The Councilors, one by one and then all together, nodded.

"The onion crop is a rock-thumping disaster," said the plumpish Digger named Pegger. He had a crooked ear that gave him a raffish happy-go-lucky look. "And the waterfall has gone dry as a bone."

"The green plants on the outer mountain have withered," said Edelbert from the neighboring chair in reproving tones, "and the river that runs through its heart has shrunk to a silver trickle over the rocks. Now that you're a Councilor, Pegger, you must really try for more nicety of diction."

"I speak as I see fit," said Pegger. "And I say what I mean. And when I say 'dry as a bone,' I mean 'dry as a bone,' and not none of your silver trickles, neither."

The black-furred Digger closed his eyes briefly. A pained expression washed across his face. *"That,"* he said, in horrified tones, "was a *triple* negative."

"Edelbert," Furgo said severely. "Pegger. Let the younglings talk."

Tad—with help from Birdie—began to tell his story. Every once in a while, a Councilor would interrupt, asking Tad to explain further or to repeat a part of the tale in greater detail.

Tad talked on. When he told about his mysterious Remembers and the blossoming of his strange new powers, a startled babble arose.

"Sagamore? . . ."

"The Sagamore! What kind of name is that?"

"I always thought that was a superstition. The belief systems of the primitive tribes . . ."

"There is a mention of a 'Sagimore' or 'Sagamore' in one of the Alternative Elder Epics, but the precise meaning of the term is a matter of debate. Only a fragment of the original text remains. It seems to have been some sort of magical fish. . . ."

"Did you say a *fish*?"

Furgo rapped his metal rod again, and the Councilors fell silent.

"You, of all Diggers, should know the tale of the Sagamore, Edelbert," said Furgo. "It appears in the third of the Original Orations, and it agrees, in all particulars, with the story we have just heard from the lips of this youngling."

Several of the Councilors nodded.

Edelbert looked furious.

"It is not a question of *a* Sagamore, Councilors. A Sagamore, if described in the ancient texts, is certainly more than a primitive superstition." It was Hadnar of the Stonecutters, in a gruff raspy voice that sounded a bit like scraping chisels. "It is a question of *the* Sagamore in the person of this boy. A boy, Excellency, and younger than my own apprentices. We all know that younglings are prone to exaggeration and that their imaginations often run away from them. You should hear my lads, with their boastings and teasings, and their tales of stonegoblins and ghosties. . . ."

"You must admit," said Gerda regretfully, "that the boy's story is a trifle hard to believe."

"If you will pardon me, your Excellency, it is *impossible* to believe." It was Edelbert, sounding as if he'd just found a bug in his dinner. "This . . . *Fisher* . . . is wholly uneducated. He is not even *clean*."

The orange Digger—Sindri of the Metalworkers—nodded.

"Surely, if there were such a mental phenomenon as this child describes, it would appear to us in a more likely form."

"Clearly a misinterpretation of the facts . . ."

They were talking about him as if he weren't even there. Tad clenched his fists.

"Form is as form does." It was Pegger, sounding angry. "Did you never see a thunder egg, Edelbert? No, you've not been down in the mines, now, have you?" He leaned toward the children, making a cupping motion with his hands. "A thunder egg is a ball of gray rock, looking like nothing so much as an ordinary stone. But if you hit it with your hammer, so"—he made a downward striking gesture—"the ball splits open, and inside, it's filled with crystals, big and bright and beautiful like none you've never seen before. You do remember that thunder egg, Edelbert, for some things you can't tell by their outsides. The Fisher sounds a truthful lad to me, and we've no call to name him liar."

"I saw him," said Birdie. Her eyes were narrowed fiercely and her lower lip was sticking out. "I was there and I saw him. Tad is just what he says he is. And if you'd been with him, you'd believe in him too. And the ha— A friend of ours says there's a shine around him. He can see it. The Shining One, he called him."

Tad rose to his feet. He straightened his back, lifted his chin, and let his gaze travel from face to face, meeting each Councilor's eyes. The Diggers stared back at him, waiting.

"I know it's hard to believe," Tad said simply. "I don't understand it all yet myself. I don't remember this place, but I know that I—or a part of me—was here once, long ago. I had a friend"—his voice caught for a moment on the word—"a friend named Burris."

Oh, Burris, if you were with me now.

Time seemed to stand still. And then the scene changed.

Trees rose dark behind him. The sky above was velvet-black, star-studded, with a thin sliver of silver moon. The campfire was nothing but red coals. He was too wound up to sleep. Tomorrow . . . something momentous would happen tomorrow. Tomorrow he would meet the Witches face-to-face. Everything depended on him. His thoughts refused to lie still.

Someone stirred beside him in the darkness.

"I've had a Foreshadow," the familiar fur-soft voice said.

His breath caught in his throat. "A bad dream, old friend." But to his own ears his voice sounded shaken. "A bad dream and Hunter firepeppers for supper."

A movement, shadow on shadow, as Burris shook his head. The warm grip of strong fingers on his forearm. "Hear me, Sagamore, and remember," the husky voice said softly.

The next words were strange words, in a language he had never heard before. He could almost *feel* these words.

Some were as heavy and thick as blocks of granite, some sharp as metal picks, some as clear as crystals.

> *Hicht yar logh und ostrem berraen*
> *Alt alben lithag rebicht ferraen*
> *Und ghawone ac averraegd*
> *Harta twinnen syntaghraegd*
> *Und ombichten clannenbain*
> *Hicht erth und hord untwinnentwain.*

"Now you," Burris said.

He repeated it back, stumbling, the foreign words awkward on his tongue.

"Again."

This time it was easier. He could understand the phrases now. They rolled from his lips like polished pebbles.

> *Though years are long and men forget,*
> *The stone-cored mountains do stand yet*
> *And, staunch as they, we do avow*
> *To keep the faith between us now*
> *And stand together, kindred-true,*
> *Though world and time divide us two.*

"What is it?" he asked.

"It is called the *Magelith*," the soft voice answered. "Spoken in the Old Tongue of the Diggers. It is a password and a pledge, taught by parents to their children generation after generation, always kept secret, known to the Diggers alone. With the *Magelith,* I make you a member of my Tribe. We are as brothers, you and I, and your sons must be as mine, for tomorrow——"

Tad thrust the words away from him in a sharp gesture of denial. "A thousand Foreshadows never come to pass," he said.

"Perhaps nor will mine," the familiar voice said, a fur-warm murmur in the darkness. "But Great Rune has whispered in my ear, old friend. Speak the *Magelith* and any Digger in the land will welcome you and give you aid, for now you, too, are of the line of Burris. Remember."

Furred fingers closed briefly over his.

"Sleep, Sagamore . . ."

Time shuddered and dissolved. He was in the Council Chamber once more, all eyes watchfully upon him, the stone floor cool under his feet. He felt dizzy and disoriented. The Remember was over. Except . . .

"Burris did me a great honor," Tad said. "He made me a member of his Tribe."

Edelbert——*It* would *be Edelbert,* Tad thought——gave an incredulous snort, as if to say that no Digger would ever stoop to such a thing.

Tad began to speak, softly at first, then louder. The foreign words this time felt utterly familiar in his mouth, as if he had recited them many times before. They echoed in the high stone chamber like chords of music, as if the stone itself recognized and welcomed them. When the last echo died away, the Councilors were staring at him goggle-eyed. Edelbert's mouth was sagging open. Pegger wore a broad gleeful grin.

"The *Magelith*," Furgo said in a shocked whisper. "How did you come to know this?"

Birdie tugged at Tad's sleeve. "The *what?*" she whispered. Tad kept his eyes on Furgo.

"I am what I say I am," he said, "and I have come to ask for help from the Diggers of Stone Mountain, as is my right as a man of the line of Burris."

"That it is," Pegger said robustly. He shot a triumphant look sideways at Edelbert, who was staring fixedly in the opposite direction and looking as if he had just stepped on a weaselpat. The other Councilors murmured excitedly among themselves.

Furgo slowly rose from his seat, stepped forward, and placed his hands on Tad's.

Then the moment shattered.

A shrill squeal cut through the air, followed by another and another. It sounded as if someone had caught a mouse and were stepping meanly and repeatedly on its tail. *Squee! Squee! Squee!*

The heads of the Councilors jerked up as if pulled by strings. Tad ducked, Pippit dodged behind his legs, and Birdie dived off the stone bench and wrapped her arms around her head. Something huge and dark flashed past, high above them. It zipped around the Council Chamber, still squealing, and then abruptly plummeted to the floor. It was a bat. Clinging to its back, looking embarrassed, was a Digger boy who seemed to be about the same age as Tad. He had rusty-red fur with brown-tipped ears and nose. An enormous bulging bundle was strapped to his back, giving him the peculiar look of a furry turtle.

"I've tamed my own bat, Grandfather!" he said. "I've tamed him! Everybody said that I couldn't do it, but I have!"

He slid awkwardly to the ground.

"He comes when I call and everything," he said. "I've named him Skeever."

"This is my grandson Willem," Furgo said. He sounded resigned.

He directed a repressive look toward Willem. "And what if you had fallen *off* the bat; had you thought of that?" he demanded sternly. "You could have been killed. Or worse, you could have fallen on top of someone else and killed *them*."

"I did think of that," Willem retorted. He reached behind him and patted the bundle on his back. "That's what this is for. I invented it, Grandfather. It works like a sort of air brake. The cloth unfolds and spreads out and just floats you down to the ground like an umbrella seed. That's what I've been calling it—a floater. Here, I'll show you."

Before Furgo could protest, he seized a cord dangling over his shoulder and yanked on it. The bundle on his

promptly exploded, spewing out enormous tangled
of cloth. Willem looked guiltily over his shoulder.

"Of course, it only works when you're up in the air."

Birdie giggled. Furgo sighed gustily.

"Sit down, Willem," he said, "and try to stay out of
trouble while we finish our business here." He gestured
politely toward Tad. "Please continue with your story."

Tad went on with his tale, taking it up where he had
left off, conscious of the bright curious regard of the Digger boy. He told of the meeting with Witherwood and
Voice and what they had learned in reading the ancient
record books.

"We think the Nixies have regained the Waterstone,"
he said. "That's how they're taking all the water. Witherwood's book said that all that time ago, the Sagamore
came to the Kobolds of Stone Mountain, and they helped
him somehow. But we don't know how. The words on the
next page—the page that would have explained it—
were all washed away. So we've come to find the Kobolds
and ask them if perhaps they could help us again."

The Councilors put their heads together. There was a
buzz of worried chatter.

"But . . . there are no Kobolds," Sindri said. "Not now.
The name is just a fairy tale for children."

"There are poems about them," Edelbert said. "They
are mentioned—in a wholly legendary sense, of course—
in the Elder Epic *The Saga of Stone Mountain*. Verses 346
to 407."

"How can they be?" asked Pegger. "What rhymes with *Kobold?*" He began to mutter to himself. "Bobold, dobold, fobold, gobold . . ."

"It's in free verse," said Edelbert coldly.

"You must forgive us, Tadpole," Furgo said. "In these modern times, we Diggers have grown away from belief in the ancient histories and the old tales. The Witches returned . . ." He hesitated. "This all comes as a shock to us."

Tad could hardly listen. He sank down on the stone bench and sat there miserably, staring at his knees. No Kobolds! Such a possibility had never occurred to him. He hadn't realized just how much he had been counting on finding them.

"But that doesn't mean," one of the Councilors was saying, "that there may not be other ways of defeating these creatures. We have, after all, made considerable technological advances over the past centuries." It was Sidda of the Engineers.

"Periscopes . . ."

"Pumps . . ."

"Mechanical arms . . . We could snatch the stone. It's a simple engineering problem—"

"Traps!" Bodric of the Leatherworkers said, sounding excited. "What do Nixies like to eat?"

They don't understand, Tad thought. *They have no idea what she's like. She's not some kind of* animal.

Then Willem spoke. He was crouched on the floor beside his bat, trying vainly to bundle the floater back together again. Billows of cloth seemed to be everywhere. "What about the faces in the rocks?"

A puzzled murmur from the Councilors.

"What do you mean?" Tad said. "What faces?"

"They're on a cliff on the outside of the Mountain," Willem said. "Faces frozen in the rock, dozens of them. Old men with beards. I used to pretend that they could come alive, that they were wizards."

"A game," Edelbert said dampingly. "A play for children."

"Faces," the burly Councilor said. Tad struggled for a moment to remember his name. Hadnar of the Stone-cutters. "I remember those faces. Masterful work. Masterful. Wasn't there some sort of story about them?"

"Pure imagination," said Edelbert tartly.

"It wouldn't hurt to take a look," said Pegger.

It was, in any case, too late to investigate today. As Pegger spoke, a reverberating gong echoed through the stone cavern.

"Day's end," Furgo said. "Time for the evening meal."

He turned to Tad and Birdie. "You will be my guests for tonight, and in the morning Willem will take you to see these . . . rock faces. And we of the High Council must discuss this further."

The Councilors, again moving as one, rose to their feet and inclined their heads toward Tad and Birdie. Tad bowed awkwardly in return. Then he turned and, with Birdie beside him and Pippit hopping awkwardly behind, followed Furgo out of the room.

Furgo's house was large and rambling. Stone rooms led into stone rooms in confusing order, and much of the furniture—large, blocky, and massive—was carved in place. Stone tables and benches seemed to grow right out of the floor. Tad and Birdie had thought that so much stone would be cold and uncomfortable, but instead the house was beautifully welcoming and warm. A fire blazed in the big hearth, and the stone seats, worn into comfortable polished hollows by generations of Digger bottoms, were invitingly heaped with squashy cushions.

The house was full of people. There were Furgo and his wife, Freyda, a comfortable round-faced Digger in a puffy cap shaped like a muffin; an elderly aunt with white circles around her eyes that gave her the look of a surprised owl; a couple of grown cousins; and Willem's mother and father and his four little sisters, who all ran around a good deal and had high piercing voices. They reminded Tad of the bat.

They were fourteen at dinner, after which Pippit fell asleep in a corner (on his back with his mouth open), and Tad and Birdie—who had eaten too much—could barely keep their eyes open. Even so, Tad, who was sharing a bed in Willem's room, found himself staying awake to talk to the Digger boy in the dark.

"The faces," Willem said softly. "Councilor Edelbert is all wrong about them. I'm sure of it."

"He didn't seem to like me much," Tad said tentatively.

"Skalds!" Willem said. "They're all like that. Snooty. And the things they make you learn in school. Verses and verses of the great epics, and if you make one little mistake . . ."

His voice trailed off.

"But he's wrong about the faces," Willem repeated. "They're not frozen all the time, exactly. I've heard them." He paused for a moment in the dark. Then he said, "They *whisper.*"

17

THE FACES IN THE ROCKS

There were hundreds of faces. They were carved in the rough brown stone of the cliff, and they looked as if they had been there for centuries. Some of the faces were so weathered that they were almost worn away, their features blurred as if someone had tried to scrub them smooth with a handful of scourweed. In some places, swallows had nested among the faces, daubing the stone heads with bottle-shaped nests made of damp clay.

Tad, Birdie, Pippit, and Willem stood looking up at them.

"They're all different," Birdie said, pointing. "Look, that one's sort of smiling. And the one next to it—the one with the big bulgy nose—just looks mean."

No two of the faces were alike. Some had wrinkled foreheads and thick bushy beards; some were bald; one or two seemed to be wearing tight caps that buckled under their chins. One had a jutting hooked nose that reminded Tad of the hawk's beak; one had a pursed-up mouth that made him look as if he had just taken a bite of a very sour pickle. Two or three had their mouths open and their eyes closed and looked as if they were asleep.

"They whisper?" Tad asked. It didn't seem possible.

Willem shrugged.

"Sometimes," he said. "At least I thought they did. I was up here at night once. It's pretty spooky in the moonlight. There were all these funny shadows and things, and all the faces looked sharper. It felt . . ." He gave an embarrassed little giggle. "It felt like they were all looking at me. All those eyes, staring. The longer I stood here, the less I liked it, and pretty soon I got so scared that I ran away. That's when I thought I heard them. Lots of little mumbly voices, whispering." He shrugged again. "When I got back home, my father said it was probably just the wind. But it didn't sound like wind. It didn't."

He looked up at the faces consideringly.

"And they move around too. At least I think they do. Every time I come here, they look a little different. See that one, with his mouth open? He wasn't like that the last time, I could swear it. *They move.*"

The little faces didn't look as if they had ever moved. They looked like rocks. Tad reached up and touched the nearest face on the tip of its beaky nose. It felt like rock too.

"Maybe we need to come back at night," Birdie said.

Tad still stared up at the crowd of faces. There were big ones, small ones, all splotched with dots of light and shadow. If he just stared at them without blinking, Tad discovered, the whole cliff began to shimmer and sparkle, and little spots jumped around in front of his eyes. Willem and Birdie were still talking behind him, but he found that if he concentrated hard enough, he ceased to hear the sound of their voices. He stared harder and harder at the sun-dappled stones. If he let his eyes drift out of focus, he found that all the little faces changed somehow: the features became sharper; the carved eyes glittered with little points of dancing light. And had one of them—two of them?—moved? He could swear the faces were shifting position, turning toward him, their empty eyes winking into awareness.

A gust of wind ruffled his hair and rattled the tall stalks of dried brown grass. *Whisper . . . whisper . . . whisper . . .*

A sudden shower of pebbles rained down from higher up on the cliff, bouncing sharply off the tops of stone heads and the bridges of stone noses, spattering across the ground at Tad's feet.

"Who are you?"

It was a rough gravelly voice that sounded as if the speaker had a throat full of dust.

Willem and Birdie gave startled exclamations and Pippit, a frightened squeak.

"Who are you, Fisher boy, that you can see beyond the stone?"

It was the closest of the faces that asked the question, a deep-lined craggy face with drooping stone mustaches and an odd little cap of rust-colored lichen growing on its shaggy stone hair. As it spoke, it seemed to move slowly forward, pulling itself farther out of the enclosing rock. Tad could see the stone lips move.

The power moved inside him, warm and strong, and he realized that he wasn't frightened at all. There was no feel of danger here.

"I am the Sagamore," he said. "I have come to seek the Kobolds, to ask their help now that the Nixies are awake."

The whisper ran through the cliffs again, but this time Tad could hear words in it.

"*Sagamore . . . Sagamore . . . Sagamore, . . .*" said the windy voices, murmuring one to the other up and down the rocky wall.

"*Nixies . . . Nixies . . . Nixies . . . awake . . . awake . . . awake . . .*"

The *S*s sounded like the dry rustling of dead leaves.

"Well, you have found them, Fisher boy," the stone voice rumbled. "Behold us, the Witches of the Mountains."

A chorus of grating voices chimed in.

"*Witches . . . Witches . . . Witches . . .*"

A final pebble bounced off an outcropping and struck Tad smartly on the top of the head.

"What help do you think we can give you, Fisher boy?"

Tad rubbed his head, wincing. He could feel a lump.

"I don't know exactly," he said. "You helped a Sagamore once before, long ago. You gave him something that helped defeat the Nixies when they were taking all the water—"

"We do not remember," a voice said sharply from high above Tad's head.

Tad looked up quickly, but he could not identify the speaker. Whoever it was, he decided, he didn't like him. The voice set his teeth on edge. It sounded like fingernails scraping on slatestone.

"Water is no friend of stone," the scrapy voice said.

"Water . . . water . . . water . . ."

The whispers suddenly sounded louder, angry. Tad took an inadvertent step back.

"Water is no friend of stone," the first Kobold repeated coldly. "Water wears the rock away and turns the boulder into dust. Water feeds the roots that crack apart the stones. Why should we help you? Let them take the water, Fisher boy."

This wasn't how things were supposed to go. Tad turned helplessly to look at Willem and Birdie. Willem stepped forward.

"That's the Great Cycle," Willem said. "It happens to everything."

Tad stared at him uncomprehendingly, trying to send questioning signals with his eyebrows. What was this? He had never heard of any Great Cycle.

"It happens everywhere," Willem said. "It has to. Even the water in your pond is part of it, Tad. The water doesn't just stay there, always the same. It turns into vapor and gets pulled up into the clouds, and then it falls back to Earth again as rain. The rain feeds the lakes and the rivers and the streams and the ponds. And then it all happens again, over and over. That's the Great Cycle. Or part of it."

He pointed down the mountainside toward the forest.

"The trees get old and die, and then they fall over, and then they rot. They turn into mold and dirt on the forest floor, and then new trees grow up where they once stood, sinking their roots into the new dirt. That's part of the Great Cycle too. The old trees die so that new trees can be born. Everything dies away and comes again, over and over."

Tad felt a pang of envy. Willem seemed to know so much more about everything than he did.

So the Sagamore is part of the Great Cycle too, he thought. *Like the old turtle said. The Mind and the Magic rest until the time is right to be born again in somebody else. Over and over . . .*

"The wet and the green, perhaps," the first Kobold said stubbornly, "but not the stone, Digger boy. Stone lasts."

"No, it doesn't," said Willem. "You said so yourself. Wind and water wear and wear on it and slowly turn it into dust."

The whispers mumbled and rumbled ominously like distant thunder.

"Dust . . . dust . . . dust . . ."

"But the dust washes down the streams," Willem said, "and piles up on the shores or settles down to the bottom of the lakes and oceans. Lots of it. And after a long long time, more time than any of us can even count, it all packs and crushes together and hardens into stone again. New stone."

The whispers softened.

"New stone . . . new stone . . . new stone . . ."

"They seem to like that," Birdie whispered.

"It's the way things are supposed to be," Willem said confidently. "If the Great Cycle stops, then everything just falls apart."

"So that's why everything is so wrong," Birdie said. "When the Nixies took the Waterstone, they stopped the Great Cycle."

The whispers sharpened into alarm.

"Waterstone . . . Waterstone . . ."

"The Water Witches may not misuse the Stone," the scrapy-voiced Kobold said from somewhere high above him. "It is against the Law."

"Well, it may be against the law," Birdie said, "but they're doing it anyway. Everything is drying up. Our pond is shrinking, and the stream above it is almost empty. *All* the ponds are drying. The forest is turning brown. Everywhere things are dying."

A buzz of whispering arose. The voices were clearer and more distinct now. There were low rolling rumbles, staccato chatters, even one high cantankerous voice that sounded a little like Grummer. They seemed to be quarreling.

"May not misuse the Stone . . . may not misuse the Stone . . ."

"Water is no friend . . . no friend . . ."

"It is nothing to do with us . . . with us . . . with us . . ."

"We helped them once . . . once . . . once . . ."

The whispering stopped.

"What's happening?" asked Birdie.

Tad shook his head.

The first Kobold spoke again. "When you came last to us, Sagamore, you walked in a different guise. The help we gave was fitting then, for you were man-grown and battle-wise. But now it is a different time, and you are not the same. You would find it of no use to you."

"A hindrance, even," a hoarse rattly voice said.

Birdie, beside Tad, bristled. "How can you be so sure he couldn't use it?" she demanded. "Whatever *it* is. You don't know what Tad can do."

A new voice answered. It reminded Tad of heavy boulders rolling. It was so deep that he could feel it vibrating inside his chest like a skin drum.

"We gave the Silent Sword," the voice said.

A Remember stirred in Tad's mind. His fingers curled as if they held a polished hilt. The blade was beaten steel set with patterns of gold. It was a beautiful thing, heavy, but not too heavy for his wrist. Once the Kobold put it in his hand, it was as if he and the Sword were one. . . .

"What's the Silent Sword?" Birdie was asking.

"The Silent Sword was forged in the long-gone days when we yet wielded hammers and tongs," the deep voice said, "and deep within its metal was set a fragment of the Earthstone. The bearer of the Sword was shielded from the Water Witches' song, and the Witches could not withstand the touch of its blade. A worthy weapon, the Silent Sword."

Birdie shot Tad a hopeful look. "It sounds the very thing," she said. "Couldn't Tad have it too?"

A buzz of mocking laughter. Tad felt his ears grow hot.

"The boy cannot use the Sword," the first Kobold said coldly. "He has neither the strength nor the skill for weapons. The Sword is not for him."

"Besides, the Sword is lost," the deep voice said.

"Lost . . . lost . . . lost . . ."

Birdie turned in dismay from Tad to Willem and back again.

"They're supposed to *help* us," she said in a distressed undertone. "They're acting like they don't even *care*."

"We cannot help you, Fisher boy," the first Kobold said. "Our day is past. We are of the stone now, rooted in the mountain. We will not walk abroad again, but will grow more and more silent. Soon we will not speak or wake at all, but will be one with the bones of the Earth."

From the face of the cliff around him came a chorus of agreement.

"Cannot help . . . cannot help . . . cannot help . . ."

"Sleep . . . sleep . . . sleep . . ."

Tad's heart sank. They had failed, then. *He* had failed. All that long journey for nothing.

"It is not so!" A new voice, its syllables sounding like a flurry of crashing hammer strikes.

Tad's head jerked up.

"It is true," the hammer voice said, "that we are bound here forever and can no longer walk about the Earth as once we did. But we are not yet powerless, brothers."

Agitated whispers.

"There have been many Sagamores," the hammer voice went on, "and no two of them the same. Each one learned to find a way. Who are we to turn our backs on this one because he is small and young?"

From somewhere deep inside, the mountain gave an angry rumble. Tad thought it sounded like a giant stomach growling.

Then there was a loud tearing sound. The cliff wall before them split open in a long jagged crack and something rolled out and fell heavily at Tad's feet. Pippit poked his head forward and nosed at it distrustfully.

"Take it, Fisher boy," the hammer voice said.

It was a fist-sized lump of dull gray stone. Tad bent down and picked it up.

"What is it?" he asked. He looked at Willem, puzzled, but Willem only shook his head.

The hammer voice gave a dusty chuckle. "A helping hand, Fisher boy."

The whispers murmured in grudging admiration.

"He's given you his right hand, Fisher boy . . . his right hand . . . with which to fight the Witch . . . to fight the Witch . . . his right hand . . ."

Tad recoiled. "This is your *hand*?"

He looked more closely at the lump of stone. At first it appeared smoothly round, but then he saw faint grooves and ridges shaped vaguely like clenched fingers, and a jutting bump that might have been the joint of an in-turned thumb.

"Your *hand*?" he repeated.

"It is the best I can give you, Fisher boy. It will help you . . . *help you* . . . *help you* . . ." The hammer voice dwindled and faded, then suddenly, as though it were making one last effort, grew stronger again. "I always loved the waterfalls," it said. "Are they still there?"

"Oh, yes!" Willem answered before Tad could speak. His eyes lit up. "They're beautiful. Like silver curtains falling over the rocks of the mountains."

Willem's face fell suddenly. Tad remembered the Diggers' motionless Waterwheel.

"At least they *were* beautiful," Birdie said, "before the Nixies stole away all the water."

Deep inside, the mountain growled.

"Take my hand, Fisher boy," the hammer voice said. "And set the Waterstone to do its work again, as is the Law."

"But how——?"

Before Tad could finish the question, the crack in the cliff sealed itself shut with a sharp snap. The whispers ceased. All in an instant, the faces froze again, seeming as they did so to blur and fade, sinking deeper into the rock.

"Thank you," Tad said into the sudden silence.

High above him a handful of pebbles rattled and fell.

Tad, Birdie, and Willem looked at one another, then looked down at the lumpy stone in Tad's hand, with its shadowy trace of stony fingers.

"But *how* will it help us?" Tad asked. "What are we supposed to do with it?" He threw a frustrated look at the silent cliff. "Why couldn't they have stayed awake long enough to explain things better?"

"Well, they seemed sure it would help," Birdie said bracingly. "And they're Witches, too; they must know more about how to fight Nixies than we do."

"Then I guess this is it," Tad said unhappily. *Why* couldn't the Kobolds have explained? "This must be what we came for."

"What do we do next?" asked Willem.

"We go back," Tad said. "We have to tell the others. We promised to meet at the Gathering of the Tribes. I told your grandfather all about it. The Gathering. The Diggers should come too; all the Tribes should be there." He hesitated. His throat felt tight. "And then . . ." He swallowed painfully. "And then I'll have to go back to the black lake. To find the Nixies."

"*We'll* go to find the Nixies," said Birdie and Willem, speaking at exactly the same time.

They hesitated, turned to each other, and made you-first gestures.

"I'm going with you," they both said at once.

Tad hesitated. It would be wonderful, he realized, to have Birdie and Willem with him. *Friends at your back,* a voice said softly in his head. Tad bit his lip.

Pippit croaked encouragingly.

"You can't," he said. "You mustn't. It's too far for you, Willem, and anyway, it's too dangerous. Besides . . ." *Can Diggers even swim?* he wondered.

"Just wait until I get my equipment," Willem said. "I have some things that should be helpful. Wait till I show you. And I have to find my bat."

He turned and began to scamper down the mountain.

"I'll meet you on the forest path," he called back over his shoulder. "The path you took when you first got here. Beyond the front gate."

"What about your grandfather?" Birdie called after him. "What about your family? What are you going to tell them?"

"I'll leave them a note," Willem shouted back.

Then he paused and turned, his bright eyes suddenly solemn.

"It's our water too," he said.

18

THE GATHERING

Squee! Squee! Squee!

Willem swooped down on them from the air. He was wearing a tight-fitting leather cap that buckled under his chin, and a pair of goggles with round dark lenses that gave him the look of a surprised bug. Skeever, the bat, wore a pair of the dark-lensed goggles, too, fastened with leather straps behind his ears.

"He won't fly in daylight without them," Willem explained. He dismounted awkwardly, crawling backward over a pair of bulky saddlebags. The bags made muffled clanking sounds, and one of them had a lot of metal tubes poking out the top.

"What's that?" Birdie asked, pointing.

"It's an invention," Willem said proudly. "I made it myself. It's a machine for breathing underwater. It—"

He stopped abruptly. The hawk had appeared at the edge of the forest.

"It's all right," Tad said hurriedly. "His name is Kral. He's a friend of ours."

The hawk advanced slowly, setting his powerful claws down delicately, his head tilted to one side to study the newcomers with a bright amber eye. Tad hurried forward to meet him.

"These are friends of ours, Kral," he explained. "This is Willem, a Digger. The bat belongs to him, sort of. His name is Skeever."

The hawk inclined his head politely. Willem, in return, gave an awkward little bow. The fur on the back of his neck, Tad noticed, was standing straight up in a stiff ruff.

"Have you found what you came for, Sagamore?" the hawk asked. His voice was the harsh cry that Tad remembered. At the sound of it, Willem flinched.

"Yes," Tad said. He patted the leatherleaf pouch at his waist that held the fist-shaped stone. "Yes, I did." *I hope,* he added to himself.

"It is well," the hawk said.

"Could you take us back now?" Tad asked. "We need to go to the Wide Clearing in the Piney Forest. There's going to be a meeting—a Gathering of the Tribes. Could you take us there?"

"By sunset as the hawk flies, little brother," the great bird answered. "Climb on my back, you and the frog and the young nestling here, and I will carry you where you wish to go. The Burrower may ride or follow."

Tad turned to the others.

"Kral will take us to the Gathering," he explained. "He'll carry you, too, Willem. Or, he says, you can follow him on Skeever."

"We'll follow," Willem said, casting a nervous glance at the towering hawk.

Kral looked back, unblinking. Then he twisted and, with a sharp tug of his hooked beak, pulled a fiery-red feather from his tail. He dropped it at Willem's feet.

"Tell the young bat-rider to carry that," he said to Tad, "and no bird of the air will harm him." He gave a sharp caw that might have been a laugh. "Tell him I do not care for Burrowers. They taste of stone dust."

Tad turned to Willem.

"He says if you carry the feather, no hunting bird will harm you," he said. "It's some sort of sign."

He decided not to relay the part about the stone dust. *There was no point,* he thought, *in asking for trouble.* Especially since the fur on the back of Willem's neck was just beginning to subside.

Tad and Birdie, entwined with a clinging Pippit, climbed onto Kral's back and settled themselves on his shoulders between the great red-brown wings. Willem, clutching the feather, wriggled back into place on Skeever's back. The hawk tensed. The bat flared its leathery wings. Then both sprang into the air and the wind took them.

The hawk set them down in a forest of pines. Massive black trunks marched away from them into the distance, as far as they could see in every direction. The ground beneath their feet was thick with brown and fallen needles, and the air smelled sharply of turpentine. The drooping branches above their heads were brittle and heavy with dust. Skeever settled beside them, darting swiftly through the trees like a flickering shadow, then plummeting abruptly to the ground. Willem climbed wearily from his back and shoved his dark goggles up onto the top of his head. The sun was just setting and the forest was growing dim.

"I will leave you here," the hawk said. He gestured with his beak. "The Wide Clearing you seek is a short walk that way."

Then, solemnly, the great bird dipped his red head toward Tad. "We will meet again, Sagamore," he said.

"Thank you, Kral," Tad said simply. "Thank you for everything."

The amber eyes looked upward briefly, toward the sky through the branches high above their heads. "Avenge my Lady, Sagamore," he said in his harsh cry. "End the Drying."

Then, with a thunderous sweep of wings, the great bird leaped into the air. The branches of the pines trembled with his passing, and a spattering of dead needles fell.

Willem whistled through his teeth. "You have a strange taste in friends, Fisher," he said.

Tad grinned at him. "So the pond folk will say, Digger," he retorted meaningfully. "And the Hunters, too, beyond a doubt, when they see your furry face."

Willem grinned back. "My friends call me Will," he said.

"Do Diggers really eat earthworms?" Birdie asked.

Willem began to laugh. "All the time," he said. "Roasted. On sticks."

"*Gick,*" Birdie said.

Tad pointed through the trees. "The Wide Clearing is that way. A short walk, Kral said, whatever a short walk is to a hunting bird. We might as well get on with it. What should we do about Skeever?"

"He'll be around," Willem said. "Bats go anywhere. He'll probably spend the night hunting. But we should take the saddlebags."

The bird's short walk was long. They followed a narrow path through the tree trunks, winding in and out among clumps of dead and crumbling ferns. They passed the shallow bowl of what must once have been a little pond. Nothing was left in it but a thin layer of bilious-colored slime and the dried body of a dead frog. Pippit gave a distressed whimper and Birdie turned her head away from it, biting her lip.

By the time they reached the Wide Clearing, the sun had nearly vanished below the horizon and evening was falling. The clearing glimmered with the lights of campfires. There was a smell of cooking in the air and a babble of many voices.

"Look, Tad," Birdie said, pointing. "There are the Fishers. They're all camped together. And that must be the Hunters over there, where all the wagons are."

Each of the tribes had its own encampment. The Fishers had built a cluster of little lean-tos, cobbled together from sticks and dry leaves, one for each family group. Each lean-to had an open front, and all seemed to contain a cramped muddle of moss sleeping pallets, leaf-wrapped packs, and baskets. A fire, carefully corralled in a circle of stones, burned before each campsite. Barefoot children in fringed tunics ran back and forth between them, dodging in and out behind the lean-tos, squealing with the excitement of seeing so many people and being allowed to stay up at night. Just last year at the Gathering, Tad thought, he and Birdie had run exactly like that, shouting and kicking fat brown puffballs, while Pondleweed chatted with friends around a wooden keg of butternut beer. Tad felt a sudden terrible pang of homesickness.

The Hunters, on the opposite side of the clearing, had drawn their painted wagons into a circle. A single great fire burned in the middle of the circle, and beside it, there was a row of people dancing. Tad could see the swirl of blue and scarlet skirts and hear the beat of skin drums, the twanging of lutegourds, and a high piping of reed flutes. The tune seemed to be one that everybody knew, since there was a lot of rhythmic clapping and every once in a while, everybody, all together, shouted, "Ho-mon-ro!"

One thing was different. The bark water buckets that usually stood by each campsite, filled to brimming, were missing. Water was too precious now to risk spilling. The camp was dry and gritty with dust, and the surrounding forest was dull and brown, ugly with the skeletons of dead trees.

"What about the Diggers?" Birdie asked Willem. "Will your family come? When will the Diggers get here?"

Willem shrugged miserably. "They might not come at all," he said. "There was a meeting last night—late, after all of us had gone to bed. My mother and father were talking about it this morning." He scuffed his feet uncomfortably, kicking at the dusty ground. "Grandfather believes in your story, Tad, and so does old Pegger, but some of the others weren't so sure. And most of the High Councilors didn't think much of this Gathering. They don't like to have much to do with the other Tribes. They say that they're all too—" He stopped abruptly, looking shamefaced.

"Too what?" Birdie demanded.

Willem scuffed a toe in the dust. "Backward," he said in an embarrassed voice. "They think you're too primitive to consult with. It's just that you don't use machines, you know, or have any kind of central government. . . ." His voice trailed off uncomfortably.

"If you think you're so much better, just because you have mechanical crossbows and dragon steam engines," Birdie began hotly.

Willem took a hasty step back, the fur on the back of his neck flaring up nervously. "It's not what *I* say," he protested. "I'm just telling you what the High Council said."

"Tad!"

Tad whirled around. Ditani was running across the clearing toward them.

"Tad!" Ditani called again. "We've been looking for you, eh? When did you get here? Where are you camped?"

She paused, skirts swirling around her slim ankles, dark eyes wide, staring at Willem.

"Are the Diggers here then?" she asked in a startled voice.

Tad shook his head. "Just Willem here—Will," he corrected himself. "He came with us." He decided not to explain just *how* they had come. He turned toward Willem. "This is Ditani, a friend of ours. She's a Hunter."

Willem put his right hand over his heart and dipped his head in a polite bow. Ditani blushed and swept back her skirt in an awkward curtsey. Tad found himself feeling annoyed. What was she blushing for?

"Is Uncle Czabo here?" he asked.

Ditani shook her head. "He comes and goes as he pleases, eh? We watch, but his wagon is not here yet.

"You're just in time for the meeting," Ditani went on. "They're planning to have an open parley—right there in the middle of the clearing next to the Speaking Rock— where those boys are putting up torches."

Several boys in fur-edged leather vests—Hunters, by the looks of them, and all a few years older than Tad— were setting torches in the ground in a wide semicircle around a low rock on the flat ground between the two encampments. Lit, the torches burned with a flickery orange flame and gave off a pleasant toasty smell of roasting nuts.

Slowly the clearing began to fill with people. They came alone or in pairs or in little family groups, drifting in quietly and settling down on mats or blankets spread out on the ground. Tad, followed by Birdie, Willem, Ditani, and a persistent Pippit, skirted the edges of the crowd, looking for a place to sit where they all would have a good view of the Speaking Rock. Finally they settled at the far left-hand end of the front row.

The first speaker was already climbing onto the Rock. It was a Fisher named Eelgrass, a tall thin man with a heavily lined face and a mouth that pulled down droopily at the corners. He held up his hand for silence and, as the voices slowly died away, began to speak.

"The ponds are drying," he began. "Doom and disaster are upon us. The Earth itself is turning to dust."

At the word *dust,* someone began to cough dustily in the front row and somebody else began to pound the cougher on the back. Eelgrass paused, looking annoyed.

Tad leaned over to whisper in Willem's ear. "I remember him," he muttered. "He always sees doom and disaster, even when everything is perfectly fine. He's the sort who can't see the blackberries for the thorns."

"I have had a vision!" Eelgrass continued, his voice growing louder. "A vision that came to me in a dream! I saw great trees, broken and falling; and the ponds, dead and empty. I heard the wind blowing across a barren land and its voice told me that this was the Great Drying, the End of All Things. Then above me in the sky, I saw the sun itself grow dim and flicker like a candle flame"—Eelgrass dropped his voice to an ominous whisper—"until at last it blinked out and all was dark forever."

A murmur of horror swept over the Fisher side of the crowd.

"Eh, it sounds like you've been eating bad mushrooms to me!" a voice called out from the center of the Hunter assembly.

As the speaker moved forward, Tad thought at first that it was Ditani's mother, Branica, but as she clambered onto the Speaking Rock, he saw that this woman was older and stouter and her braid was flecked with gray. She wore an orange dress belted with red and green, and heavy dangling necklaces of carved bone beads.

"I am Enelda of the Hunter Tribe," she announced, "and I have seen more summers and winters than many, some dry and some in floodtime, some fat and rich, some poor and thin. There are good years and bad years, eh? This Dry, it too will pass over, no matter this Fisher doomsaying about the end of days. You pond folk take the dismal view, no?"

She nudged Eelgrass in the ribs with her elbow, and he looked outraged.

"And if it doesn't pass?" he demanded in an affronted voice. "What then, Hunters?"

"Yes, what then?" someone else echoed.

"We move!" It was another Hunter. "Up caravans and on to greener forests beyond the reach of the Dry! What else?"

A babble of protest arose from the clustered Fishers.

"Move?"

"Move?"

"Leave the ponds?"

"Move?"

Birdie turned to Tad. "Can they do that?" she whispered. "Move out of the Nixies' reach? If the Waterstone is as powerful as Treeglyn said . . ."

Willem had gotten to his feet. There were cries of surprise as he climbed onto the Speaking Rock.

"A Digger!"

"Eh, are the *Diggers* here, then?"

The voices quieted as Willem began to speak.

"The Drying isn't just here," Willem said. "It's everywhere. You can't move away from it. Even many leagues from here on Stone Mountain, the land is dry and the rivers are empty."

Eelgrass looked smug.

"But that doesn't mean it's the end of everything," Willem continued.

Enelda nodded in agreement and threw a triumphant glance at Eelgrass.

"We think we know what's causing the trouble," Willem said.

"The Diggers always think they know everything," someone said from one of the front rows.

"Mad," said someone else firmly. "All of them, mad. Mad as May mosquitoes."

"And where are the rest of them, I ask you? Not one Digger here but this lad, barely half grown."

"Too good for the likes of us, those Diggers."

The tip of Willem's nose had turned pink.

"And we may know how to stop it," he said loudly.

The voices hushed.

Willem turned toward Tad.

"Tell them, Sagamore," Willem said.

19

THE BAND OF FOUR

Tad knew that they hadn't believed him.

He could see it in their faces, Fishers and Hunters alike. Almost all wore identical expressions: skeptical and suspicious. Here and there was a face with an angry, scornful expression, and one or two looked amused, as if they had just been treated to a foolish, but entertaining, tale. Many were talking in low voices among themselves.

"Moonshine and shadow, that's what I call it. Not a particle of truth about it . . ."

"Hardly a time to be joking, with the streams dried up and the ponds as low as a grass snake's belly . . ."

"Fishers. What can you expect, eh? Living as they do, never budging from the banks of their ponds, raised with their heads in water . . ."

"Never heard of such things, not in all my born days. Sagamores and invisible witches and shiny magicstones . . ."

A few—a very few—faces looked thoughtful, as if they were seriously considering what Tad had told them. An old Fisher magicker—an ancient woman, wrinkled as a walnut—claimed to remember an old tale about the Sagamore, but her story became more and more confusing and finally trailed away altogether. Anyway, she seemed to think that the Sagamore had been a giant white squirrel.

"Eh, then, Fisher boy, if you have such a knack for magicking, show us!"

It was a tall sullen-looking Hunter with shaggy black eyebrows and stripes of yellow paint on his cheekbones, wearing floppy scarlet pantaloons. His voice was mocking and hostile. "Show us how you plan to fight this witch, Fisher!"

Tad stood on the Speaking Rock, the uncomfortable center of all eyes. The voices of the crowd swirled around him.

"Deluded . . ."

"Poor lad, he lost his father. . . ."

"I've said it before and I'll say it again: No boy never made a magicker . . ."

Tad caught sight of Ditani and Birdie, sitting side by side on the ground below. Ditani's face was filled with sympathy and concern. Birdie looked mad and her lower lip was sticking out. Pippit was trying to climb into her lap.

The sullen-looking Hunter laughed, nastily.

Tad felt a wave of despair. How could he ever make them understand?

"So bring the rain, then, Fisher!" someone shouted from the rear of the crowd. "If this Sagamore has such special powers, use them! End the Dry!"

"I can't end it that way," Tad said. "No one can bring the rain. The water's gone. There's nothing there, so long as the Nixies have the Waterstone."

From the crowd, there were cries of anger and disgust. Scattered arguments began to break out, mostly among the younger men, some of whom were shouting and shaking fists at each other. People stood up slowly, gathered up children and sitting mats, and turned their backs on Tad, heading back toward the campsites, muttering unhappily together. Tad caught bits and pieces of disjointed conversations as they passed.

"Waste of time, this is, a three-days' journey and naught but flitty-headed fairy tales at the end of it . . ."

"Water on the brain, those Fishers; daft as the Diggers, if you ask me, Bevo . . ."

"Mayhap tomorrow we'll have talk with some sense to it, and no more youngers, who ought better to stay home and tend the minner nets. . . ."

In hardly any time at all, it seemed, the torches had been extinguished and the clearing was empty. Tad slid down from the Speaking Rock and sank miserably to the ground.

"They didn't believe me," he said.

"Stupid as pillbugs," Ditani said stoutly.

Pippit grakked loudly as if in agreement.

Willem shrugged. "People believe best what they're used to believing," he said. "New things take time, Tad. It's always the way."

Birdie nodded at him vigorously. "Like the story about Driftbud the Windmaker," she said. "Nobody believed her at the beginning, and they all laughed and laughed, and then she put the green sail on her boat and whenever she called, the wind would come and take her wherever she wanted to go."

"Exactly," said Willem, nodding back.

"Or the Magic Mudhopper," Birdie said.

Willem stopped nodding and looked confused.

Tad was too worried to discuss the Magic Mudhopper.

"It doesn't really make any difference," he said. "I have to go to the black lake whether they believe me or not. I still have to go after the Waterstone."

"But *how*?" Ditani asked. She threw her dark braid back over her shoulder and shook her head at Tad. "Fleet as you pond folk are as swimmers, you are not fishes, eh? How will you go into the dark water and not drown?"

"Like this!" Willem reached for his bulky saddlebags. Hastily he unfastened their flaps, turned the bags upside down and shook them. A tangle of metal tubes and coils tumbled out, with an awful clanging and clattering sound.

"It's a breathing machine," Willem said. "I brought two of them."

He scrabbled through the mass of metal, wrenched out an odd-shaped piece, and waved it in the air.

"You put this part over your nose and mouth like this. It buckles in the back." It was a cup-shaped metal mask with leather straps and a pair of waving hoses that curved back over the ears. "Then you fasten it to this tube"—as he gestured enthusiastically, the tube unwound itself unexpectedly with a loud *sproing*—"and the tube connects to a canister of pressurized air. You wear it on your back. It lasts for hours."

He dropped the tube, picked up the metal mask, settled it over his nose, and buckled it behind his head. It made him look like a furry grasshopper with a pair of bobbing silver antennae. His voice became muffled.

"Mtt mmt mmppttee," Willem said.

"What?" Tad said. "We can't hear you. What did you say?"

Willem snatched off the mask. "I said it works perfectly," he said. "I tested it in the bath-pools at home."

Ditani muttered something under her breath in which Tad could only distinguish the words *Digger* and *mad*.

"We'll be fine if we wear these," Willem said confidently. He held the mask out toward Tad.

Tad took it gingerly between two fingers and dangled it in front of him. The hoses bobbled foolishly. Birdie giggled. When he finally met the Nixies, Tad reflected dismally, he was going to look awfully silly.

The stars were out, silver-bright in the black sky. Directly overhead, through the opening in the trees, Tad could see the handle of the Fishing Net and the brilliant blue-white star that the Fishers called Rune's Kindlestick. The Hunters, Ditani said, called it the Firefly.

Behind them, in the encampments, people were settling down for the night. The campfires were banked and the blanket bundles rolled out. A breeze set the bells of the Hunter wagons chiming, and from one of the Fisher lean-tos came the sound of someone softly singing a lullaby. It was the song about the silver moonfish that Tad's mother used to sing when he and Birdie were little. Hearing it made Tad's throat feel tight.

Birdie, Willem, Tad, and Ditani were still sitting on the dusty ground, their backs against the Speaking Rock. Pippit crouched sleepily beside them, his bulgy eyes slowly drooping shut. Every once in a while he gave a sighing little croak, seeming to say that it had been a long day for a small frog. Willem, with extravagant hand gestures, was telling Birdie about the Winter Festival inside Stone Mountain, and Birdie was looking suitably awestruck and asking lots of questions. Ditani was sitting silently, her arms wrapped around her ankles and her chin resting on her knees. They had been making plans. It was decided that they would leave for the Nixie's lake at daybreak of the coming morning. It was not yet decided who was to go.

For a moment a silence fell. Then Birdie leaped back into the unfinished argument.

"Of course Ditani and I are going too," she said. Her lower lip was sticking out. "There should be more than just the two of you. What if something goes wrong and you need help? It's not as if there's anybody rushing to back you up."

That was right enough, Tad thought.

Ditani pulled herself upright.

"Cowardy as deermice, the lot of them," she said scorn-fully. "And stupid as toadstools, to boot. Why shouldn't I be there, eh? A Fisher and a Digger to go, but none of the Hunters?"

"Willem only has two breathing machines," Tad said. "Enough for just two of us. There's no point in more going." He paused, trying to make his argument more convincing. What had the hawk said? "It's foolish to take risks unnecessarily."

"Among the *Hunters,*" Ditani said, looking outraged, "friends do not stay with the wagons when friends are in danger."

"Among the *Fishers,*" Birdie said, in a voice that Tad immediately recognized as unpeaceful, "they say that only a fool goes into deep water without a friend to watch on the bank."

Pippit, abruptly awakened, chimed in with a protest-ing bleat.

Tad looked from one to the other.

"You don't understand," he said. "It's so dangerous. I remember terrible things. We could die, any one of us. You know what happened to Father, Birdie. If anything happened to you too—" He made a gesture of despair. "Not even Willem should go," he said.

Birdie shook her head. "You can't choose for other peo-ple," she said. "You have to let us choose for ourselves, Tad."

Ditani stretched out her hand, palm upward.

"I choose," she said.

Willem leaned forward and laid his hand on Ditani's.

"In the Epics," he said, "they will call us the Band of Four. There will be many stanzas written about us in bad Digger verse, and our story will be recorded in the House of Skalds."

Birdie put her hand on Willem's.

"They will sing about us around the campfires," she said. "Beside all the ponds on summer evenings."

"Eh, they will," Ditani said. "And beside the caravans."

Pippit butted his green head against Tad's knee.

Tad found that he couldn't speak.

So instead he stepped forward and laid his hand on top of theirs.

20

THE PARLEY

The black lake lay to the west.

They had left before sunrise, creeping stealthily out of the still-sleeping camp. No one woke to see them go. *Probably,* Tad thought glumly, *no one cares.* The early morning air was chilly, and each wore, warmly draped around his or her shoulders, a mouseskin cloak, fur side in. The cloaks had been borrowed the night before from Plumrose and Wallow of Deep Pond. Plumrose and Wallow had talked a great deal, nervously avoiding all mention of Nixies, Waterstones, or Sagamores.

The four children walked along the forest path in single file, with Ditani in the lead. She had abandoned her scarlet skirts and was dressed in loose silkgrass trousers, a belted blouse, and soft leather boots. The painted stripes on her cheekbones were scarlet instead of turquoise-blue, and there was a red feather tied in her braided hair.

"Battle colors," she said, when Tad asked. "When the Hunters fight, they paint in battle colors and wear the blood feather."

A bow was slung across her back. In one hand she carried a wickedly pointed spear; in the other, an acorn lantern that contained the flickering stub of a beeswax candle.

She was followed by Birdie, who carried a small bow and a bark quiver filled with red- and blue-feathered arrows; then came Willem, burdened with his clanking saddlebags; and finally Tad, with an anxious Pippit, bringing up the rear. They trudged along silently in the predawn darkness, each lost in thought. Tad kept his eyes on Ditani's lantern flame, bobbing dizzily up and down, up and down, like a pond-sick firefly. Then Tad heard the singing.

It was a single flutelike voice, singing a melody so simple, so haunting, and so piercingly sweet that it brought tears to Tad's eyes. Now that he had heard it, he realized that he had never known true music. The tune tugged at his heartstrings, sang in his blood. He would do anything, *anything,* to hear more of that silver fairy music. It was almost more than he could bear.

Ahead of him the lantern light vanished abruptly. Ditani had blown out the candle. Tad tripped over a root and almost fell on his face. The music stopped dead. Tad moaned aloud in dismay. What had happened? Into his mind crept a whisper of cold laughter.

This time you cannot win, Sagamore. Come listen . . .

With an effort, Tad shut the voice out. He could have kicked himself for being such a puddleheaded idiot. Tumbling into the Nixie's trap like a fat buzzfly into a spider's web. He called himself names, silently. *Mudhead. Wormbrain.*

In the gray half-light of almost-dawn, they paused by the side of the path for breakfast: cold bread and a swallow of tea. Everyone was quiet and subdued. Even Pippit was silent, crowded behind Tad, nervously rolling his eyes. A faint rustle of wings above them signaled Skeever the bat, prowling watchfully overhead.

"How much farther?" Birdie questioned.

Tad shrugged.

"Not very," he said. "Not much longer now."

He reached out cautiously with his Mind, questing, like a shellfish poking out a curious tentacle. He could *feel* the black lake. He could sense a presence in the near dis- tance—cold, wary, hungry. Determined to survive.

Azabel?

The sense of presence sharpened, turned toward him, but before it could come closer, Tad jerked his Mind away.

"We have to talk," he said. "Before we go any farther."

Quickly—as best he could—he explained about the singing.

"You wouldn't be able to help yourselves," he said. "It pulls at you. You feel as if you'd do anything in the world to just keep listening to it, forever. My father heard it"— his voice wavered—"and he just walked into the black lake. When we get closer, close enough for you to hear them, it could happen to you too."

They sat silently, looking at one another.

"I should never have let any of you come," Tad said. He felt awful. "I don't know what I was thinking."

"Eh, we could give them a song of our own," Ditani said stoutly. "Singing, all four of us, we could drown out the sound of yon fishy ladies."

She began to sing at the top of her voice.

> *There was a deermouse in the grass*
> *A deermouse, fat and sweet.*
> *A Hunter crept up with her bow*
> *And took it home to eat!*
> *Oh ...*

"Come on, sing."

Pippit began a rhythmic blatting.

"Deaf-man's leaf," said Birdie.

"What did you say?" Tad said.

"There was a deermouse in the grass—"

"Deaf-man's leaf," repeated Birdie, louder. "Stop it, Ditani. Pippit, stop. That's a dreadful song."

"What's deaf-man's leaf?" asked Willem.

"It's for poisons of the ears," Birdie said. "It's a little creeping plant, so big"—she measured with her fingers—"with blue flowers. You chew the leaves. But they taste good. Sweet, like wintermint." She sounded knowledgable, confident. "It's good for earaches, but it does other things too."

She scrambled to her feet. "I'll show you. I saw some, just down the path."

She was back almost immediately with a handful of small pointed leaves. The Drying was killing them—all had withered stems and shriveled brown edges—but there remained a stubborn heart of dark green. Tad took one and put it in his mouth. Cautiously he bit down. It crunched unpleasantly. Then—Birdie was right—it tasted sweet and minty.

"It's good," he said, munching. "Try it."

Birdie, Ditani, and Willem popped leaves in their mouths and chewed.

"Better than firepeppers, eh?" Ditani said.

Tad made a face at her. He helped himself to another leaf.

"But how do you know it will help?" he asked.

Birdie looked puzzled.

"Somebody must have told me," she said blankly.

She dangled a leaf temptingly at Pippit. "Here, Pippit, pretend it's a fly."

Pippit threw her a scornful look.

"Poisons of the ears," Will said. "Well, it makes sense. *Poison* sounds like Tad's Witches, right enough." He winked at Tad.

"Not *my* Witches, you rock-headed earthworm-eater," Tad said smiling.

By the time they reached the edge of the forest, the sun was well above the horizon. The lantern was long out, and the cloaks, now grown too warm, were folded and stuffed bulkily into Willem's bags. The path opened before them, and then, abruptly, ended. Before them lay the shore of the black lake.

They crowded together, peering out from under a concealing clutter of dead leaves and bracken. The water of the lake looked as thick and black as tar. The water's edge was strewn with bones, large and small—the great bones of deer, the tiny remains of birds, mice, and squirrels. Half buried in mud was a broken wooden wheel.

Ditani gave a horrified gasp of dismay. The spokes and rim of the wheel were painted in bright alternating stripes of yellow, red, and green. Tad had seen that wheel before, parked beside a campfire in the forest, while an old man pulled berries out of nothing and turned scarves into butterflies.

"Uncle Czabo," Ditani whispered.

They stared miserably at the broken wheel.

"He must have heard her," Birdie said in a small voice. "Heard her singing and just pulled his caravan right into the water."

"May Death wait on her wagon step," Ditani said fiercely. Her eyes were bright with anger. "He was my blood kin, of my clan and Tribe, a cousin. I shall avenge him."

Willem put a warning hand on her arm.

"Not now," he said quietly. "Don't make any noise." He tugged at Tad's tunic sleeve and pointed. "Look at that," he said, barely moving his lips. Tad followed the direction of Willem's pointing finger.

They were not alone.

Some distance away, a crude fortress had been erected on the lakeshore. It was surrounded by a palisade of saplings that had been stripped of bark and branches and shaped to vicious points. On either side of the entrance gate stood a pair of armored soldiers, stiffly at attention. They wore leather helmets, leather jerkins stitched with disks of iron, and tall leather boots with iron buckles, and they carried shields and spears. Slung across their backs were bows — strung and ready — and quivers full of black-feathered arrows.

"Sentries," Willem whispered.

Tad nodded. "Grellers," he whispered back.

As if on some unspoken signal, the sentries, in unison, took two steps forward, turned sharply to the right and left, facing away from each other, and marched briskly to the corners of the palisade fence. Then, still in unison, they reversed themselves and returned to their original positions.

"Keeping watch," Willem muttered. "How will we be able to get to the lake's edge without their seeing us and raising the alarm? It's all open ground from here to there, flat as a rock-thumping fry-pan cake."

Tad nodded, frowning.

The sentries, moving like automatons, repeated their inspection of the perimeter, then returned to their posts.

"Could we do it while they're turned away?" Tad asked. "If we put on the breathing tubes and things here in the forest and made a run for the water just as the sentries reach the farthest point of their patrol? They'd never reach us in time."

"They'd never reach you at all," Ditani said. "Not with me and Birdie to cover your backs."

Willem looked doubtful. "We'll clank," he said. "They'll hear us. And we won't be able to run very fast. They have a long range with those arrows."

"So do we have a long range with ours," Ditani said ominously.

Tad could think of no better plan.

"Then let's get ready," he said. "Quietly now. You'll have to show me how to put it on, Will."

"Wait a minute," Birdie said. "Something's happening."

The doors of the fortress were opening. As they swung wide, the sentries leaped back, snapped smartly to attention, and thumped the hafts of their spears on the ground. A small procession moved past them. It was led by a Greller in a long black robe with a hooded cowl pulled so far forward that his face was hidden in shadows. Behind him marched four more robed figures, walking two by two, their faces disguised by narrow black masks embroidered with silver. The procession advanced steadily down the lakeshore toward the children's hiding place. As the Grellers drew nearer, Tad could see that the leader carried a roll of parchment in one hand.

"I wonder where they're going," Willem whispered.

Tad had a foreboding feeling that they were about to find out.

The procession halted some twenty paces from the bracken pile where the children crouched, and arranged themselves in a line with the hooded Greller in the middle. Pippit, crouched at Tad's feet, began to mutter and twitch nervously. Birdie put a warning hand on his head. Then the leader raised the hand holding the parchment, threw back the folded hood of his robe, and took one step forward.

"I bear a message for the Sagamore," he cried in a loud voice.

Birdie gave a gasp of horror and clutched Tad's arm.

"They have our scent," Ditani whispered urgently. "They know we're here. What are we going to do?"

"I bear a message for the Sagamore!" the robed Greller cried again.

Then his voice changed. It grew higher, colder, clear as a bell made of Hunter steel and black ice. The black-masked Grellers fell to their knees and dropped their foreheads to the ground.

"Come out, Fisher, and parley!"

Tad's heart began to pound. Slowly he straightened.

"It's no good," he said. "She knows I'm here. I might as well go out and talk."

"Don't be a hollow head," Birdie whispered at him angrily. "The frog doesn't parade itself before the heron."

"Nor the mouse before the fox." Ditani backed her up.

"I am not a mouse," Tad said. He had a sudden vision of the fallen deermouse, dead, Nobono's arrow lodged in its chest.

"I am not a mouse," he repeated.

A Remember answered from somewhere deep within his mind, a voice tinged with amusement. *No more you are, lad.*

Or was it Will's voice? Tad hesitated, caught for a confused instant between past and present. Will, feeling Tad's eyes upon him, shifted a worried expression to a defiant grin.

"We're more than a match for Grellers," Will said bravely. "They're all thick as posts." He let his mouth sag open in a vacant stupid expression and crossed his eyes. "That's what my grandfather always says about them. Too dense to tell gold dust from mustard seed, he says, and fools enough to follow a blind mole. Let's go see what they want."

Tad started to protest that he didn't want company, but Willem waved him aside.

"He has his followers," he said, "and you should have yours. Come on, Tad, don't keep them waiting. You're the Sagamore. You go first. I'll be right behind you."

They thrust the tangle of leaves and twigs aside and strode out into the open. The morning air was growing warmer and the breeze off the lake carried a smell of rotting meat. The masked Greller stood motionless, watching Tad and Will walk toward him across the packed sand and dead grass.

"It has been a long time, Sagamore." The Nixie's high cold voice sounded almost wistful behind the blank fish-scale mask.

"Aye, Lady," Tad said. "A long time."

"The offer still stands." A barely perceptible note of music had crept into the cold voice. It sounded like silver syrup.

"What offer?"

The masked Greller thrust the rolled parchment into his hands.

"Our terms," the Nixie said.

Tad unrolled the parchment and held it out so that Willem could see it too. It was covered with writing in silver ink and stamped on the bottom with a black wax seal.

"I can't read it," he muttered to Willem under his breath. He felt as if he were confessing a shameful secret.

"I can't either," Willem muttered back. "I've never seen anything like that before. It doesn't look like letters. It looks like crab tracks."

Tad handed the parchment back to the waiting Greller.

"Tell us what it says," he said.

Laughter. A cascade of silvery notes like fat raindrops falling into a silent pool.

"So forgetful, Sagamore? Perhaps I can help you."

"Help me how?" Tad demanded suspiciously.

You are not as they are, the voice went on, secretly, sweetly, inside his head. *They do not believe in you, Sagamore. They scorn you. They will never accept you. Your gift will set you apart. You will be envied, hated, feared. You will be alone. The Tribes will not unite for you, Sagamore. They are lost to you. Leave them behind. Leave them.*

Faintly, as if it were very far away, a voice began singing.

Come and be a king in the deep water. You will have a castle of coral and pearls and a throne of crystal and gold. You are of our kind, Sagamore, not theirs.

The singing swelled up, an enchanted cascade of indescribably beautiful sound. But somehow it had lost its power. *It is poison,* Tad thought.

Do you accept, Sagamore?

Accept! Accept! Accept! The music urged him.

"No," Tad said.

Ah, the Nixie's voice said. *Ah, I see. You miss your pond. That little driblet of water.*

Scornful laughter like silver bubbles.

But I could spare it for you, Sagamore. Cease to trouble me and go home, and all will be as it was before. Your pond will fill.

"What about all the other ponds?" Tad said. "What about the forests? And the Diggers' waterfall?"

The singing faded to a tuneful murmur.

What does it matter? the Nixie whispered conspiratorially. *What will you see of it, Fisher? Stay at home by the banks of your pond and let the world beyond go by as it will. It is nothing to do with you.*

"You mean go by as *you* will," Tad retorted.

The singing rose again, piercingly sweet, but it bothered Tad no more than the buzzing of a honeybee.

Save yourself, the Nixie murmured seductively. *You, Sagamore, you shall have water. Your tree will remain green. Go home.*

"No," Tad said again. "There's water enough for all of us, Azabel. Give it back. Give up the Waterstone."

For a long moment nothing happened.

Then die!

The masked Greller tipped back his head and gave a long howl of fury. Behind him Tad heard Pippit squawking hysterically and Ditani frantically shouting a warning. As if the howl had been a signal, the wooden gates of the Grellers' fortress slammed open and a horde of armed warriors poured out, bows and spears at ready. The bowmen in the lead broke ranks, stepped smartly to the side, and dropped to one knee, taking aim.

"Tad! Will!" It was Birdie, shrieking. "Look out! Run!"

A bowman fired.

The arrow flashed through the air, but it never reached its intended target. There was a blow against Tad's back as he was violently thrust aside, out of harm's way. It was Will, shouting a warning—and Will, crying out and falling backward, a black-feathered arrow protruding from his shoulder.

21

THE RALLYING OF THE TRIBES

AaaaOOOOaaaa!

From the edge of the forest came the wail of a snail-shell horn. A Fisher horn.

AaaaOOOOaaaa!

Tad looked up, astonished, from where he had dropped to his knees at Willem's side. The roots of the great trees were suddenly alive with moving figures. There were Fishers in battle dress—vests and helmets awkwardly cobbled together from sheets of birch bark. They carried bows, fishing spears, and stone hatchets sharpened to a razor's edge. Among them were the tense crouched forms of Hunters, their dark faces fierce with stripes of scarlet paint, bows and bone-handled knives in their hands.

The Greller army halted in its headlong rush down the shore. This was a far more formidable force than they had expected and they were no longer sure what to do. Soldiers in the rear—still charging blindly forward—crashed heavily into soldiers in front of them, who were suddenly charging backward. There was a flurry of contradictory orders. There were cries of "Forward, Grellers, forward!" and, at the same time, shouts of "Back, men, back!" Grellers in the very middle of the formation, who had been bumped into the hardest and from both sides, had turned angrily and started fighting with their neighbors.

In the resulting confusion, Fishers and Hunters attacked. They burst from the cover of the woods and raced toward the fort, shrieking at the tops of their lungs.

"Water-thieving swamp pigs!"

"Eh, stand and fight, you fur-faced traitors!"

"For the ponds and forest!"

"For the Tribes! For the Tribes!"

In the midst of it all, the wail of the snail-shell horn sounded again.

AaaaOOOOaaaa!

Arrows filled the air.

Tad crouched at Willem's side.

"I thought they weren't coming," he said.

Willem gave a ghost of a grin.

"I guess they weren't so cowardly after all," he said faintly. "I thought that Hunter in the red pants — the one who gave you such a hard time, Tad — was looking pretty ashamed of himself at not offering to help. Some of the others were too."

He gave a gasp of pain. "Some of them believed in you," he said. "Don't think they didn't, Tad. They just had to hammer it out a bit, that's all. Like the story of what's-his-name, Birdie's Magic Mudbug."

Tad laid a hand on his arm.

"They'll have brought healers with them," he said. "People who can help you. I'll go find one of them, Will."

Willem shook his head.

"No," he said. "You have to go now, Tad. It's a diversion they've made for you, don't you see? It's your chance to get to the lake. But you have to go *now.* Take the breathing tubes."

"I'm not leaving you like this," Tad said.

Another voice, a remembered fur-soft voice, now choked and twisted with pain, spoke in his ear.

Go now and do as you must, old friend, and we will meet again around a campfire in Great Rune's garden.

Tad's eyes filled with hot tears. Burris. And now Willem. The tears spilled over and ran down his cheeks.

"I'll stay with him, Tad." It was Birdie. "I'll stay with him until you get back."

Ditani stood behind her, arms awkwardly filled with metal tubes and dangling hoses. "And I'll go with you," Ditani said, struggling with the tangled breathing tubes. "I have no powers like yours, but I am of the Blood, and mayhap you'll have need of a good Hunter spear." She wrenched at the tubes, pulling one set free. "Here, put this thing on."

"Do it, Tad," said Willem.

Tad reluctantly buckled the odd-shaped goggles behind his ears, settled the air hoses, and strapped the air canister over his shoulder, while Ditani did the same. *We sure don't look like warriors,* Tad thought ruefully. *We look like a pair of bulgy-faced waterbugs.*

Ditani kicked off her leather boots.

"I'm ready," she said.

The shouting grew louder near the gates of the fortress, where Fishers, Hunters, and Grellers clashed in battle. The dusty ground was scattered now with crumpled bodies.

"I wish the Diggers had come," Willem said weakly. "I would have liked to have seen a true rally of the Tribes, like they had in the olden days. You'll have to tell them about this, Tad, back at Stone Mountain. Tell them what happened."

"You can tell them yourself," Tad said.

The corners of Willem's mouth twitched in the beginning of a smile.

"You look like a couple of big bugs," he said. "Put the mouthpieces on."

Tad and Ditani did as they were told.

Birdie suddenly flung her arms around them both in a crushing hug. "You're braver than Bog the Weaselkiller," she said huskily. "Both of you."

She stepped back quickly and made Great Rune's sign—a circle in the air in front of her face. "Great Rune keep you safe," she said.

"He won't have a chance to if they don't get going," Will said.

He tried to lift his head, but fell back, grimacing with pain. Tad winced in sympathy.

Hall-ooo!

A shrill metallic call rang out above the commotion of the battle. A black-clad trumpeter stood on the battlements above the palisade, sounding an alarm. As if in answer to a command, a group of Greller soldiers broke loose from the throng and began to trot purposefully toward the children, spears threateningly lowered.

"Go!" Birdie shouted.

Tad and Ditani turned toward the black water. The troop of Grellers picked up its pace. A spear whistled over Tad's head. The trumpet sounded once more, and the gates of the fortress crashed open, revealing a mass of Grellers hauling on thick ropes. A massive catapult lumbered ponderously into view. Its great wooden throwing arm was bent back, loaded, and ready to fire.

Tad and Ditani seized hands and began to run. The trotting Grellers, moving as one, veered to pursue them. They were coming even faster now. Tad's heart thudded wildly in his chest. He and Ditani sped toward the water, the Grellers pounding at their heels. He stubbed his toe on something unspeakable. Ditani stumbled and almost fell, pulling him awkwardly with her. The Grellers came on.

Then from behind them and over their heads came a terrifying earsplitting screech. In spite of himself, Tad stopped and looked up. A rock the size of a rock bass was plummeting toward him, straight out of the sky. It was moving as fast as a Hunter's arrow, faster than a Fisher's spear. Ditani, muffled behind Will's mouthpiece, gave a strangled scream. Tad stood frozen, staring in horror. He resigned himself to being squashed. At least it would be quick, he reflected, so it could hardly hurt much. One thwack and then dead.

The rock struck.

It landed with a tremendous thump on the lakeshore, just short of the water. The ground shook with the impact, and black mud splattered up in fountains. The rock had dropped with awful precision directly onto the troop of pursuing Grellers. Two or three of them were quite thoroughly gone—*Flat as lily pads,* Tad thought queasily—beneath the fallen rock, and the rest, babbling in terror and casting horrified looks at the empty sky, were in retreat, thundering back the way that they had come. Tad stared after them. Back at the entrance to the fortress, the Grellers of the catapult crew were shouting furiously and waving their fists in the air. One Greller, protesting, was pulled off the back of the machine and flung to the ground. The rest, still shouting, seemed to be stomping on him.

The battle was just beginning. Hunters scattered across the lakeshore, sheltering behind rocks and rubble, springing out suddenly to hurl short spears or—with deadly accuracy—to shoot red-feathered arrows from their bows. Fishers formed themselves in ranks, shoulder to shoulder, spears bristling outward, and advanced—*Moving like a pike,* Tad thought, *into a school of sticklebacks.*

From behind the Greller fortress came a measured beating of skin drums. Tad felt Ditani, beside him, tense and raise her spear. It was the weasels. They paced forward, black heads darting to and fro like snakes, long sinuous bodies hugging the ground. Their riders sat motionless, frowning in concentration, controlling their steeds with prods of their metal-tipped whips. A ripple of fear ran through the gathered ranks before them. Suddenly one weasel broke loose from the pack and leaped forward, snarling. It arched its back, reared, and then fell upon a crouching Hunter. There was a flash of fangs and a shriek. The Hunter, flung to one side, lay crumpled and still. Two more weasels sprang forward and began prowling toward a little cluster of frightened Fishers. As the weasels, in unison, moved forward, the Fishers—in unison—moved back.

From behind them, a black streak rocketed from the forest—fangs bared, paws hardly seeming to touch the ground.

"They're trapped!" Tad cried in horror. "Weasels on both sides of them . . . they're trapped!"

Then, above the noise of the throng, he heard Birdie's voice, shouting in excitement.

"It's Blackberry!" Birdie cried. "It's Blackberry!"

The new weasel sped toward the embattled Fishers. Now Tad could see that it had a rider clinging to its back. It was Voice, with a look of grim determination on his face. His flaming hair blew out behind him, and in one hand he brandished a spiked thornbush club. Blackberry soared over the backs of the startled Fishers and struck at the throat of the lead Greller's mount. The two animals fell together, rolling, clawing, tearing. Voice vanished from sight. Another catapulted rock screamed overhead.

I have to help, Tad thought, and he heard a chime of silver music echo: *Help.* He took a step back toward the battle, and then another.

Something else was happening too. Tad felt it before he saw it. It was moving toward them, threading like a dark shadow through thickets and between tree trunks. A wave of hatred swept before it, and an overpowering lust for blood. A gray wolf stepped out of the wood. It towered above the battle, lips peeled back to show pointed teeth, red tongue hanging down.

The wolf growled low in its throat, a long threatening reverberation like a hundred skin drums beating all at once. Tad's blood ran cold.

A silver whisper slipped into his head.

Your friends need you, Sagamore. Would you abandon them? Go to them. Fight with them. Fight the Wulv.

Tad took another half step, tugging to undo the straps of his goggles. The wolf paced forward. Shrieking Grellers raced away before it. It clawed them aside, barely looking at them. Its hot red eyes were fixed on a little group of frightened Fishers. Its dark mind gave a heave of pleasure. Gloatingly, it licked its lips.

HOLD! Tad's mind bellowed a command.

The wolf's head snapped up. Its eyes narrowed to red-pointed slits. Its head turned, searching, and then, above the roiling tangle of fleeing fighters, its gaze locked with Tad's. Tad caught the echo of an icy whisper.

Yes, Wulv! There, Wulv! Good blood! Sweet blood!

The wolf crouched. Its haunches tensed and quivered. Then it launched itself over the heads of the rival armies in a single soaring lunge. Its clawed feet dug trenches in the lakeshore. Its mind was a black bottomless well. A snarl bubbled from its throat.

Yes, Wulv! Sweet blood! the Nixie urged.

The wolf moved toward Tad. Then its ears twitched. Distracted for a moment, it looked uneasily toward the sky. Tad had heard it too. The high shriek of a stooping hawk.

Leave this to me, Sagamore. He heard the voice as clearly as if he were riding on the bird's broad shoulders. *Your battle is not here.*

The wolf reared up on its hind paws, screaming in fury, as the hawk plummeted toward it out of the sun.

Tad seized Ditani's arm and ran toward the black water.

22

THE NIXIE

The water felt awful. Oily, filthy, and *warm*. It was exactly the temperature of blood. He hated wading in it. Nothing could be seen below the black surface.

The water closed around their ankles, then their knees. Soon it was up to their waists. Tad had never been so scared in his life. His heart was thumping so hard it hurt, and his stomach felt as if it were full of firepeppers.

Malawissa. The word crept softly into his mind. *Malawiss-aaah.* It sounded like one of Treeglyn's words, a word in the leafy wind-language that he had first heard in the little tree cottage in the forest. He groped for his leatherleaf pouch and fumbled for the stick of oak that was Treeglyn's gift. The very touch of the wood was reassuring. Strength flooded into his fingers. Suddenly— incredibly—the fear was gone. He felt solid, indomitable, unbending. Like an oak tree. Then the meaning came to him. *Malawissa*—when a tree stands straight in a storm, defying thunder and lightning.

This is it, Tad thought. He reached out and took Ditani's hand. Together they dived. The black water closed over their heads.

They found themselves in a vast underwater world. Beneath the black surface, they found that they could see great distances into the farthest reaches of the lake. There were towering black boulders and forests of undulating weeds with stems as thick as a man's arm, and—between the forests—long empty stretches of trackless sand. The lake was utterly dead. Nothing moved in it, not a fish or a frog or a waterworm. All was perfectly still except for the *whoosh*ing of the breathing tubes.

Tad touched Ditani's arm and pointed, forward and downward. They began to swim. Tad's webbed feet flared wide and swept smoothly through the water. He found that he had to pause at intervals, paddling, waiting for Ditani to catch up. *She is still the prettiest girl I've ever seen,* he thought, *but she'd never make a Fisher. She swims like a sick duck.*

Down they went, and deeper down. The light grew grayer. They circled an immense mound of rock, a craggy underwater mountain. On the far side of the mountain was an entrance to a grotto. There was a sense of watching now, the cold feel of an alien presence. She lived here. This was the place. Tad signaled to Ditani, who nodded and gestured with her spear. Slowly they swam forward and entered.

Glowworms in fish-bone cages lined the stone walls, giving off an eerie bluish light. It made the whites of Ditani's eyes look phosphorescent through her goggles and turned Tad's skin the color of a clam. They swam slowly inward, barely kicking their feet. The grotto narrowed to a hallway, its floor paved with tiles cut from shimmery rainbow-colored shells. They passed through an open doorway at the end of the hall and found themselves in a great arching chamber. It was like a palace in one of Pondleweed's fairy tales. The walls were studded with richly colored jewels: blue, green, crimson, and deep brown-gold. There were hanging tapestries, beaded with seed pearls and embroidered with colored silks, and stone urns filled with sprays of coral.

Tad and Ditani slid downward through the water, landing feet first on the shell-tiled floor. Before them was a high-backed stone chair, inlaid with silver and aquamarine. On the seat of the chair lay a white crystal. It glowed in the dimness with an inner light all its own, and it seemed to pulse rhythmically as if it had a heartbeat, as if it were alive. The Waterstone.

Ditani tugged impatiently at Tad's elbow, jerking her head at the Stone. Then, before he could stop her, she lunged forward, reaching out a hand to seize it. There was a brilliant flash of light and a loud crackle. Ditani, clutching her hand to her chest, was hurled backward through the water. Tad sprang to help her, but before he reached her, she had already struggled back to her feet. She shook her head at him, silently telling him that she was all right. Her hand was red and angry-looking, as if it had been burned.

One of the tapestries began to heave and sway as if caught in an invisible current of water. A hidden hand swept it aside. Beside him, Tad felt Ditani—still nursing her hand—give a start of surprise. The Nixie was beautiful.

The creature before them had the body of a beautiful young woman above the waist, and below, an iridescent green fish's tail. Her long silver-green hair floated out behind her in the water. She had a pale lovely face and strange slanting silver eyes with long straight pupils like those of a huntercat. Her skin glistened faintly in rainbow colors like mother-of-pearl. She wore a jerkin of pearl-embroidered fish skin, and a necklace of coral beads. Circling her head was a fine silver chain from which hung—precisely in the middle of her gleaming forehead—a single teardrop-shaped pearl.

She moved gracefully toward the children, swaying lightly back and forth in the water. Suddenly she smiled, and Tad saw that her mouth was full of needle-pointed teeth.

Azabel, he whispered in mind speech.

So we meet, Sagamore, the Nixie said. Her *S*s sounded like hissing snakes. She looked Tad and Ditani up and down, and her lips bubbled with laughter.

And this time you come in the form of a half-drowned rat. It was not so in the old days, Sagamore. Then you walked in honor, a giant among men. You are not what you were, Sagamore. You have fallen.

A faint music began, a sweet silvery hum.

Doubt swept over Tad. He felt ignorant, awkward, and small. No, smaller than small—*puny*. Of course he wasn't fit to be the Sagamore. How could he ever have thought so?

And what is this that you have brought with you?

The Nixie undulated closer until she hovered face-to-face with Ditani. She thrust her head closer and peered into the goggles. Ditani stood her ground.

A mouse-eater?

Ditani's fingers tightened on her spear—and then, with a muffled gurgle of horror, flung it away from her. The spear had turned into a squirming snake. It slithered across the floor and vanished through a pearl-hung doorway.

And what is this?

The straps that held Ditani's goggles came undone. The breathing tubes were jerked away. Ditani flailed wildly and gulped water.

The Nixie laughed mockingly.

Is she precious to you, Sagamore? What will you do to save her?

Furiously Tad tore at the straps of his own breathing tubes. He ripped his mouthpiece off, clapped it over Ditani's mouth, and slid his air canister over her shoulders. He was so angry that he had hardly realized what he was doing. But he was all right. He was breathing normally, as if the water were air, or as if he were a fish. He could feel his nose flaps flutter.

You can't stop me, Azabel, he said. *You know you can't touch me. I've come for the Waterstone.*

The Nixie reared up in the water, growing taller and more menacing. Everything about her seemed to swell up and grow larger. Her hair stood out like silver-green spikes. She stretched her hands toward Tad, and he saw that her fingers were tipped with pale green claws.

We will make a bargain, Sagamore!

Slowly, hypnotically, the Nixie began to sway back and forth, supple as an eel. The silver humming grew louder.

Leave the Stone! Go and never return, and you shall have the girl! And I will give you . . . this! The Nixie pulled a tapestry aside.

Tad gasped. There, behind a door of fish bones bound together with silver wire, floated Pondleweed. He was enclosed in a crystal bubble that floated midway between the chamber floor and ceiling, just barely bobbing up and down as if little waves were bumping against it. His eyes lit up at the sight of Tad and his lips shaped soundless words.

Leave the Stone, and you and he will go home again, the Nixie's syrupy voice whispered. *You and your father will go back to your pond. Is it a bargain, Sagamore?*

Tad struggled with shock. He had never expected anything like this. He had thought he would never see his father again. Now he felt joy, amazement, horror, and despair, all muddled up at the same time. His mind felt like boiling soup.

And if I don't agree?

The Nixie bared her pointed teeth.

Then he will drown! she hissed.

She pointed a finger at the bubble. Water began to seep slowly into it, forming a puddle around Pondleweed's feet.

No! Tad cried. *Stop! Let me speak to him!*

The door is not locked, the Nixie said sweetly. *The water is jail enough. Go to him, Sagamore. See what he says.*

Tad tore the cage door open. The skin of the bubble stretched and wrapped around him, sealing him inside. He flung himself into his father's arms. For one glorious moment, all trouble seemed to disappear.

But there could be no real joy in this reunion. Tad felt as if he were being torn in two. He couldn't let Pondleweed drown. But he couldn't let the Nixie keep the Waterstone. Everything would die then—*everything*. He had promised to seize the Stone and restore the water. That was his trust. But this was *Pondleweed*. As he struggled to explain all that had happened, his father held him at arm's length, just looking at him, as if he were drinking the sight of him in. When Tad finished, he slowly shook his head.

"If it weren't such a short time since I saw you, lad, I'd swear you'd grown taller," he said. "Your mother would be so proud."

Tad felt as if he were choking. Hadn't his father listened? Didn't he understand?

Then Pondleweed pulled him close again, turned him away from the watching Nixie, and spoke softly in his ear.

"Son, once you know what's right, there's nothing for it but to do as you must, no matter how bitter a brew it is to swallow. And that's what we will do together, you and I, you as the Sagamore, and me—well, me as a common man of the Fisher Tribe."

Tad's eyes burned with tears.

"It's hard for you, young as you are," Pondleweed said, softer yet. "But you'll find your way, son, never fear. Care for Birdie now. You two will have to help each other."

The water in the bubble was rising higher.

Choossse! the Nixie cried.

Pondleweed met her eyes over the top of Tad's head.

"We have chosen!" he said loudly.

Then he stepped back and smiled at Tad, a smile so filled with love and pride that Tad felt as if his heart might break in two.

"We will meet around a campfire in Great Rune's garden," Pondleweed whispered. Then he grasped the walls of the bubble in both hands and tore it wide open. A blinding rush of silver water swept past them, bursting the bone door and tumbling Tad head over heels out onto the floor of the Nixie's chamber.

When Tad's vision cleared, Pondleweed was gone.

23

THE MIND AND THE MAGIC

"Free me!"

The voice seemed to come from the level of Tad's waist. From his pouch. Frantically he tore open the leather-leaf flap and groped inside. His seeking fingers encountered the misshapen lump of rock that was the Kobold's hand. As he touched it, it squirmed. Tad snatched it out of his pouch and stared down at it in alarm. The rock writhed and wriggled, then abruptly pulled itself free of Tad's grasp. It hung impossibly in the water for a moment, as if it were as light as a bubble or a bladderpod. Then it opened. Fingers unfolded one by one, shaking themselves free of the confining stone, spreading wide. The hand had short stubby fingers, and the first finger seemed to have a frayed bandage wrapped around the knuckle. The bandaged finger pointed directly at the Nixie, and a shadowy shape began to take shape around it—the half-transparent image of a little bearded man. His expression, what could be seen of it, was outraged.

"You have broken the Law, Azabel!" the Kobold said sternly. It was the hammer voice, Tad realized, harsh with anger. The Kobold's image rippled as if little waves were sweeping through it.

"The Stone is mine!" the Nixie cried, her voice rising. "You have your Stone, Beziel! This one is mine! *Mine!*"

"It is not yours!" the Kobold bellowed.

Tad's pouch thumped insistently against his side. He reached inside again and pulled out Treeglyn's oak stick, with its faint tracing of a wild-haired little face. The stick trembled and shivered, and then suddenly jerked itself out of his hand and hovered in the water. Above it formed the translucent image of a woman, her hair as tangled as a bird's nest, her eyes brilliantly blue.

The Nixie smiled nastily. "Beziel," she said, "and now Treeglyn. I thought *your kind* were long gone."

"Not yet," Treeglyn's image snapped.

"Not hardly," the Kobold rapped out.

"But you are both alone," the Nixie said. "You are the last." Her voice began to croon. "As I am alone. My sisters are gone, gone, into the deep sleep, taken from me forever, gone, gone." The croon sharpened into a silvery hiss. "Taken from me, Sagamore! And I will have my revenge! You are no longer what you were, Sagamore. Your world will die. And *I will have my Stone.*"

She undulated forward, rearing up in the water, swelling until she was twice—three times—her former size. She bared her pointed teeth, and her silver-green hair flared out around her shoulders as if blown by an invisible wind.

"You should have bargained when I offered," the silver voice said. "For now there is no turning back. I will destroy you, Sagamore!"

A triumphant ripple of music echoed through the chamber.

"I have made a pact with Ohd!"

The Dryad and the Kobold recoiled. They wobbled queasily in the water, staring at the Nixie in horror. Watching them made Tad's eyes go out of focus.

The Nixie reached out her claw-tipped fingers and beckoned, and the Waterstone shot across the chamber like a slippery fish. The Nixie caught it in both hands and raised it high above her head. The Stone's soft glow grew brighter, and it began to pulse—dim, bright, dim, bright—in rhythm. Dim, bright, dim, bright. Tad could hear it. It sounded like a beating heart. *His* heart. The Stone and his heart were beating together. He felt a terrible tugging in his chest.

"Your body will die, Fisher boy," the Nixie belled. "Your body will die and the Sagamore will be caught in the Stone. The Mind and the Magic will belong to Ohd."

The Dryad and the Kobold turned their wavery faces toward Tad. The world burst into unbearable brilliance and went dark.

He was hanging in the middle of nothing. There was nothing to see but dark, a dark so deep that Tad could almost feel it. Blackness was all around him. He was as blind as a mole. Then a voice from somewhere out of the darkness spoke directly in his ear. Whose voice?

Use the Gift, Tad.

The Gift. But how? What to do with it? Tad felt nothing but anguish and confusion. If only he were older, bigger, stronger. If only he had a sword.

Use the Gift.

An idea flickered. It had something to do with rocks rolling, one of Pondleweed's sayings. "If enough push all together, the largest rock will roll." The flicker steadied and grew stronger.

Your Talent, said Witherwood, *is speaking mind to mind.*

"I would have liked," said Willem weakly, the Greller arrow in his shoulder, "to have seen a true rally of the Tribes."

Pull free, a weasel said.

"Brother," said the hawk.

Your Talent, said Witherwood . . .

It was as if all the pieces of a complicated puzzle had finally fitted together. The idea became an understanding, and then a certainty.

Then he was back—or had he ever left?—in the Nixie's blue-lit chamber. The Nixie swayed before him in the water, the Waterstone clutched in her claw-tipped fingers. Her lips curled in a mocking smile. Tad took a deep breath—it made a glubbing sound in the water—and deliberately reached out with his Mind.

I stand for the Fishers! he cried into the silence and emptiness. *Who stands with me?*

The Kobold and the Dryad spun around in the water. Their images heaved and shuddered. Tad reached—and felt their minds joining with him, strange and unfamiliar minds, but deep and old and strong.

I stand for the Kobolds! the hammer voice thundered. *I stand for the rock of the Earth! Who stands with me?*

I stand for the Dryads! Even Treeglyn's mind voice was a screech. *Who stands with me?*

Ditani's eyes flashed through her buglike goggles. *I stand for the Hunters!*

The Nixie laughed. Her cat's pupils had dilated until nothing was left around them but a thin silver rim of iris. Her eyes looked like black pools.

"It is not enough," the Nixie said. A strain of music crept into her voice. "Your bond is not strong." The music grew louder and sweeter. "You cannot win, Sagamore."

I can, said Tad.

His Mind reached farther, calling, and he felt other minds—first startled, then listening, then rushing to join with him. Fisher minds. Hunter minds. Digger minds, sturdy as the stone of the mountains. A flurry of small green minds. *Pippit?* Tad thought. *Frogs? Or are those the leafy voices of trees?* The soft twining minds of weasels—*Not slaves!*— the chittering minds of squirrels, the proud wind-clean minds of hawks. Minds that barked and yelped in a defiant chorus. *Foxes.* Foxes, red and gray, calling to him from the hills and the dark of the forest. *The Dens stand for Rune!* Long cool minds, striped with danger, but now joining with him, sharp with purpose. *Snakes,* Tad realized, with a thrill of wonder. *We ssstand with you, Sssagamore!*

Then, from a great distance, a new mind turned toward him.

I am Gorma, Sachem of the Mogs. What need have you, Sagamore?

In his mind's eye, Tad saw the great black bear heaving herself erect, shaggy paws lifted to the sky. She wore a collar of gold nuggets around her neck, beaten into the shape of curved claws.

Join us, Tad answered.

The Nixie had gone silent and watchful. Suddenly she looked afraid. She held the Waterstone high over her head and cried out, "Ooo-hd!"

Tad felt as if he were at the center of a whirlwind. He was *malawissa*—a tree in a storm, standing firm against thunder and lightning. He was the rock in the mountain's heart; he was the water that fed the ponds. He was the wind that held the hawk. He was the Sagamore.

Like an angler reeling in a fish, he pulled the minds together, all of them, large and small, young and old, weak and strong—but even the weakest of them was strong when all stood like this, together.

I defy you, Ohd, Tad's thought whispered. *I stand for Rune.*

I, too, a mind voice said beside him.

I stand for the green. For the mountains. For the forest.

I stand for Rune.

I stand.

I defy.

Tad gathered the minds together, stronger, brighter, a blaze of belief and determination. Pictures flashed through his Mind. The empty bowl of a pond, fish rotting on its banks. A shriveled grove of dead trees. A fallen nest filled with the stiffening bodies of baby birds. The pictures crowded upon one another. A broken wagon wheel, half buried in black mud. A child crying with thirst. Pondle-weed, imprisoned, drowned.

We defy.

The Nixie was wailing, her cry rising higher and higher, until it sounded like one of the Diggers' scream-ing engines. Then the water began to swirl tightly in circles around her. Her hair coiled upward over her head like gleaming smoke.

The water swirled faster. She looked as if she were wrapped in whirling mirrors. Her features began to blur. It was hard to see her now. She was encased in a silver funnel of water. The funnel spun faster and faster, dizzy-ingly fast, tossing out a frothing spray of foam.

A despairing silver voice touched Tad's mind.

Ooohd . . .

And then in an instant the roiling whirlpool vanished, taking the Nixie with it. The wailing stopped abruptly as if an immense stone door had slammed shut upon it. The Waterstone dropped to the shell-tiled floor and rolled to rest against Tad's feet.

•   •   •

The minds were gone. Or rather not gone altogether but dispersed again, gone their separate ways. For a moment, all was silent except for the teakettle sound of Ditani's breathing tubes.

Then the water trembled and a Presence entered the chamber. The Mind that touched Tad's now was infinitely immense and terrifyingly alien. It made him think suddenly of the huge uncanniness of space and stars—but at the same time, there was something comfortably familiar about it. There were green edges to it, and little glints of merriment that reminded him of sunbeams dancing on pond water. He was filled, all at once, with fear and welcome and gladness and awe.

"Well done, Sagamore," a deep green voice said.

The images of the Kobold and the Dryad rippled joyfully. Ditani was looking around confusedly in all directions.

"And you, Witches," the green voice said. "You, too, have done well. You have kept your trust, wielding your Stones wisely through the ages." It paused, then a note of amused admiration crept into it. "Hummingbirds," it said. "Very clever. And those striped rocks—excellent. What are you calling them?"

"Agates," the Kobold mumbled. He sounded pleased, but embarrassed.

"But it has been a long and heavy trust," the voice continued, "and you must be tired. Should you wish to do so, when you find worthy successors, I give you permission to pass on the Stones. There are many among the newer peoples who are wise and deserving with whom the Stones would be safe."

The Kobold nodded slowly. "I have such a one in mind," he said.

The Dryad gave an assenting squawk.

"And you, little Hunter," the deep voice continued. "It was a brave thing you did, to accompany the Sagamore."

Ditani shook her head, as if to say that she hadn't done anything brave at all. The breathing tubes bobbled.

"The heart is more important than the hand," the voice said, "and your heart, little Hunter, is loyal and valiant. You will have bright days and fine hunting and smooth ground beneath your wagon wheels."

The water trembled again and, for an instant, Tad saw the Kobold and the Dryad bending their heads in reverence, and Ditani looking buggily surprised. Then, between one breath and another, they were gone.

"And as for you, Sagamore"—the green voice sounded regretful—"I would like to tell you the same, that all will go well with you, that your days will be filled with sunlight, fat fish, and clear water. But you are the Sagamore, the guardian, and your path is hard and lonely. Your loss is already great. Now you will watch from the shadows and they will forget you. Not all that you have done, but much, and that is for the best. Do you understand?"

"I'm not sure," Tad whispered.

The deep voice gave a ghost of a chuckle.

"Oh, you'll be a hero for a bit," it said kindly. "But they won't get your story right. At least most of them won't. It's too much for them, if you see what I mean. It's like your young friend told you. People believe best what they've always believed.

"It's not always easy, the Gift," the voice went on. "But you'll grow into it. You'll see. And in the meantime . . ."

There was a flash of light from the white crystal on the floor of the Nixie's chamber, and the Waterstone floated upward into Tad's hand.

"Take it," the deep voice said. "Take it home to your pond. It's yours now. Guard it carefully."

Suddenly the voice changed, sliding into a husky whisper. Tad's eyes widened in amazement. It was a voice he recognized—the voice of an ancient turtle resting on white rocks beside a still blue pool. The embroidered tapestries billowed, and the jeweled chamber began to blur and fade. He felt as if he were falling into a long, long tunnel. There was a light at the end of it; first a pinprick in the distance, then steadily growing bigger, closer, and brighter. He rushed toward it.

Great Rune's last words whispered in his ear: *"Use the Gift wisely, Tadpole of the Fisher Tribe."*

24

BIRDIE'S TALENT

Tad was lying on the lakeshore. All around him was a buzz of activity. Feet pounded past him, and there was a confusion of shouting.

"It's gone blue, I tell you! Blue as a blooming blueberry!"

Tad sat up.

The black lake had changed color. Shore to shore, as far as the eye could see, it was now a cool clear blue. A handful of ex-fighters, wet to the skin, were splashing in it. As Tad watched, a Fisher, attacking from the rear, pulled an unwary Hunter under the water. The Hunter emerged spluttering, water dripping from his braids. He gave a mock roar and pounced on his assailant. The Fisher fell over backward, web feet flailing, shouting with laughter.

Tad looked behind him. The walls of the Greller fortress had fallen. Rows of Greller soldiers were sitting on the ground in front of the broken gate, their hands tied behind their backs and their legs stretched straight out in front of them. They looked hot and angry. Between the fortress and the beach, a great fire was blazing, tended by a scattering of Fishers, Hunters, and Diggers—Diggers!—armed with long poles. Grellers, under guard, dragged sledges toward the fire, laden with debris and dead branches.

From the opposite direction came what sounded like a series of thunderous explosions. Tad whirled around. A great bear, attended by a yapping train of foxes, was tearing down the dam. Rocks toppled, crashing alternately into the brimming lake (with volcanic splashes) and into the dried riverbed (with earsplitting bangs). Onlookers along the shore who had ventured too close squealed and retreated. Those who didn't retreat fast enough became suddenly dripping wet. Nobody seemed to mind.

The bear's massive shoulders heaved as great chunks of the stone barrier fell. The bear roared in triumph. The water burst through, freed at last, fountaining over the parched rocks, rushing gloriously away southward. The watchers on the shore sent up a chorus of cheers. Fishers, Hunters, and Diggers jumped up and down, yelling, hugging, and pounding one another ecstatically on the back. In the midst of the excited crowd, Tad could see Eelgrass standing on a hummock, waving lanky arms in the air. He was shouting a dismal warning about mudslides and floods.

The cascading water glittered in the sunlight like a leaping school of gold-and-silver fish. Somewhere far away, Tad knew, that foaming water would gentle and slow as it filled the streams and tributaries, bubbled over the little waterfalls, and swirled into the rock pools until finally, gratefully, it poured with a musical trickle into a green pond by an old willow tree. The bear roared again, a gleeful bellow.

It is well, Sagamore?

It is well, Tad answered.

A pair of excited arms seized him from behind and pulled him into a rib-cracking hug. It was Voice, bruised and battered but glowing with delight. His orange hair looked incandescent.

"You did it, Tad! It's all thanks to you!"

"And you and Witherwood," Tad said. "And Blackberry." Voice gave a sheepish grin. "It's thanks to so many people." *Most of all to Pondleweed,* he thought, but he found that a lump rose up in his throat at the memory of his father's name. "To the Kobold—Beziel—and Treeglyn, and Kral, the hawk. And Ditani and Willem. You haven't met them yet. Willem is a Digger and he has a bat of his own. . . ."

The words trailed off as Tad remembered. *Willem!* He had left him on the shore, the battle raging around him, a Greller arrow in his shoulder. Had the healers found him? Was he all right? Pulling Voice behind him, he rushed toward the place where he had last seen his friend, lying on the dusty ground with Birdie standing guard. Fishers, Hunters, and Diggers fell back before him.

Will was still there. His head was pillowed on a folded cloak. Birdie and Ditani crouched over him, faces filled with worry, while Pippit lolloped anxiously from one to the other. They leaped up joyfully at the sight of Tad— Pippit went into a frenzy of croaks and leaps—but all soon turned back to the young Digger. Will's eyes were closed.

"How is he?" Tad asked apprehensively. "Is he all right?"

An elderly Hunter woman knelt at Will's feet, packing clay jars into a small basket. She had removed the arrow from Will's shoulder and smeared the wound with a pinkish salve. She looked up as Tad spoke and nodded briskly.

"He will do, your strange friend," she said. "He loses much lifeblood, but he will recover. Give him food, eh?"

Tad took Will's hand between his own. The fingers felt limp and cold.

"Will?" Tad said.

Will moved his head weakly and muttered something under his breath.

"Will?" Tad said again.

"Peaberry," Birdie said suddenly. "That's it. Peaberry."

She sprang to her feet and took off at a run, her bare feet pounding the ground. Over Willem's silent body, Tad and Ditani exchanged puzzled glances.

"Peaberry?" said Ditani. "What is peaberry? Where does she go?"

Birdie was back, panting, her hands filled with aromatic herbs. There were long stems hung with tiny bell-shaped blossoms—withered, but still smelling sweet—a scattering of round reddish leaves shaped like mouse ears, and some short stalks hung with fruits that looked like peas. Birdie crushed the fruits in her fingers, making a green paste that she patted gently over Willem's wound. Then she broke a few leaves and held them under his nose.

"This will make him feel better," she said. "And the leaves are for making tea too. He should drink it when he's feeling stronger."

She sounded calm and confident. *Almost like an older,* Tad thought. *A real healer.* And then the realization burst upon him. *Birdie has the Talent.* Just like Granny Thimble-berry. Or maybe it's green blood, like Treeglyn said.

Will's hand felt warmer. His breath came stronger now and more evenly. Birdie crushed more leaves, shaping a poultice that she bound in place with a strip of silkgrass torn from the hem of her tunic.

"It's for shock and loss of blood," Birdie said softly. "There's an old name for this plant—spearleaf. Not because the leaves are shaped like spears, but because warriors once used it for battle wounds."

Will opened his eyes. The corners of his mouth tight-ened in a ghost of a smile.

"You're back!" he said faintly. "Did we win?"

Tad's eyes met Ditani's and then Birdie's.

"Oh, yes," he said. "We won."

They were, of course, the talk of the Gathering. The story of the meeting with the Nixie was told and retold, by Tad and Ditani in turns. Their audience, crowded spellbound around the Speaking Rock, gasped, squealed, and cheered in all the right places, and all clustered around Tad and Birdie in long minutes of silent mourning for Pondleweed. Even as he told it, though, Tad could feel bits of the tale slipping away. It wasn't that things changed, exactly, but that some things just weren't talked about. People skirted around those somehow, looking uncomfortable, asking instead what the Nixie looked like, or wanting to hear about the Grellers' catapult or the bear.

Willem, still heavily bandaged but sitting upright now, recounted the events of the battle with the Grellers on the lakeshore. His favorite part was new to Tad: the account of the arrival of the Diggers on their fleet of transport bats, armed with incendiary bombs. Willem could talk almost indefinitely about how the bombs were made and how best to go about dropping them, but he was continually interrupted by shouts from the Hunters, who only wanted to hear about the defeat of the wolf by the hawk.

Birdie's budding Talent was a source of awe and admiration, and she was peppered with requests for help and advice. She was also followed everywhere by a train of small children begging to hear the tale of how she had tamed the weasel. Blackberry and Voice, both heroes themselves, were made much of by everyone—and though Voice still claimed to have crawly feelings about weasels, Tad had seen him more than once affectionately scratching Blackberry under the chin. Voice was to accompany Tad and Birdie home to the pond—"To help you settle," he said diffidently—and it was clear to Tad that Blackberry was to come, too, as a permanent member of the family. He hoped that Pippit wouldn't take it too badly.

Werfel and Grummer—who had both been in the battle—stopped by to offer their congratulations, though the occasion was somewhat marred by Grummer fainting dead away at the sight of Blackberry. He was revived by Voice, and taken away, mumbling disjointedly about ferrets, to be fortified with butternut beer.

The entire Digger Council arrived in state, carried on a fleet of elite transport bats decked out in black leather harnesses trimmed with silver. Fishers and Hunters were nervous around them at first, but the ice was broken by Pegger, who not only had an endless supply of funny stories but could make puppets out of silkgrass handkerchiefs and play the stickpipes (slightly off-key).

Pegger performed at the dance on the final night of the Gathering, at which everyone—young and old, Hunter, Fisher, and Digger—joined in a great revolving circle, clapping their hands over their heads and shouting "Ho-mon-ro!" Everyone agreed that he was a great success.

Nobono and Branica, both ready to pop with pride, would hardly let Ditani out of their sight.

"What a trade we make for her!" Nobono told all who would listen. "She will have the best of everything, my first daughter!"

"My father and mother, they mean well," Ditani told Tad later. Her dark eyes flashed a challenge. "But me, I find my own boy. When I am ready."

As the last notes of the music died away, there was a flurry of leave-taking. People began to drift back to their campsites. There were children to put to bed, and packing to be done, and preparations to make for the long journey home. Tad and Birdie, Willem and Ditani lingered behind in the deserted clearing. Tad, who for so long had wanted only to get back home, found that he could hardly bear to say good-bye. All four faces were glum. Pippit, who couldn't seem to keep still, circled them unhappily, making damp dismal sounds. Tad knew just how he felt.

"I won't see you in the morning," Willem said. "We'll be leaving as soon as the transport bats are ready. They don't like to fly in sunlight, you know, so we're going tonight. Besides, a lot of people are in a hurry to get back to Stone Mountain. It's been fun, they're saying, but they've had enough of sleeping above ground, out in the open air."

"We go at first light," Ditani said. "The caravans have been resting long enough. Time to set them rolling, eh?"

"We go at sunrise," Birdie said. "We're going to ride Blackberry—Voice and Tad and me and Pippit."

Nobody spoke for a long depressed minute.

"Things will be different now," Willem said. "The Diggers are coming to the next Gathering, did you hear? It will truly be a meeting of all the Tribes. We'll see each other then."

"And maybe we can see each other in between," Tad said. "Or we could send messages. We might spend the winter with Witherwood. Voice promised to teach me how to read and write." He paused, looking from face to face. "But I'm going to miss being the Band of Four."

"We'll always be the Band of Four," Willem said.

25

RETURN TO THE POND

Tad lay drowsing in the sun.

From behind him came the busy scraping sounds of Birdie working in her garden. He didn't know about any green blood, Voice said, but Birdie certainly had green fingers. Just beyond the garden's stick fence, Blackberry lay sleeping, curled in a furry ball with his tail over his nose. He was making a contented snoring sound. Voice, whistling through his teeth, was working on the frame of a new—and bigger—boat. Pippit was helping by croaking encouragement and stepping on things.

On the surface everything was almost the same as it had always been—*and yet,* Tad thought, *so different.* Now there was the aching hole made by Pondleweed's absence. Even all the new friends they had made—even Tad's Gift—couldn't make up for that, though Witherwood had said that it would get easier with time. *Maybe it's another of those things that I'll have to grow into,* Tad thought.

He closed his eyes and let his Mind roam free. His powers were growing now, just as the old turtle had said they would. He could reach farther and farther. He stretched, searching, until he felt the hawk's presence.

I see you, Shining One, the hawk's harsh voice told him.
I see you, Wolf-slayer, Tad replied. *Is all well?*
All is very well, the hawk answered.

Tad pulled his Mind away, calling a farewell. He had a task to finish. He scrambled to his feet and scampered out onto the half-submerged log that extended into the pond. Frogs, lounging on the lily pads, glugged in greeting, and blue-tailed hoverflies darted before him. He crouched at the end of the log, peering down into the clear sunlight-striped depths. Sun warmed the back of his neck. Far beneath him fish fins flickered.

Tad reached into his leatherleaf pouch and pulled out the white crystal, shimmeringly threaded and veined with silver. The Waterstone. It seemed to glow with a soft inner light, and when he held it to his ear, it made a musical bubbling sound like the rush of little runlets over river rocks. As his fingers tightened around it, the sound grew louder. The stone seemed to pull against his grasp, urging him toward the water. *That's where it belongs,* Tad thought. *That's where it's supposed to be. It wants to go home.* But still he continued to hold it, running his fingers over its gleaming surface. He had lost so much for it, given so much to keep it safe. Regretfully he shook his head. Then he leaned over and dropped the Waterstone into the pond.

The stone spiraled slowly downward, trailing a tail of glittering bubbles. Tad watched it go. It seemed to shine brighter and brighter as it fell, slipping through the water as smoothly as a silver sunbeam. It fell faster and faster. Then it dropped from sight and the light vanished. Tad held his breath. For a moment he felt a sharp pang of loss.

Then the pond turned deeper green as if in welcome, and the warm wind suddenly smelled sweet with rain.

**Look for _The Return of the Dragon,_
also by Rebecca Rupp**

"So who lives in those tents?" Zachary fretted. "And
where are they? They could be anywhere. _Spying._"

"Oh, do be quiet, Zachary," Hannah said. "Let's
climb."

They scrambled up the steep slope of Drake's Hill
until they reached the enormous pile of rock, layered like
gigantic steps, that crowned the hilltop. Carefully they
began to climb, feeling for remembered hand- and foot-
holds. At last they edged around a final rocky ledge to
stand on a wide platform overlooking the ocean. At the
back of the platform gaped a dark opening that led, the
children knew, to a hidden cave. The very sight of it made
their hearts beat faster. Before them was an endless stretch
of deep blue water, lashed by the wind into white-capped
waves. And just off the shore of the island —

"Look at _that_!" gasped Zachary, pointing downward.

Below them, a great white boat lay at anchor.

"A yacht," said Hannah in an awed voice.

"I'll bet that's who's camping on the beach," Zachary
said.

He fumbled in his backpack and pulled out his own
small pair of binoculars. He put them to his eyes, focused,
and slowly swept the length of the boat, from bow to
stern.

"Funny," he said. "It doesn't have a name. Most boats
have names. Even Mr. Jones's little boat has a name

painted on it. But this one doesn't say anything. It's just plain white."

"Let me see," said Hannah, reaching for the binoculars.

She put them to her eyes and studied the silent floating yacht.

Then, as the children watched, a doorway opened and a man appeared on the yacht's polished deck. He was broad-shouldered and deeply tanned, with closely clipped iron-gray hair. He wore dark trousers and a heavy white sweater. He stood for a moment gazing out to sea, then slowly turned toward the island. A seagull glided past, sun glinting off its white wings. The man lifted a pair of binoculars to his eyes. Hastily the children dropped down behind a pile of concealing boulders.

"*He's watching F's cave*," Zachary said. "He suspects something."

"How could he?" Hannah said in disgusted tones. "You're nuts, Zachary. He was watching that gull."

"It gives me the creeps," said Zachary. "That boat. Those tents. People snooping around."

Cautiously he poked his head above the rocks and peered toward the white yacht. The gray-haired man had lowered his binoculars and was scribbling something in a small notebook.

"You see?" Hannah said. "He's a bird watcher. They take notes all the time. About the kinds of birds they've sighted."

"I think he's going below," Zachary said. "There— he's walking across the deck—he's gone."

"Let's go see Fafnyr," Hannah said. And then, as Zachary frowned and opened his mouth: "I *know*, Zachary, but all this F stuff is getting silly. We'll ask him if he knows anything about the boat. And the camp."

Zachary dropped the binoculars back in his pack and pulled out his flashlight.

"Let's go," he said. "I'll lead the way."

One by one, the three children ducked into the cave. As they entered, they smelled the special scent remembered from last summer—a spicy mix of wood smoke, incense, and cinnamon. The cave was much larger than it looked from the outside. Zachary's flashlight threw eerie shadows on the stone walls. As they edged farther into the cave, the sounds of the outside world were suddenly silenced. The whistle of the wind and the rhythmic crash of the waves ceased abruptly. All was utterly quiet. The cave led farther and farther downward, deep into the center of the hill.

"The cave seems bigger than it used to," Sarah Emily said. Her voice quavered a little. Sarah Emily was afraid of the dark.

"It's all right," Zachary said reassuringly in front of her. "We're almost there."

Just as he finished speaking, the flashlight beam glittered in the darkness, reflecting brilliantly off a broad expanse of shining golden scales.

Sarah Emily caught her breath.

It was a dragon.

And don't miss the early adventures of
Zachary, Sarah Emily, and Hannah in

The Dragon of Lonely Island!

ISBN 0-7636-0408-9 (hardcover)
ISBN 0-7636-1661-3 (paperback)